戏剧翻译中的对话与诠释

李 丽 ◎著

中国书籍出版社
China Book Press

图书在版编目(CIP)数据

戏剧翻译中的对话与诠释 / 李丽著. -- 北京：中国书籍出版社, 2024. 11. -- ISBN 978-7-5241-0074-4

Ⅰ. I046

中国国家版本馆CIP数据核字第20243SM853号

戏剧翻译中的对话与诠释

李 丽 著

丛书策划	谭 鹏 武 斌
责任编辑	张 娟 成晓春
责任印制	孙马飞 马 芝
封面设计	博健文化
出版发行	中国书籍出版社
地 址	北京市丰台区三路居路97号（邮编：100073）
电 话	（010）52257143（总编室） （010）52257140（发行部）
电子邮箱	eo@chinabp.com.cn
经 销	全国新华书店
印 厂	三河市德贤弘印务有限公司
开 本	710毫米×1000毫米 1/16
字 数	238千字
印 张	15.25
版 次	2025年1月第1版
印 次	2025年1月第1次印刷
书 号	ISBN 978-7-5241-0074-4
定 价	98.00元

版权所有 翻印必究

序

在20世纪文学的璀璨星河中，塞缪·贝克特的《等待戈多》无疑是一颗独特而耀眼的星辰。自1969年贝克特因其荒诞派戏剧的巅峰之作《等待戈多》荣获诺贝尔文学奖以来，这部作品便以其深邃的哲学意蕴和独特的艺术风格，对西方乃至全球的文学和戏剧产生了深远的影响。在这部戏剧的传播和翻译过程中，中国学者和艺术家们也对其进行了深入的探讨和多样化的诠释，使其在中国的文化土壤中生根发芽。

本书旨在通过对《等待戈多》六个中文版本进行比较研究，探讨戏剧翻译中的哲学和文化适应问题。本书选择了对话理论、改写理论和叙事学理论作为分析框架，以期从不同的角度审视翻译过程中的内在动机、外部影响和舞台表现性。在对话理论的视角下，关注译者在戏剧翻译中的主体性，以及他们如何在多重对话关系中扮演角色。改写理论则让笔者洞察到目标文化对翻译过程的规范和约束，以及意识形态、诗学和赞助人这三个关键词如何影响译者的改写策略。叙事学理论则引导研究戏剧翻译中的表演方式，以及如何在目标语言中构建叙事。在书的最后部分，展望了翻译和戏剧改编的未来，强调了学术界在探索新方法、伦理标准和合作方式方面的重要性。

这部作品的撰写过程中，得到了众多学者、翻译家和戏剧工作者的支持和启发，对他们的贡献衷心地表示感谢。此外，期待读者能够通过阅读本书，对《等待戈多》的中文翻译有更深入的理解和欣赏。最后，由于笔者的研究能力，书中难免有不足之处，期望读者予以批评指正，以便在今后的研究中予以完善和改进。

是为序。

目 录

序   1

Ⅰ   引言   1

Ⅱ   文献综述   **13**
    2.1   戏剧翻译研究   13
    2.2   贝克特戏剧翻译在中国的研究   25

Ⅲ   对话理论视角   **34**
    3.1   角色对话   42
    3.2   舞台描述   66

Ⅳ   改写理论视角   **86**
    4.1   意识形态   99
    4.2   诗学   115
    4.3   赞助人   131

Ⅴ   叙事学理论视角   **139**
    5.1   时间和空间框架   146

5.2	选择性挪用	155
5.3	标记	160
5.4	参与者重新定位	165

VI 文化适应挑战   171

6.1	成语表达	173
6.2	文化参照	177

VII 翻译和戏剧改编的未来   180

7.1	翻译和戏剧改编的演变	182
7.2	新兴趋势和技术	184

VIII 结论   194

参考文献   200

附录   213

附录 I	213
附录 II	221

目 录

Abstract	1
I Introduction	1
II Literature Review	13
2.1 Researches on Drama Translation	13
2.2 Previous Researches on Samuel Beckett's dramas translation in China	25
III Analysis of Four Translated Versions in the Viewpoint of Dialogue Theory	34
3.1 Characters' Dialogues	42
3.2 The Stage Description	66
IV Analysis of Four Translated Versions in the Viewpoint of Rewriting Theory	86
4.1 Manipulation of Ideology	99
4.2 Manipulation of Poetics	115

4.3	Manipulation of Patronage	131

V Analysis of Two Theater versions in the Viewpoint of Narratology Theory — 139

5.1	Temporal and Spatial Framing	146
5.2	Selective Appropriation	155
5.3	Labelling	160
5.4	Repositioning of Participants	165

VI The challenges faced by translators in adapting cultural nuances. — 171

6.1	Idiomatic Expressions	173
6.2	Cultural References	177

VII The Future of Translation and Theatrical Adaptation — 180

7.1	The Evolution of Translation and Theatrical Adaptation	182
7.2	Emerging Trends and Techniques	184

VIII Conclusion — 194

Bibliography — 200

Appendix — 213

  Appendix I — 213
  Appendix II — 221

I Introduction

Samuel Beckett, the renowned Irish playwright, straddled linguistic boundaries, crafting his literary works in both English and French. His magnum opus, *En attendant Godot* (translated as *Waiting for Godot)*, exemplifies this bilingual prowess. Premiered in French, it later found its English voice under Beckett's own translation for performances in England. The impact of this play has been nothing short of seismic, resonating across time and space.

Beckett's life unfolded against the backdrop of France, where he spent a significant portion of his existence. His immersion in French culture and language deeply influenced his creative process. *En attendant Godot*, first staged in Paris in 1953, defied linguistic boundaries. Beckett's choice to write it in French was deliberate—a testament to his artistic fluidity. Later, he meticulously translated it into English, capturing its essence while adapting it for English-speaking audiences.

In 1969, Samuel Beckett received the Nobel Prize in Literature—an honor that reverberated through literary circles. His recognition was not solely for *Waiting for Godot*, but this play played a pivotal role in shaping his legacy. The Nobel Committee acknowledged Beckett's ability to distill existential themes, human absurdity, and the essence of existence into powerful narratives. *Waiting for Godot* epitomized these qualities.

Waiting for Godot stands as a beacon of modern theater. Its sparse setting—

a desolate landscape with two characters, Vladimir and Estragon—becomes a canvas for profound exploration. The play's existential musings, its blend of humor and despair, and its portrayal of the human condition resonate universally. The characters' futile wait for an enigmatic figure named Godot becomes a metaphor for life's uncertainties.

Since its premiere, *Waiting for Godot* has disrupted theatrical norms. Beckett's minimalist approach—sparse dialogue, circular structure, and a sense of timelessness—defied traditional storytelling. The play challenged audiences to question reality, purpose, and the very act of waiting. It invited introspection, leaving space for interpretation and debate.

More than half a century after its debut, *Waiting for Godot* remains relevant. Its impact extends beyond the stage, infiltrating literature, philosophy, and popular culture. Directors, actors, and artists continue to grapple with its enigma. Its legacy persists, urging us to confront our own existential dilemmas. In the barren landscape of *Waiting for Godot,* Beckett captured the essence of human existence—the waiting, the uncertainty, and the quest for meaning. His bilingual journey, Nobel recognition, and enduring masterpiece ensure that Samuel Beckett's legacy endures, forever challenging the boundaries of artistic expression.

Samuel Beckett's *Waiting for Godot* stands as a beacon in the literary landscape—a work that transcends time, language, and cultural boundaries. Through the seemingly mundane act of waiting, Beckett weaves a tapestry of existential musings, absurdity, and the human condition. Let us delve deeper into the layers of meaning within this enigmatic play.

The Endless Wait: Vladimir and Estragon, our protagonists, inhabit a desolate landscape. Their existence revolves around waiting—for Godot, a mysterious figure who never arrives. The futility of their vigil underscores the absurdity of human behavior. Beckett masterfully balances tragedy and comedy. As Vladimir and Estragon engage in trivial conversations, their banter veers from poignant to farcical. Their futile efforts to fill time—changing shoes, contemplating suicide, and discussing turnips—highlight the human tendency to seek purpose even in the void.

I   Introduction

The Absurdity of Existence: The unavoidable conclusion emerges human life itself is absurd. The characters' routines—waiting, questioning, and forgetting—mirror our own existence. Their circular conversations echo our perpetual quest for meaning. The theater of the absurd, of which Beckett is a key figure, rejects traditional narrative structures. Instead, it exposes the absurdity of our routines, rituals, and societal norms. In Waiting for Godot, the stage becomes a mirror reflecting our own absurd lives.

The Folly of Seeking Meaning: Godot remains elusive—an enigma. Is he a savior, a metaphor, or an illusion? Vladimir and Estragon's desperate yearning for him parallels our own search for purpose beyond the mundane. The play's title itself invites interpretation. "Godot" sounds like "God," hinting at religious or existential implications. Yet, Beckett leaves us hanging, questioning whether meaning exists beyond our immediate reality.

Uncertainty and Time: Time, a recurring motif, haunts the play. The characters wait, unaware of its passage. Estragon's boots, Vladimir's hat, and Lucky's rope—all markers of time—become absurd symbols. The tree, leafless and unchanging, embodies stagnation. Its cyclical growth and decay mirror our own futile cycles. Beckett reminds us that time marches on, indifferent to our struggles.

Global Impact and Oriental Influence: *Waiting for Godot* reverberates far beyond Western literature. Its themes resonate with audiences worldwide. In China, it has sparked scholarly debates and adaptations. The play's universal questions—about existence, purpose, and the void—transcend cultural boundaries. Its influence on Oriental drama underscores its timeless relevance. In this existential theater, Beckett invites us to confront our own absurdity. As we wait for our own metaphorical Godots—be they love, success, or enlightenment—we grapple with the same uncertainties. *Waiting for Godot* remains a mirror, reflecting our shared human journey—a waiting room where we ponder the unanswerable. And so, we wait, filling the void with laughter, tears, and the quest for meaning.

Theatrical Revolution: *Waiting for Godot* defied conventions, challenging the accepted norms of traditional theater. Beckett's minimalist approach—sparse stage design, repetitive dialogue, and a sense of timelessness—upended expectations.

The play's circular structure mirrors the human condition—a perpetual cycle of waiting, questioning, and seeking meaning. By stripping away excess, Beckett forces us to confront the essence of existence.

Characters as Archetypes: Vladimir and Estragon, with their contrasting personalities, embody universal archetypes. Vladimir, the thinker, grapples with philosophical questions. Estragon, the doer, focuses on immediate needs.

Pozzo and Lucky, the secondary characters, represent power dynamics. Pozzo, the oppressor, treats Lucky as a mere tool. Their absurd interactions reveal the absurdity of hierarchy and exploitation.

Language and Silence: Beckett's mastery lies in what remains unsaid. The pauses, the silences—the pregnant moments—speak volumes. The characters' inability to communicate effectively underscores the human struggle. The play's sparse dialogue forces us to listen intently. We become attuned to the gaps, the nuances—the existential void that language fails to fill.

Cultural Adaptations: *Waiting for Godot* transcends borders. Its themes resonate across cultures. In China, it has inspired adaptations, sparking discussions on existentialism, absurdity, and the human quest for meaning. Directors and actors worldwide grapple with its challenges. How does one portray waiting? How does one convey the weight of existence? The play's universality ensures its relevance.

Legacy and Unanswered Questions: Beckett leaves us with questions. Who is Godot? Is he salvation, illusion, or a metaphor for our own yearnings? The play's open-endedness invites interpretation. As we wait alongside Vladimir and Estragon, we confront our own uncertainties. Perhaps Godot is not a person but a state of being—an elusive hope that keeps us going.

In the barren landscape of *Waiting for Godot*, Beckett beckons us to reflect on our own absurdity. The theater of the absurd becomes a mirror, reflecting our shared humanity—the waiting, the questioning, and the search for meaning. As the curtain falls, we remain suspended, caught in the act of existence, waiting for

I Introduction

our own Godots.

While literary criticism has long dissected Samuel Beckett's iconic play *Waiting for Godot*, the field of drama translation studies remains relatively unexplored. This book aims to rectify this oversight by delving into the six Chinese versions of the play. By doing so, it sheds light on the nuances of adaptation and provides fresh perspectives for enhancing drama translation. To explore the play's translation issues in detail, it is worth devoting some time to check the previous research on its enjoying reception and critical reception in China diachronically.

In the 1960s, Beckett and other absurd writers began to be studied critically in China. Dong Hengyi（董衡异）, in 1963 briefly introduces the plot and theme of Beckett and his work *Waiting for Godot*. In 1964, Ding Yaozhan（丁耀瓒）gets "Avant-garde Literature and Art in the Western World（西方世界的"先锋派"文艺）" published and this article introduces the plot and significance of Beckett and his works *Waiting for Godot* and *Krapp's Last Tape*. In July 1965, the first Chinese version translated by Shi Xianrong（施显荣）is published in the form of yellow book as an internal reference. In 1969, Qiu Gangjian（邱刚健）publishes his translated version in Tai Bei. Although the play is published in a separate edition, it has little influence on Chinese literature at that time because of its small circulation.

In 1980, Shi Xianrong's version is collected in the drama *Collection of Absurd School*（《荒诞派戏剧集》）published by Shanghai Translation Press for the first time. In the 1980s, restricted by the historical conditions, there are few researches on Beckett in China. Most of the papers discuss the wilderness, such as "Tragedy of Nothingness and Despair（无与绝望的悲剧）" by Cui Chengde（崔成德）. There are also comparative studies, such as Ludan's（卢丹）"Overlapping, Parallel and Overlapping: Reflections on O'Neill and Beckett's Plays（重叠，平行，交叉——关于奥尼尔与贝克特创作的点滴思考）"; Wang Yanling's（王艳玲）"Pursuit and Waiting: A Comparison between Passers-by and *Waiting for Godot*（追寻与等待——过客与等待戈多之比较）"; and Jin Sifeng's（金嗣峰）

"Theatre of the Absurd and Chinese Theatre of the Absurd（荒诞派戏与中国的荒诞戏）".

In the 1990s, *waiting for Godot* are more and more frequently adapted for theater. In 1991, it is directed by Meng Jinghui（孟京辉）, and it is performed in the auditorium of the Central Academy of Drama（中央戏剧学院）, which is the first stage version in China. In the play, Meng Jinghui transforms the two prototypes of tramps into two unemployed young people in the Chinese context, which tells the theme of ideal and disillusionment. This version continues the connotation of Beckett's repression. Strictly speaking, Meng Jinghui's version is just a campus drama, but it causes a sensation in the Chinese drama circle at that time, and it has an important impact on the development of Chinese experimental drama. In 1998, Ren Ming（任鸣）directs the drama version, which shows the loneliness, loss and helplessness of modern people from the contemporary perspective. At the same time in 1998, the director Lin Zhaohua（林兆华）cleverly spliced Антон Павлович Чехов's *Three Sisters* and *Waiting for Godot* into a feminist *Waiting for Godot*, explaining the theme of different times, similar destiny. It can be seen that this play has a deep influence on the contemporary Chinese avant-garde drama directors. The angle of studying this play has been expanded. People are no longer obsessed with the judgment of its political value, but hold a positive attitude towards its artistic value. They admire the artist's courage and charm of bold innovation by the play's poetic language and refreshing expression. Such as Shu Xiaomei's（舒笑梅）two articles："On the Space-Time Structure in Beckett's Dramatic Works（试论贝克特戏剧作品中的时空结构）", and "Poetic, Symmetrical and Absurd: the Main Features of Beckett's Dramatic Language *Waiting for Godot*（诗化·对称·荒诞——贝克特〈等待戈多〉戏剧语言的主要特征）". At the same time, the scope of comparative study has been expanded.

Since the 20st century, the understanding of this play in China has been further deepened. In 2004, the Gate theatre from Ireland stages it in Beijing Capital Theatre（北京首都剧场）, which makes Chinese audiences appreciate the authoritative Beckett drama. In 2006, Beckett's centenary birthday, a series of commemorative activities is held in China. Five volumes of *Beckett's selected works* translated by Guo Changjing（郭昌京）and Yu Zhongxian（余中先）, are published by Hunan Literature and Art Publishing House（湖南文艺出版社）. It is the largest translation collection of Beckett's plays so far. In 2007, Meng Jinghui's comedy of *Two Dogs' Opinions on Life*（《两只狗的生活意见》）premieres successfully and has been staged ever since. The drama expresses people's feelings through the perspective of dogs and satirizes the ugly phenomenon in society. In 2008, Liao Yuru（廖玉如）publishes her translated version（等待戈多·终局）. In August 2016, the world's first complete works of Beckett is finally published by Hunan Literature and Art Publishing House in the form of Chinese translation. In May 2019, the Chinese version, the only script authorized by midnight press[①], is recompiled by Yi Liming（易立明）. Beckett's centenary birthday in 2006 pushed Beckett's drama research to the climax again, and the multi-perspective and multi-dimensional criticism system for Beckett's drama has basically formed. Some scholars interpret Beckett's drama from the perspective of time-space relationship. The interpretation of time-space style is a literary criticism methodology with advantages of both form criticism and theme research, which paves the way for further study of complex and obscure drama.

Although the research of *Waiting for Godot* in China has got great achievements, systemic study on its Chinese versions is scarce. Owing to different historical backgrounds and social environments, Chinese versions have large differences between each other. Some translators follow the page at every step, so their translations are made for the target readers to read. Some translators pay attention to the performance of drama that their translations highlight more acting on stage than language on page. This book selects six versions of *Waiting for Godot*. Among them four Chinese versions translated by Shi Xianrong, Liao

---

① The copyright owner of *Waiting for Godot*

Yuru, Yu Zhongxian and Qiu Gangjiang and two Chinese versions directed by Wu Xingguo（吴兴国）and directed by Yi Liming. They are all unique. Shi's version is the first Chinese version; Liao's version is the first translated by a female translator; Yu's version takes Beckett's French version as source text; Qiu's version is the first bold translation; Yi's version is the first to be authorized by midnight press and Wu's version is the first added Peking Opera elements.

Based on the reception of Beckett's *Waiting for Godot* in China, this book adopts Mikhail Bakhtin's dialogic philosophy, rewriting theory, and narratology as its theoretical foundation, to conduct an examination of the six Chinese versions. The reasons to choose these three theories are explained by the following contents.

Dialogue theory focuses on the translator subjectivity as the internal influence in drama translation process. In the intricate dance of translation, the translator emerges as a central figure—a participant rather than a passive conduit. Drawing from Bakhtin's Dialogic theory, we recognize that the translator's subjectivity shapes the interplay between source text and target readers. Let us explore this dynamic further. According to Bakhtin's Dialogic theory, the translator is an active participant. Gone are the days when translators were mere "transparent bodies". Instead, they engage in a dialogue—an interpretive dance—between languages and cultures. Bakhtin's theory emphasizes the dialogic nature of communication. The translator, like an actor on stage, brings their own voice, experiences, and biases to the performance. The translator's purpose becomes paramount. Why translate? What drives their choices? These subjective elements influence the final product. Whether preserving the original's nuances or adapting for cultural resonance, the translator's subjectivity shapes the trajectory of the translation. There is no doubt that the translator shall be taken as the subject of translation because the translation purpose and strategies adopted by him exert influence on translation practice. This book puts forward that a new hermeneutic cycle comes into being when the translator interacts with the original text and the target text. When the translator interacts with the source text, a new hermeneutic cycle unfolds. Interpretation begets creation. The translator becomes a bridge—

a mediator—between worlds. Their choices echo across linguistic boundaries, creating a double-voiced text. The translator grapples with linguistic nuances, cultural gaps, and artistic fidelity. Each decision—word choice, tone, rhythm—ripples through the translation. The hermeneutic cycle demands reflexivity. How does the translator interpret ambiguity? How do they balance faithfulness with creativity? In this dance of subjectivities, the translator becomes a co-creator—a vital force shaping cross-cultural understanding. *Waiting for Godot,* like all great works, thrives on this interplay. As we ponder Vladimir and Estragon's existential waiting, we, too, wait—for meaning, connection, and the next act of translation.

The book underscores the significance of rewriting theory—a lens that directs our attention to the norms and constraints of the target culture during the translation process. This theory, representing external influence, sheds light on the intricate dance between source and target languages. It represents the external influence. Lin Ping（林萍）, echoing this perspective, emphasizes the role of mainstream ideology and poetics in shaping translation dynamics. Rewriting theory transcends mere linguistic equivalence. It delves into the cultural fabric—the unspoken rules, expectations, and nuances that govern how a text resonates in its new context. By acknowledging these external factors, we move beyond literal translation. Rewriting becomes an act of cultural negotiation. Also, it emphasizes the role of mainstream ideology. Ideology permeates every layer of communication. When translating, we encounter dominant ideologies—social, political, and artistic—that shape our choices. Rewriting theory prompts us to question: How does the target culture perceive certain concepts? What values underpin its norms? Poetics—the art of language—plays a pivotal role. Translators grapple with rhythm, tone, and stylistic nuances. Rewriting theory invites us to explore: How do we capture the original's poetic essence? How do we adapt it for a new audience? Rewriting extends beyond words. It involves performance—the actor's delivery, the director's vision, the audience's reception. As we rewrite, we negotiate meaning, context, and artistic fidelity. The play becomes a living entity, shaped by our subjectivity. Rewriting theory reverberates across time.

Adaptations—whether for stage, screen, or literature—extend the cycle. Each iteration reflects the translator's legacy. How does the play evolve? How do audiences reinterpret it? In this dance of rewriting, we honor Beckett's legacy while weaving new narratives. *Waiting for Godot*, like all great works, thrives on this interplay.

Narratology, a powerful lens in translation studies, illuminates not only linguistic choices but also the performative aspects of drama. By examining narrative characteristics and individual variations, narratology unveils the rule system governing storytelling. Narratology extends beyond words. It invites us to view translation as a performance—an act that transcends mere linguistic fidelity. In *Waiting for Godot,* the translator becomes an actor, embodying the characters' voices, rhythms, and emotions. The stage is the page, and the audience—the readers—await their cues. Narratology studies the way of performing in drama translation. It cannot only lead us to view the unique scenery of drama translation, but also give us the ability to construct an image of performance. The translator's choices—what to emphasize, what to omit—become frames that shape the narrative. Each frame invites interpretation. Because narratology "studies the common narrative characteristics and individual differences in all forms of narration, and aims to describe the rule system related to narration in controlling narrative process"(Prince 3). Furthermore, translation is seen as a frame, whether in its literal or metaphorical sense. Translation itself is conceived as a framing process. *Waiting for Godot* becomes a canvas. The translator, like an artist, paints with words, colors, and cultural nuances. By using these three theories, the book presents an interpretation of the six Chinese versions from three aspects, internal cause: The translator's subjectivity—their purpose, ideology, and poetics. external cause: Cultural norms, reception, and adaptation. and stage externality: How the translated text performs—on stage, in readers' minds, and across time. It is expected to achieve the unification of external and internal research on *Waiting for Godot*'s Chinese translations. By weaving these perspectives, we achieve a holistic view. The translator, as both subject and performer, bridges the gap. *Waiting for Godot*, reframed through narratology, becomes a living dialogue—a play within a play.

More specifically, this book explores following three dominant issues by examining six Chinese versions of *Waiting for Godot*. The first issue is the philosophy on drama translation in the perspective of Dialogism. The second issue is the Manipulation of the works in translating from English into Chinese. These two issues are related with the translation of the text for reading. The third issue is focused on the translation for performance. It deals with the construction of the narrative in the target language.

To do this study, Chapter one introduces the research background, literature review, research questions and research approaches. To be more comprehensive and convincing, existing research associated with the issue are mostly obtained. Thus, this part shows what has been achieved and where needs improvement. Besides, an outline of structure and research method are included.

Chapter two explores examinations related with the translation of the text for reading by analyzing four Chinese versions translated by Shi Xianrong, Liao Yuru, Qiu Gangjian and Yu Zhongxian through dialogue theory. It makes the dialogue theoretical analysis from two aspects. One is characters' dialogues and the other is stage description. The comparisons of typical examples are given to better render the explanation of different treatment undertaken by different translators. The four translated texts are created as double-voice texts.

Chapter three is to examine the same four versions. This book applies Andre Lefevere's rewriting theory to the study of the comparison of four Chinese versions, and that of how poetics, ideology and patronage influence the translation activities, and thereby quite different stylistic versions are produced.

Chapter four is to check the theatrical versions for performance by analyzing two versions adapted by Wu XingGuo and Yi Liming through narrative translation analysis. This book focuses on how to make it performable by temporal and spatial framing, selective appropriation, labelling and repositioning of participants. By analyzing the readability and performability of Chinese versions of *Waiting for Godot*, we can better understand the diversity and unity of the drama translations.

Chapter five makes it clear that in the realm of translation, accessibility can also involve developing scripts that are sensitive to cultural differences and inclusive of diverse perspectives. This means not only translating the language but also considering cultural nuances, idioms, and context. It could also involve adapting content to be more inclusive.

Chapter six indicates the future of translation and theatrical adaptation is a fascinating topic that intersects with various disciplines, including linguistics, cultural studies, and the performing arts. As we look ahead, we can anticipate several trends and developments in this field:

Chapter seven is the conclusion of this book. Within its framework. the discussions of Chinese versions of *Waiting for Godot* can be more comprehensive and systematic. The book breaks down the traditional study aiming at providing a new perspective for further improvement of drama translation.

II Literature Review

Before starting to explore the Beckett's dramas translation issues in detail, it is worth devoting some time to point out the researches on drama translation and previous researches on Samuel Beckett's dramas translation in China.

2.1 Researches on Drama Translation

Hans Sahl, a drama translation theorist, defines drama translation as the act of performing a play in another language and researchers are pushing back the frontiers and opening doors to reveal what's drama translation and how drama translation work. These studies have already thrown up some interesting results by the five aspects of semiotics, dramaturgical analysis, stylistics, cultural school and playability. The following contents will clearly illustrate this point.

2.1.1 Semiotics

The semiotic study of drama can be traced back to the Prague School of the Czech Republic in the 1930s. During this period, there were a group of literary critics who analyzed the composition of drama from the perspective of structuralism and semiotic system, such as Otamar Zich, Jan Mukarovsky, Jiri Veltrusky, Jindrich Honzl and Peter Bogatyrev. Among them, Zich and Mukarovsky have the greatest influence. In his book Aesthetics of the Art of Drama, Zich claims that there are various systems in drama, and that each system is related to each other and affects each other, so there is no priority. Like other systems, drama text is an integral part of the whole performance system. Mukarovsky applied Saussure's symbolic definition to literature art, and thought that the life of an art work lies in the collective consciousness of the public. Here, signifier can refer to the work of art itself, and signified refers to the aesthetic goal. Therefore, in his view, drama performance is an organic whole, a large system formed by the cooperation of different subsystems, and the audience is the creator of the overall system meaning. Thus, the understanding of drama semiotics accords with the epistemology of dialogic philosophy.

In the 1960s and 1970s, dramatic semiotics developed further, among which Kowzan and Ubersfield's contribution is outstanding. Kowzan established 13 drama symbol systems of auditory or visual symbols and he emphasized the attribute of the written text as the performance component, therefore, he plays an important role in the redefinition of the position of a written text. Ubersfield in 1978 wrote the book of Lilre le théatre and raised two noteworthy questions: "first, on any concept of drama the connection between the written version and the performance should be considered as permanent; secondly, the written version is incomplete" (see Nicolarea 2008). Later, Elam (1980) and Parvis (1989) raised drama semiotics to the height of paradigm and affirmed its value as a research method. It is because of the multi-level and multi angle interpretation of the drama text and the analysis of various symbols in the drama system that the drama translator takes into account all the factors that need to be translated into the target language script, audience and culture as much as possible. Che Suh (2005: 56) pointed out that landouceur (1995: 35-36) established the descriptive comparative analysis model of translated drama based on the translation description model of Lambert and van Gorp (1985: 52), and studied the relationship between the translated script and the target philology and the whole social and cultural system.

2.1.2 Dramaturgical Analysis

The history of dramaturgical analysis can be traced back to the beginning of drama performance, because the audience will always comment on some factors in the play after watching a play. Hence, whether from the general audience or literary critics, these feedbacks and comments effectively promote the development and improvement of drama art.

Erving Goffman, a sociologist, erected a doctrine of dramaturgical analysis and he is widely known for developing the dramaturgical perspective with analyzing the social interaction and regarding that people lived their lives like actors performing on a stage. In the book of Dramaturgical Analysis of Social Interaction, Hare, A. Paul and Blumberg, Herbert H. make further explanation from the standpoint of the language of the theater to describes social behavior.

In the 1960s, this kind of description mode gradually monopolized the study of drama because of its wide field of vision, sophisticated argumentation, and finding a balance between subtle observation and subjective interpretation. The most famous scholar is Pavis. By examining the concretization process of the original script on the stage of the target language, he (1989: 29) thought that drama translation involves T1 (translation in the general literary sense), T2 (translation for stage performance) drama art analysis, T3 stage performance and T4 audience appreciation. He believes that drama translation suitable for performance cannot be simply regarded as the product of linguistics, but also the product of drama art activities.

Although this perspective cannot exhaust all fields of drama research, it provides the research with a comprehensive means to study drama performance and avoid one-sided understanding of Drama.

2.1.3 Stylistics

Stylistics was born in the early 20th century and flourished in the 1960s and 1970s. Before the end of the 1970s, poetry was the main study object. Since the 1980s, the study of novel style has been paid more and more attention, and less attention has been paid to drama although in 1962 Austin proposed that discourse analysis could be the theoretical guide of drama language. Some stylisticians, equipped with pragmatics and discourse analysis, have been trying to change the situation (Short, 1989, 1996, 1998; Simpson, 1989; Leech, 1992). Until the 1990s, the dramatic study becomes attractive. Bassnett (1985: 102) stressed that drama translators should focus on the language structure of the text and pay special attention to the text symbols, including the deictic units, the shifts of tone of register, the pauses and silences, the problems of intonation patterns and the speech rhythms, that is, the language and paralanguage factors of the text. Based on the particularity of drama language for taking the dialogue of characters as the main body, which emphasizes the colloquialism, individuation and action of language. the researchers should focus on the dynamic process of the generation and understanding of the meaning in context and interaction. In order to achieve the explanatory adequacy, how drama dialogue language is expressed for the dramatic conflict and how drama dialogue language reveal characters image and personality should be analyzed by the research of drama language. By treating the analysis of dramatic text as a valid way of understanding drama, they form a striking contrast to traditional dramatic criticism which holds that the significance of drama lies in the performance and the only proper way to approach it is to be in the theatre.(封宗信，2002: 42)

In the 1980s and 1990s, the rapid development of pragmatics and discourse analysis has been widely used in the analysis and research of English drama language, which has constructed the theory and method of English drama stylistics (Yu Dongming, 1996: 103). Western scholars such as Carter and Simpson (1989), Bennison (1993) and Herman (1995, 1998) have made fruitful efforts in this regard.

2.1.4 Cultural School

The cultural turn in the field of translation studies also affects drama translation. Many researchers have explored drama translation from a cultural perspective. In the late 1980s, in cross-cultural drama translation, Parvis (1989: 83) summed up two opposite tendencies. One is to try to preserve the cultural features of the original language in order to highlight the differences between the original language culture and the target language culture. The other is to try to resolve the incomprehensible differences in the original culture in translation. According to Parvis, both of them are not ideal. He proposed a "middle road", which uses translation as a conductor to connect the two cultures, so as to deal with the relationship between the two cultures. On this basis, Parvis demonstrated the universality of culture and a universality of culture. Taking the translation of Mahabharata as an example, Carriere and brook, as translator and director respectively, successfully translated the myth only through the actions and words of the actors shown in the drama text. According to Brooke, the language of stage enables translation. Therefore, Parvis affirms that the action of drama is not limited to its social function, but a universal encounter among actors of different cultures (ibid: 40) . While Pavis analyzed the composition of drama translation, he pointed out that a translation always consists of a part of source text, a part of target text and target culture, because any transformation involves changing many aspects of the source text in order to adapt to the target language and target culture. In view of this, Pavis believes that drama translation is a kind of interpretative behavior, because its main purpose is to pull the source text to the target language and culture (from Nicolarea, 2008).

In the 1990s, Bassnett raised the issue of assimilation in drama translation. She believes that drama translation is influenced by both the source culture and the target culture, and assimilation is inevitable because "translation is not carried out in a vacuum, translation always takes place in a continuum, and the context in which translation takes place inevitably affects translation practice, Just as the norms and restrictions of the source culture play a role in the source text, the norms and restrictions of the target culture must play a role in translation" (Bassnett, 2001: 93). In addition to Pavis and Bassnett, Aaltonen also makes an in-depth study of drama translation from a cultural perspective. Aaltonen (1996) believes that the translation of drama involves cultural transfer or manipulation, and which elements will be moved in and how to move in are related to the audience's awareness of cultural customs and the awareness of the dramatic functions of specific cultural elements in shaping characters and constructing plots, themes and styles. Since there are many ways to interpret cultural elements, manipulation and migration are necessary strategies. The audience is not attracted by the heterogeneous culture and only the issues of common concern of human beings have real attraction. In order to make the audience interested, the drama should first approach the real life, that is to say, "the audience must be able to establish a connection with the unfamiliar reality, so it is necessary to manipulate the cultural characteristics, so that the culture and plot in the drama can have enough common ground"(ibid.: 118).

Aaltonen (2000: 53-63), based on the multi-system analysis method of Zohar, analyzes the specific performance of cultural transplantation in drama translation from the perspective of drama reception and the performance consists of compatibility, integration and alterity. In addition, based on the relationship between the two cultures, the causes of adaptation are analyzed in detail from reverence, subversion, rebellion, art, community, etc., and the complicated performance of cultural transplantation in drama translation is demonstrated.

Aaltonen (1993, 1996, 2000) always thought that cultural transplantation was inevitable in drama translation, and it was more prominent than other styles. She believes that drama translation is egotism from the beginning, and the purpose of drama translation is rarely to introduce the other and let the audience understand the foreign tradition; on the contrary, it is to use this tradition to serve the social culture of the target language. The centrality of the target system in cross-cultural drama translation is also highly praised by Lichte (2004: 284). In her opinion, the starting point of cross-cultural drama performance is not the foreign script or foreign culture, but the needs of her own drama and culture. The choice, transformation and transplantation of foreign scripts and their drama traditions depend on their relevance or integration with their own drama traditions. Brisset (1996: 158) also believes that the choice of script in drama translation should focus on whether its language organization strategy is in harmony with the performance norms in the target language society.

2.1.5 Playability

Playability is also a term derived from the theory of dramatic art. It is the most important feature that distinguishes drama from other literary genres, and it mainly manifested in the action and colloquialism of drama. Crystal (1997: 75) once pointed that "Drama is neither poetry nor novel. It is first and foremost dialogue in action". In fact, the exploration of "performability" runs through the whole development period of drama translation research. In the past 30 years, drama translation scholars have had a heated discussion on whether drama translation should follow the standard of performability including Anderman, Coelsch-Foisner& Klein, Zatlin, Snell-Hornby and so on. Among them, the change of Bassnett's dramatic translation thought from the late 1970s to the early 1990s has aroused strong repercussions.

In the late 1970s, Bassnett drew on the semiotics of theatre believing that the text of drama is incomplete, and that the text and performance are inseparable and organic. Usually, a play is used for performance. Therefore, drama is not only a literary discourse, but also a combination of language and action in a harmonious time frame. (Bassnett, 1978: 161) Therefore, Bassnett believes that drama translation should follow two principles different from poetry and novel translation, namely "performability" and "text function of drama translation". Among them, the second principle is the derivation of the first principle. At the same time, Bassnett's emphasis on the concept of "performability" has two important implications for the translator: first, performability shows that the concept and performance of the text are two different aspects; second, there are some "performability" features implied in the drama text-the action of language (1978: 161-176). Therefore, she believes that "performability" is the first principle that a drama translator should follow. This point of view has a profound impact on the study of drama translation and has become the core of drama translation studies.

After the mid-1980s, Bassnett's view began to change gradually. The fundamental reason for the change is that she gradually realized that if the performability is involved, a series of problems faced by the drama translator are impossible in her eyes, such as, in addition to the drama text, the translator will also face a number of factors, including the super language factor and the action factor. The more extensive symbol system is limited by the performance tradition of the target language and the differences of audience expectations. Moreover, the term "performability" has not been defined for a long time. Sometimes, it seems to mean that the translated drama text should read fluently, and the actors should not have trouble in speaking lines in the performance; sometimes, it refers to a series of cultural domestication strategies, such as replacing the dialect in the original text with the dialect in the target language, or deleting the non-transplantable part rooted in the original culture. (1985: 90-91) therefore, she believes that performability is just an excuse for many translators to find various language strategies in their translation, which should not be regarded as the standard of drama translation, and translators should pay more attention to the language structure of the text itself. In this period, she still affirms the incompleteness of the drama text and admits that the text and the performance are inseparable; however, the translator should start from the script, because all kinds of performable factors are encoded in the script. But at the same time, she points out that there are countless ways to decode the performable elements of any script, and the translator's work can only start from the language structure of the text itself. (ibid: 101-102) it can be clearly seen that Bassnett's transformation aims to simplify the task of the translator, free the translator from the constraints of the drama system, and fully focus on the language structure of the drama text. It is this simplification and one-sided emphasis on the role of the text that makes her research gradually fall into contradiction.

In the 1990s, Bassnett's thought was more radical. Although he could not completely deny the dialectical relationship between drama text and performance, he began to advocate the reduction of drama translation to the field of literature. She tried to find support from Veltrusky (1977). According to Veltrusky, not all plays are created for dramatic performance, and other types of texts can also be used for performance. "Although not common, sometimes narrative literature such as prose and novels can be used to accomplish this function (for performance). Therefore, it is wrong to regard the characteristics of drama text as inseparable from performance. The theatre is not a literary genre, but an art, and language is only a part of it. While in the drama included in the literary genre, language is all of them — although each genre organizes language in a different way (Bassnett 1998: 98)." Veltrusky regards drama as a literary genre and drama text is also regarded as literature for readers to read. As for the stage of drama, it goes beyond the scope of literary consideration. He further points out that "all plays, not only the library plays, are for people to read, just like novels and poems. There is no actor or stage in front of the reader. There is only written language in front of him. Most of the time, readers doesn't think of the characters as stage images or the places where the behaviors take place as scenes on the stage. Even if the reader wants to imagine these scenes on the stage, the difference between the drama text and the performance will not change, because in the imagination, these have no meaning, but in the performance, these become the carriers of ideas." (ibid: 99) Hence, Bassnett believes that once we admit that the drama text is only a factor in the performance system, it means that the translator, like the author, does not have to consider how to organically combine the script with other symbol systems, which is the task of the director and the actor. (1998: 99) obviously, this is a one-sided understanding of the drama text, which separates the various symbol systems in the drama system, denies the organic connection between the script and other symbol systems, and provides an excuse for her drama literariness. Then, she questioned the universality of "performability", holding a negative attitude to the fact that the multi-layer structure of drama has cultural commonness and can go through different cultures (1991: 107). According to the viewpoint of drama anthropology, Bassnett thinks that culture has its particularity and drama "performability" has no universality. She quoted Melrose's point of view and objected to the deep structure of drama text, the commonness of drama culture and the inner language action. Based on Melrose's point of view, Bassnett concludes that "performability" is a term without credibility, an illusion of free human thought and an excuse for translators to justify their own translation strategies. (1990: 77; 1991: 110; 1998: 95-96)

Many scholars criticized this. In the late 1980s, Pavis opposed Bassnett on many issues. First of all, Pavis supports the criterion of performability, and believes that the factors of performance must be taken into account in the exploration of drama translation (Weissbort & Eysteins-son, 2006: 558). Secondly, Pavis believes that the whole instruction system is an action structure embedded in the written text. Moreover, Pavis was in favor of "the universality of movement and the universality of culture" (Nicolarea, 2008). In addition, in order to achieve performability, Pavis emphasizes the principle of brevity in drama translation.

In the mid-1980s, Snell Hornby further described the characteristics of dramatic texts. She developed Reiss's view and classified drama text as "multimedia text". She (2007: 108) believed that multimedia text was different from novels, short stories and lyric poems, and the text was only a part of a larger and more complex whole. Moreover, multimedia texts, including drama scripts and opera lyrics, have the same characteristics, that is, they are all specially created for the live performance on the stage, and they are all music scores that can play their full potential only when performing.

Snell Hornby (2006, 2007) continued to explore the issue of performability and once again stressed that dramatic texts are the basis of performance, just like "music score". The translator should pay attention to the performability and speakability of the translation, and pay attention to the singing when translating opera. On this basis, Snell Hornby put forward his own standards of performability: first, stage drama dialogue is an artificial language with special text cohesion and mutual indicative vitality; second, performability is characterized by the interaction of multiple perspectives; third, language can be seen rhythmic and progressive potential actions, in which rhythm not only refers to the stress pattern in the sentence, but also includes the internal rhythm of the plot or drama action, including the alternation of tension and relaxation, suspense and calm, etc.; fourth, lines form the actor's personal dialect, which is a tool to convey emotion through the actor's voice, expression, gesture and action Fifth, watching a performance is a personal experience, but the audience is not just a spectator, but a certain response to the performance. At the same time, Snell Hornby also stressed that it is impossible to formulate specific and universal rules (2006: 86-87, 2007: 111-112).

Assimakopoulos (2002) uses relevance theory to study drama translation. He believes that a drama is a dynamic text type whose main purpose is not to be read, but to be performed. In translation, all dimensions of drama should be fully considered, not only the text itself. From the perspective of translatology, the performability factor is a constant in the study of drama translation. Marco (2003: 58) also believes that stage restriction is crucial for drama translation, because performance is the ultimate goal of drama translation. For example, the coordination of words to the action, the sense of rhythm of delivery and orality are all the concrete manifestations of performability. Therefore, drama text should be regarded as a seed that sprouts and blooms in stage performance, not just a static literary work.

After the above discussion, the study of drama translation under the philosophy of dialogue is rarely involved, so this research intends to provide a new perspective for drama translation from the perspective of Bakhtin's dialogue theory. Dialogue theory provides a scientific and effective epistemological platform for drama translation studies. First of all, dialogue theory provides a scientific and effective guiding ideology for drama translation studies. The research shows that the understanding of drama translation from a dialogic and dynamic perspective is an effective way to reveal the essential characteristics of drama with both literariness and stage, and also the key to resolve the many disagreements that have plagued drama translation studies for a long time. Drama is different from other literary genres. It is the essence of drama to put on a perfunctory performance. The colloquialism, action, disposition and literariness of drama translation are the embodiment of dialogism in drama translation, and also the accurate grasp of the dual nature of literariness and stage in drama translation. Secondly, dialogism emphasizes that the cognitive process of human beings is the process of the interaction between the cognitive subject and the surrounding environment (object). It is of great significance to scientifically define the multiple dialogues among the translator, the reader and the text in the process of translation, and also provides a reference for the perspective of Beckett's drama translation. Thirdly, dialogism considers that the better the dialogue between the subject and its surroundings, the higher the value of the subject. Finally, dialogism provides us with strong methodological support for the research methods of macro and micro studies, qualitative and quantitative analysis, and horizontal and vertical comparison. On the basis of theoretical construction, the text selection, translation theory, translation practice and cultural value of Beckett's drama translation are systematically examined, combed, studied and investigated.

2.2 Previous Researches on Samuel Beckett's dramas translation in China

Beckett's drama began to achieve worldwide fame in Europe and soon extended to the American continent. Gradually it became the classic of western drama. In 1953 the French version of Waiting for Godot premiered in Paris. Two years later, the English version of Waiting for Godot premiered in London. Since then, Paris and London have become the birthplaces of Beckett's plays and these two cities have gradually pushed Beckett to the center of the world stage. In Germany, Waiting for Godot also achieved great success. In a sense, the play fits the psychology of the German people after the war, because most Germans are still immersed in the feelings of failure, division, confrontation and frustration. At this time, Godot is no different from the redemption of their hearts. After its premiere in London, Waiting for Godot soon spread to Beckett's native Ireland. Dublin has become an important Beckett research center in the world. In 1960, Greece, the ancestor of Western drama, staged Endgame, marking that Beckett began to be accepted by the European orthodox drama circle and gradually entered the classic ranks. Beckett's plays came out of Europe and were soon accepted by the mainstream of American society: Waiting for Godot in Miami in 1956, in San Francisco in 1957 and in New York in 1961. So far, the tentacles of Beckett's plays have extended to the western people of different cultures and backgrounds, and have entered the western mainstream world. Since this book only discusses the Chinese translations of Samuel Beckett's dramas so the acceptance of Samuel Beckett's works in China will be introduced.

2.2.1 The enjoying reception

As a world-famous literary master, Beckett's dramas have been translated into many languages, including Chinese. This research will comb the enjoying reception of dramas in China diachronically.

In the 1960s, China adopted a critical review of Beckett and other absurd writers. Dong Hengxun, in the eighth of front in 1963 wrote on the fall of Dramatic Art—on the French anti drama school and briefly introduced the plot and theme of Beckett and his work Waiting for Godot. In 1964, the 9th of world knowledge published Ding Yaohu's avant-garde literature and art in the western world, introducing the plot and significance of Beckett and his works waiting for the ending of Godot and Krapp's Last Tape. Meanwhile, as an internal publication, the Foreign Drama Materials made a brief introduction to Beckett's Waiting for Godot in the 11th of 1964. In July 1965, Shi Xianrong's Waiting for Godot was published in the form of yellow book as an internal reference. Although Waiting for Godot was published in a separate edition, it had little influence on Chinese literature at that time because of its small circulation.

In the1970's—1980's, Zhu Hong published Review of Absurd Drama in the second issue of world literature in 1978 and he introduced "the meaning of absurdity", "Beckett and the absurdity of existence", etc. In 1980, Waiting for Godot, translated by Shi Xianrong, was included in the drama collection of absurd school published by Shanghai Translation Press for the first time. In 1981, Beckett's Endgame (translated by Feng Hanjin) and Happy Days (translated by Xia Lian, Jiang Fan) were published in the second issue of Contemporary Foreign Literature. In January 1982, the anthology of foreign intellectual novels published by Huacheng publishing house included Beckett's novel The Wronged (translated by Zhang Zhaoxiang). In August 1983, The Drama of the Absurd published by foreign literature press included Beckett's Waiting for Godot (translated by Shi Xianrong) and Happy Days (translated by Jin Zhiping) and Waiting for Godot (translated by Shi Xianrong) is included in the third volume of Selected Works of Foreign Modernists published by Shanghai Literature and Art Publishing House in 1984. Before the play, there is an introduction written by Shi Xianrong, which introduces Beckett's life, works and his contribution to the literary world. In the fourth volume, there is Beckett's novel Self Narration of the Absurd Guest (translated by Tu Lifang). All of these publications made Chinese youth in the 1980s who love Drama saw the light of western new drama, which opened the heyday of Chinese avant-garde drama. Therefore, it can be said that the translation and introduction of Beckett in China reached a climax in the early 1980s.

In the 1990s, various western literary trends and modernist writers' works poured into China, while Beckett's translation and introduction were somewhat unsatisfactory. In 1991, Waiting for Godot, directed by Meng Jinghui, who was a student of the Central Academy of Drama at that time, was performed in the auditorium of the Central Academy of Drama, which is the first stage version of Waiting for Godot in China. In the play, Meng Jinghui transforms the two prototypes of tramps into two unemployed youth in the Chinese context, which tells the theme of ideal and disillusionment, and continues the connotation of Beckett's repression and resistance to repression. Strictly speaking, Meng Jinghui's Waiting for Godot is just a campus drama, but it caused a sensation in the Chinese drama circle at that time, and had an important impact on the development of Chinese experimental drama. In 1992, the fourth issue of Foreign Literature published Beckett's work Krapp's Last Tape (translated by Shu Xiaomei). In August 1992, China Social Sciences Press published Beckett by A. Alvarez (translated by Zhao Yuese). In August 1995, Lu shuimao et al. translated Beckett's Sedative, Home and Exile into Chinese published by Henan University Press. In October 1995, Changchun Publishing House published the biography of Beckett, the great master of absurd literature (by Jiao ER and Yu Xiaodan). In 1998, Ren Ming, director of people's art, directed the drama version Waiting for Godot, which shows the loneliness, loss and helplessness of modern people from the contemporary perspective, and explains the "waiting" of modern Chinese version. At the same time in 1998, the director Lin Zhaohua cleverly spliced Антон Павлович Чехов's three sisters and Waiting for Godot into a feminist Waiting for Godot, explaining the theme of "different times, similar destiny". It can be seen that Beckett and Waiting for Godot have a deep influence on the contemporary Chinese avant-garde drama directors. In addition, in December 1998, China social Publishing House published the Nobel Prize bank for literature, in which the first volume briefly introduced Beckett's life and creation, and Waiting for Godot (translated by Shi Xianrong) was included in the third volume. In the seventh issue of today's pioneer in 1999, a translator retranslated tranquilizer.

Since the 21st century, the understanding of Beckett in China has been further deepened. In 2000, Shanghai foreign language education press introduced the original edition A Cambridge literary guide—Beckett edited by John Pilling which contains several papers on Beckett's drama research by contemporary western scholars, making the domestic academic circles have a better understanding of the current situation of Beckett's drama research. In January 2002, People's Literature Press published Waiting for Godot in the form of separate edition (translated by Shi Xianrong) and in March of the same year, the British Volume of chronicle of foreign short stories in the 20th century was published by People's Literature Publishing House. The volume contains a short novel a night (translated by Qiu Zhikang). In 2003, Hebei Education Press published Martin Eisling's classic work theatre of the absurd (translated by Hua Ming), which is of great benefit to Beckett's drama research. In the same year, Meng Jinghui planned to rehearse a hundred person version of Waiting for Godot. On the premise of maintaining the style of the original work, he used hundreds of actors, and used a lot of experimental elements in music, stage image, etc. to perform another kind of play Waiting for Godot, later due to the outbreak of SARS, the performance failed. In 2004, the Gate theatre from Ireland staged the original Waiting for Godot in Beijing Capital Theatre, which made Chinese audiences appreciate the authoritative Beckett drama. In 2005, the Shanghai Drama Art Center staged Endgame directed by German director Walter ASMS, which is the second Beckett drama performed in domestic theater after Waiting for Godot. In 2006, Beckett's centenary birthday, a series of commemorative activities were held in China. Five volumes of Beckett's selected works, translated by Guo Changjing and Yu Zhongxian, were published by Hunan Literature and Art Publishing House, which contains three complete plays and several short plays, i. e. Waiting for Godot, final and freedom. It is the largest translation collection of Beckett's plays so far. At the same time, Shanghai People Press published Portrait of Beckett and the book is divided into two parts, one is a large number of stills and Beckett's personal photos, the other is three commemorative articles written by James Norsen (translated by Wang Shaoxiang). In 2007, Meng Jinghui's comedy of two dogs' opinions on life premiered successfully and has been staged ever since. The drama expresses people's feelings through the perspective of dogs and satirizes the ugly phenomenon in society. Meng Jinghui said frankly that two dogs is Waiting for Godot. In 2008, Shanghai foreign language education press introduced Ronan McDonald's monograph of Samuel Beckett in its original edition, for which Wang Lan wrote a guide. The publication of these bibliographies has provided a good foundation for Beckett's drama research in China, and has made great contributions to the in-depth and systematic study of Beckett's drama. The fate of the deconstruction and reconstruction of Beckett's plays in China is caused by the differences of cultural demands between the east and the west, as well as the product of specific historical context. In this sense, it is necessary to restore the reception process of Beckett's drama in China in the historical and cultural context.

2.2.2 The Critical Reception

The translation and research of Beckett's plays started relatively late in China. Attention being paid to Beckett's drama in China, which began in the late 1970s and the early 1980s, flourished in the 1990s, and fully developed at the turn of the century. In the early days of China, the research of Beckett's drama was mainly focused on absurdism and existentialism, with a single perspective; with the arrival of the climax of Beckett's translation in the 1980s, the study of his works also appeared in various journals.

In the 1980s, restricted by the historical conditions and research vision at that time, there were few researches on Beckett in China, and to some extent, the understanding of the master came from foreign researches. AI maolai's Theatre and film of the absurd: Eugene Eunice and Samuel Beckett (world film, 1982 (06)), Jan Monaco's how to interpret a film (5) — Chapter Six media (world film, 1986 (06)). And Samuel Beckett, a writer of absurdity who is full of disappointment about existentialism, written by Elizabeth B. buz (world culture, 1988 (02)), most of the papers discussed the wilderness in general and discussed the theme of Waiting for Godot, such as tragedy of nothingness and despair by Cui Chengde (foreign literature research, 1985 (03)). There are also comparative studies, such as Ludan's overlapping, parallel and overlapping: Reflections on O'Neill and Beckett's plays (Journal of Jianghan University. 1985 (02), Wang Yanling's pursuit and waiting: a comparison between passers-by and Waiting for Godot, Journal of human studies of Tianjin Normal University, 1987 (04)). Jin Sifeng's Theatre of the absurd and Chinese Theatre of the absurd (foreign literature research, 1989 (04)).

In the early and middle period of 1980s, there were two kind of attitudes towards Beckett's dramas for domestic scholars. On one hand, when it comes to his using absurd forms to represent the social reality of the west, scholars believed that objectively played a role in arousing people from nightmares, so the dramas are the "persuasive" and "positive". But on the other hand, scholars thought that he observed the world from the point of existentialism, so it was negative and not desirable. Because Its obscure works tend to harm people's understanding and transformation of the world. Therefore, we can't copy the artistic technique of Waiting for Godot, but should develop our own national style in the broad background of revolutionary realism and revolutionary romanticism. We must not follow the absurd drama and other modernist culture and art without analysis. On account of Beckett and other absurd writers, they had a great impact on the practice of drama creation in China in the early 1980s. Among the researches, the comparative study of Beckett earlier is another major feature of Beckett study in the Chinese academic circle.

In the 1990s, the researches on Beckett in China go a step further. The angle of studying Waiting for Godot has been expanded. People are no longer obsessed with the judgment of its political value, but hold a positive attitude towards its artistic value. in Waiting for Godot Beckett deeply reflects the spirit of the 20th century western crisis era, and successfully captures the unique fear and confusion of the modern West. His poetic language and refreshing expression make us admire the artist's courage and charm of bold innovation.

The discussion on the theme of Waiting for Godot mainly focuses on the meaning of waiting, the meaning of Godot and the existentialism. In addition, people began to pay attention to the analysis of the artistic form of this work, such as Li Weifang's Circulation: Waiting for Godot, Journal of Henan University, 1993 (02), Zeng Jun's Waiting for Godot and Beckett 's language strategy (Journal of Jingzhou Normal University, 1994 (06)), Sun Yan's hope in tomorrow— on the concept of time in the absurd drama Waiting for Godot (Shanghai artist, 1998 (03)), etc. on the space-time structure in Beckett's dramatic works (Shu Xiaomei, foreign literature research, 1997 (02)), poetic, symmetrical and absurd: the main features of Beckett's dramatic language Waiting for Godot (Shu Xiaomei, foreign literature research, 1998 (01)). There are only two works about Beckett's Novels: one is Lu Yongmao's in the dark kingdom of the subconscious—on Beckett's Novel Molloy (Journal of Henan University, 1995(02)), focusing on Beckett's single works; the other is Hou Weiri's containing truth in Absurdity: on Samuel Beckett's absurdity novel (Journal of Hangzhou University, 1998 (04)) to discuss his novel creation from a macro perspective. At the same time, the scope of comparative study has been expanded. Zeng Jun's "Rhapsody of the absurd world" — from confinement to Waiting for Godot (Journal of Yangtze River anthropology, 1992 (02)), He Changyi's seeking and waiting: the old man and the sea and Waiting for Godot (Journal of Yunnan Institute of people, 1994 (04)).

Since the 20th century, the research on Beckett's drama has gradually enriched from part to whole in the Chinese academic circle, making important breakthroughs in methodology and drama concept; Beckett's centenary birthday in 2006 pushed Beckett's drama research to the climax again, and the multi-perspective and multi-dimensional criticism system for Beckett's drama has basically formed.

Among them, the representative articles are: Ran Dongping (2003) published an artical in foreign literature to discuss Beckett's theory of still drama.; Beckett: the rewriting of the novel by Drama (He Chengzhou, contemporary foreign literature, 2003 (04)) has investigated the cross stylistic characteristics of Beckett's drama from the perspective of intertextuality. The study of Beckett's metadrama (He Chengzhou, contemporary foreign literature, 2004 (03)) discussed the plot characteristics, structural principles, metaphor and other artistic features and innovations of Beckett's drama from the perspective of dramatic structure; the duet of male and female voices in Beckett's Drama — on the last tape of Clapp and happy days (Shen Yan, foreign literature review, 2007(03)) studied Beckett's drama from the perspective of language and art; roar in the skull: spatial analysis of Beckett's Finality (Zhang Shimin, He Shu, foreign language research, 2009 (04)) and others interpreted Beckett's drama from the perspective of time-space relationship; the interpretation of time-space style is a literary criticism methodology with advantages of both form criticism and theme research, which paves the way for further study of complex and obscure drama. Li Danxia (2011), based on the art form of "chaos" and combined with Bakhtin's theory of space-time body, She made a detailed analysis of the time, space and structure of space-time body in Waiting for Godot, revealing the main form of artistic innovation and the uniqueness of space-time structure of Beckett's drama. In the paper of The meta dramatic reference of artistic creation, Liu Lixia (2011) used the meta drama theory to analyze the meta drama reference of Beckett's two plays speech and music and cascanto to the artistic creation itself. In the two plays, Beckett vividly presents two problems in the creation process in the form of drama. One is the relationship between speech expression and emotional expression in the process of creation; the other is the creation mission that perplexes the author himself, which is "unable to continue, but has to continue". Therefore, the two works are about creation. Zhang Yu and Wang Tianhao (2012), through interdisciplinary semiotics research, analyzed Waiting for Godot with the code of time, name, social meaning of objects and characters' behaviors, so as to provide readers with a new interpretation method of drama.

The pragmatic studies of Beckett's plays are mostly from the perspective of relevance theory, such as the absurd effect of Beckett language in Waiting for Godot by Li Lumin and Kang Haihong, and the conversational relevance and absurd theme in Waiting for Godot by Tong Xiaoyan. Wang Shujuan (2012) explored a new research perspective from the key concept presupposition of pragmatics. He analyzes Beckett's drama from the perspective of presupposition in pragmatics and finds that the author constructs an absurd world through the cancelability of presupposition and professional terms, which conveys his philosophy of the world.

In recent years, the whole research of Beckett's drama in China has gained a lot. Liu Aiying, Cao Bo and others have made a stage arrangement and summary of the achievements and main features of Beckett's drama research in China, which is helpful to grasp the trend and direction of Beckett's drama research in China from the macro level.

Generally speaking, the research of Beckett's drama in China has experienced a process from scratch, from small to large, from single to diversified. After a certain period of academic exploration and accumulation, we can finally learn from the essence of the Western Beckett drama research, and the domestic Beckett drama research has basically realized the docking with the western mainstream academia. From the restriction of absurd criticism to the construction of multi criticism system, Beckett's drama research is about to usher in a qualitative leap and that's why the author does the important work of filling in details of existing researches.

III   Analysis of Four Translated Versions in the Viewpoint of Dialogue Theory

This chapter is set to examine four Chinese versions of *Waiting for Godot* by Shi Xianrong, Liao Yuru, Qiu Gangjian and Yu Zhongxian under Bakhtin's dialogue theory. Bakhtin expresses his view of dialogue through the analysis of Dostoevsky's novels, which is an important part of his whole ideological system. "Any utterance, whether spoken or written, that people use in communication with each other is internally dialogic"(72). The most important function of language is its communication function. Bakhtin's study of language in human life and communication reveals the nature of dialogue in language.

What is dialogue? From the general language point of view, as long as there are advices and adoptions with the external form of talking with each other, there is a dialogue, while monologue talking to oneself is not dialogue. From the perspective of poetics, whether it is a dialogue or not does not depend on whether there is an intuitive form of advice, and some monologues can also be a kind of dialogue.

Example 1, Plato's dialogue collection *Critto*:

Socrates: Critto, isn't it early?

Critto: It's still early.

Socrates: About what time?

III Analysis of Four Translated Versions in the Viewpoint of Dialogue Theory

Critto: It's almost dawn.

Example 2, Dostoevsky's *Записки из подполья*:

I am a sick person ... I am a fierce person. An unpleasant person. I think my liver is sick, but I don't know anything about it. No one is sure where I am sick. I have never been to a doctor, and I have never been to a doctor, although I respect medicine and doctors ... No, I don't want to cure because of anger. (translated by the author)

From the perspective of general linguistics, Example 1 is a question-and-answer dialogue, which has an intuitive form of dialogue. From the perspective of poetics, the situation is just the opposite; Example 1 is not a dialogue, but Example 2 is a dialogue. Because dialogue can only be produced in the full presentation of self-awareness, and produced in the process of consciousness itself is not self-sufficient in value, which leads to interrogative words. Example 1 is nothing more than one person saying: I don't know the time, just ask Critto; Another person is saying: I know. I told him to come on. Such a pragmatic dialogue discourse does not have the dialogue function of meta-linguistics at all. It is two monologues with self-sufficient value talking, and it is a monologue in a dialogue environment. Example 2 is a kind of soliloquy in appearance, but it is full of doubts caused by the self-sufficiency of the protagonist's own value. All questions and talks are about the nature of his own existence from various angles. It is a dialogue in a monologue environment. Therefore, from the perspective of poetics, no matter whether the discourse has the intuitive form of dialogue or not, as long as the discourse itself is not self-sufficient and in doubt, it constantly decomposes itself and constantly explains itself, so that such a discourse has the meaning of dialogue. Therefore, we introduce Bakhtin's dialogue theory.

Dialogue first appeared in the *Apology*, Ph. do and Crito. Dialogue thinking is a philosophical way of thinking. Bakhtin expressed his view of dialogue through the analysis of Dostoevsky's novels, which is an important part of his whole ideological system. He stressed that endless dialogue is the only form of resorting to language in real life. He thinks that the formalists focus on how the language of poetry evokes people's new feelings of life, so as to penetrate the consciousness that conceals the truth of existence. Therefore, they pay attention to the signifier of words and make use of the arbitrariness of the signifier to achieve the effect of defamiliarization. For example, a voice of praise and prayer, a burst of passionate singing and a shuddering exclamation, these words must ask people to listen, and cause shock effect. But what can it do for those who don't listen and are not shocked? Therefore, Bakhtin's theory focuses on the "dialogism" of the novel language, hoping to arouse people's listening and recalling through dialogue. Therefore, his theory pays more attention to the signified of words, and makes use of the "difference" of the signified to create an endless process of dialogue. It is precisely because of the differences in the meanings of words that dialogue has an indeterminate character. This is the ultimate meaning of the theory of dialogue. This kind of dialogue in "difference" makes discourse not only express a voice of praise, prayer and exclamation, but also a kind of "conversation" that is constantly negotiated and agreed in the collective, and a kind of "dialogic" language that has gained social significance. Bakhtin believes that this "dialogic relationship is beyond the field of linguistics". Therefore, his central concern is not the phonetic, lexical, grammatical and rhetorical problems in general linguistics, but the language types (i. e. dialogue types) composed of various language materials according to different dialogue angles.

In his opinion, "dialogue" is the natural existence of human-being. "Language can only exist in the dialogue between speaker and listener while dialogue communication is the real existence in language. The entire life of language, no matter which the fields, penetrates the dialogue relationship"(Bakhin, 1988: 224), then "all is attributable to dialogue or dialogue opposition, which is the center of everything. Everything is approach but dialogue is the purpose. A single voice can't finish and also cannot solve. Two voices are not only the minimum conditions of life but also the lowest survival conditions" (Bakhin, 1998: 340). Based on the discourse, "Dialogue" points to the open communicative process between subjects. The nature of dialogue origins from the lack of relationship

III Analysis of Four Translated Versions in the Viewpoint of Dialogue Theory

between "self" and "the other" and often exists in the self-consciousness. In recent years, it has been attached more and more attentions in translation that the achievement in the interpretation of the language nature by the philosophy of language—dialogue theory. The dialogue theory provides a new point of view to translation theories, practices, and the construction of translation criticism.

As we know, translation is a kind of cross language and cross-cultural communication activity, in which the translator plays the role of "intermediary"; this seems to have been a consensus in the field of translation. However, behind this "consensus", there are still a series of problems to be solved: what is the nature of this communication activity? Who participates in it? What is the relationship between the participants? What factors or forces dominate this communication activity? How do these factors or forces affect this communication activity? Linguistic school, functional school and cultural school have given different answers. According to the linguistic school, translation is a process of information transmission through language conversion. The translator is the speaker and spokesman of the author of the original text. He decodes the original text and then encodes it into another language to convey the author's intention to the target readers faithfully and accurately. According to functional school, translation is a purposeful cross-cultural communication behavior authorized by the client or sponsor. According to the translation purpose, the translator chooses the corresponding translation strategy to achieve the specific expected function. The cultural school regards translation as an event of cultural exchange under the macro social, historical and cultural background. The translator manipulates and rewrites the original text under the control of ideology, poetics and patronage. These three schools respectively focus on the study of abstract concepts such as "equivalence", "function" and "norm", emphasizing the restriction of external factors on the translator's translation activities, while neglecting the translator's personal initiative and creativity. Evidence of a lack of dialogic thingking can be found in the following citation:

The mainstream western translation theories only mentioned the ideal condition of translation, but they were away from translation practice and ignored the specific interpersonal interaction in the situation of translation (Robinson 1991: 38-63).

Therefore, "human" is the center of translation studies. From the perspective of practical translation activities, translation is regarded as a dialogue between the author of the original text, the translator and the target readers, crossing the barriers of language and culture. This dialogue is a kind of "double voice" dialogue (Robinson, 2003: 113). "Double-voicedness" is a term used by Bakhtin to describe the language features of the novel. The characteristics of this language are: "it immediately serves two speakers and displays two different intentions. One is the direct intention of the protagonist; the other is the author's intention reflected. There are two voices, two meanings and two modalities in this kind of discourse (Bakhtin, 1998a: 110). Based on Bakhtin's theory, translation is also regarded as an activity event with the characteristics of "double-voicedness"; thus, the translation also shows two different intentions: one is the intention of the author of the original text, the other is the intention of the translator reflected, and the translation also contains two voices, two meanings and two modality. Robinson also uses Bakhtin's Dialogism in chapter two of Translator's Appearance to explain the causes of "double-voicedness" in translation dialogue. These reasons can be summarized as follows: (1) language has "intrinsic dialogism" and "Self discourse" is always intertwined with "other's discourse". Discourse exists and forms in the dialogic environment, and the speaker does not fully possess the meaning. Bakhtin pointed out that discourse lies in other people's discourse and contains the intention of dialogue: "in fact, language, as the real and concrete existence of social thought, at the same time as the opinion of miscellaneous language, is of great significance to individual consciousness. It is at the juncture between self and others. Half of every word in a language is someone else's word. It is only when the speaker adds his own intention, his own intonation, and grasps it, so that it can acquire its own meaning and modality, then the word can become its own. Before becoming its own, a word does not exist in a neutral and impersonal language; it lives on the mouth of others, in the context of others, and serves the intention of others." (Bakhtin, 1998a: 74) Since words do not belong to anyone and are not private property that can be distributed, stolen or infringed upon, but can be freely circulated in the dialogic public sphere, there is no pure, perfect and ideal boundary or correspondence between texts. Therefore, the translator cannot establish the objective text equivalence or reader response equivalence between the original text and the target text (Robinson, 1991: 101-104). In this way, Robinson dispels the ideal pursuit of "equivalence" in traditional translation theory, and highlights the individuality of the translation, that is, the translator's personality and voice. (2) The "inherent dialogism" of language determines that understanding is not "copying" but dialogue. Bakhtin believes that discourse is always targeted, and any expression of the speaker is aimed at getting an answer. Therefore, it is inevitable to guess the response of the hearer and organize this conjecture into his own expression in advance: "the real speech in conversation, a direct and unabashed reply that points the target to the next step. It stimulates answers, guesses answers, and organizes itself by taking into account replies. Discourse is formed in the atmosphere of what has been said, and at the same time, it is determined by the unanticipated reply. This is true of all realistic dialogues." (Bakhtin, 1998a: 59) in this sense, any expression seems to be a mini dialogue, in which the speaker's interpretation of "what has been said", the speaker's new intention, and the listener's "reply" in speculation all exist in the expression. Therefore, to understand the text—to understand the author's expression—is to enter the context of dialogue in the text. Understanding is not to passively understand the literal meaning of text symbols, but to actively dialogue with the author, ask questions to the author and respond or agree or refute the author, reach agreement with the author on some issues, gain understanding, and incorporate what is understood into his own things and emotional world. The translator's understanding of the original text is the same. Therefore, this book emphasizes that the translator talks with the author of the original text. At this time, the translator no longer regards the original text as the object, but as the subject. The relationship between the translator and the original text is no longer "I-it" (subject-object) mode, but "I-You" (subject-subject) mode. The original text is no longer the object of the translator's experience and utilization, but a partner of equal dialogue with the translator (Robinson, 1991: 96). (3) The translator is not a neutral and impersonal tool for language conversion. The inherent dialogism of language determines that the translator's voice can only be suppressed or covered up, but not completely eliminated. Traditional translation theories tend to regard the translation as a kind of "object language". The task of the translator is merely to convey the words of the original author in another language. The translator should not mix his own voice with the voice of the original author. In fact, it's just an illusion. Before translating, the translator should first understand and interpret the original text, and if he wants to understand and interpret the original text, the translation will inevitably appear the feature of "double voice". According to Bakhtin's Dialogic theory, understanding "other people's words" is to transform other people's words into self's "others' words"; Bakhtin's dialogical thinking about their relationship is right on the nail: "after other's words are incorporated into our own language, we must get a new understanding, that is, our understanding and evaluation of things, that is to say, to turn them into two-voice words." (Bakhtin, 1998b: 258)

Therefore, this book will adopt the dialogue theory which is not only a mode of artistic thinking, also a kind of philosophy and humanistic spirit to analyze the drama translation.

This book holds the view that this philosophy of language starts from the social attributes. This book delves into the philosophy of language, tracing its roots to social attributes. Emphasizing language symbols, it transcends the confines of modern linguistics, venturing into the realm of endless dialogue. At its core lies the belief that everything—our thoughts, interactions, and existence—ultimately boils down to dialogue. Modern linguistics dissects language into systematic structures, formal logic, and grammatical rules. But this philosophy dares to venture beyond those boundaries. It recognizes that language is not a sterile construct; it breathes,

III Analysis of Four Translated Versions in the Viewpoint of Dialogue Theory

evolves, and thrives through human interaction. Bakhtin's assertion— "Everything comes down to dialogue and is attributed to dialogue" (Bakhtin, 198b: 338)—resonates. Dialogue, here, transcends ordinary conversation. All about this theory is about "dialogue", but here the dialogue does not necessarily refer to the ordinary conversation. It emerges from real-life verbal exchanges—the banter, the debates, the shared silences. This everyday communication becomes an abstract literary term. Dialogue, fundamentally, is a dance between "self" and "the other". It mirrors our relationships, our conflicts, and our shared humanity. Whether spoken or unspoken, dialogue reflects our inner dialogues—the conversations we have with ourselves. In literature, dialogue becomes a powerful tool. Characters converse, revealing their depths, their desires, and their contradictions. The form of dialogue—the pauses, the interruptions, the subtext—shapes our understanding of the narrative. Each choice—the nuances, the idioms, the rhythm—creates a double-voiced text. The hermeneutic cycle continues.

In recent years, dialogue theory has emerged as a powerful lens for understanding language. By delving into the philosophy of dialogue, it sheds light on translation, offering fresh perspectives and enriching the field. This book embraces dialogue theory, recognizing it not only as an artistic mode of thinking but also as a profound humanistic spirit. Dialogue theory transcends linguistic analysis. It delves into the essence of communication—the interplay of voices, perspectives, and shared humanity.

As we translate, we engage in a dialogue—a dance between source and target languages. The characters' voices echo across cultural boundaries. Translation theories often focus on linguistic fidelity. Dialogue theory shifts our gaze. It invites us to consider not just words but the spaces between them. How do characters converse? What nuances lie in their pauses, interruptions, and subtext? These questions become our compass. Dialogue, here, extends beyond ordinary conversation. It becomes a form of artistic expression—a canvas for cultural negotiation.

As we analyze drama translation, we recognize that the translator is both artist and philosopher. Each choice—the rhythm, the idioms, the stage directions—shapes the narrative. Characters' dialogues reveal their depths—their desires, fears, and contradictions. The stage, too, becomes a character—an active participant in the drama.

By examining both, we unravel the threads of meaning. How does language perform on stage? How do characters' voices resonate? In this exploration, dialogue theory becomes our guide—a lantern illuminating the path. In the following, it explores examinations related with characters' dialogues and the stage description.

3.1　Characters' Dialogues

As a literary genre, drama is mainly composed of two parts: dramatic dialogue and stage description. With the help of dialogues, the playwright depicts various characters showing their psychological activities to reveal their inner world. Dramatic dialogue has different language expressions, for example: dialogues and monologues. These two expressions are selected by this book to prove characters' dialogues in *Waiting for Godot* of four Chinese translations which have the feature of double-voicedness. Act one of this play is filled with the dialogues between Estragon and Vladimir when they are waiting for Godot beside a bare tree. They start to talk when they meet each other. While waiting, they talk about the two thieves crucified at the same time as Jesus Christ, recall their old days, argue for whether they are waiting for Godot or not, comment on the taste of turnips and quarrel with the order for hanging. Estragon continuously tries to take off his boot and pulls it with his hands, while Vladimir continuously takes off his hat and peers at it as if there was something inside.

III Analysis of Four Translated Versions in the Viewpoint of Dialogue Theory

In the desolate landscape of *Waiting for Godot*, Vladimir and Estragon—two vagrants—engage in a poignant dance of contrasts. Their interactions reveal not only their individual quirks but also the essence of human existence. Vladimir, the thinker, clings to the past. Memories haunt him—the echoes of better days, lost hopes, and unfulfilled promises. His mind is a repository of moments—both joyous and painful. He weaves narratives, seeking meaning in the fragments of time.

Vladimir's remembrance contrasts Estragon's Forgetfulness. Estragon, on the other hand, lives in the present. His memory is fleeting—a butterfly flitting from flower to flower. Each moment slips through his fingers, leaving no trace. He forgets as soon as it happens, like sand slipping through an hourglass. Estragon shares his dreams—fragments of imagination, perhaps an escape from their bleak reality. But Vladimir cannot bear to listen. Dreams, like memories, are ephemeral. They tease us with possibilities, then vanish into the recesses of our minds. Estragon grows weary of life's monotony. The food, the routines—they all become tiresome. His impatience mirrors our own. Vladimir, pragmatic, adapts. He gets used to things—the tasteless meals, the endless waiting. Survival demands resilience. Estragon claims to be a poet—a dreamer, perhaps. His words flutter like leaves in the wind. But Vladimir, more grounded, feels the weight of their poverty—their empty pockets, their threadbare existence. While waiting, they meet two passers-bies, Pozzo and his slave Lucky. Pozzo, the talker, engages with the vagrants. His words flow, filling the void. Lucky, tied to a rope, dances and thinks. His words, however, prove meaningless—chronic echoes of emptiness. In this existential dance, Vladimir and Estragon embody our contradictions—the longing for meaning, the struggle against forgetfulness, and the absurdity of existence.

Samuel Beckett set the main characters in *Waiting for Godot* as two pairs—Gogo and Didi,[①] Pozzo and Lucky. These two pairs form a cooperative and dialogic relationship with the characters, however, the dialogues in the whole play

---

① Gogo is Estragon and Didi is Vladimir.

are absurd and unconventional. In other words, the dialogues seem to have not connected with each other in meaning. As Esslin points out, absurdist plays can only "be reflections of dreams and nightmares" (13). Accordingly, the dialogues of the characters are incoherent babblings. The following is a good example to show the dialogue is impossible to convey any significant meaning.

ST:

Estragon: Taking off my boot. Did that never happen to you?

Vladimir: Boots must be taken off every day, I'm tired telling you that. Why don't you listen to me?

Estragon: (feebly). Help me!

Vladimir: It hurts?

Estragon: (angrily). Hurts! He wants to know if it hurts! (Beckett: 13)

The above quotation takes a common question-answer form between Estragon and Vladimir. Their special relationship brings a certain psychological fluctuation in their speech. As their dialogue though seems to be not communicative, disclose their psychological state. It is one of the major features of dramatic dialogues. In this quotation, Estragon tries to take off his boots but failed for several times, so he asks Vladimir for help. However, Vladimir doesn't do him a favor. Instead, he asks Estragon a question "It hurts?". For this declarative clause Estragon becomes angry when he hears what Vladimir has said. But he doesn't answer Vladimir's question directly. On the contrary, he also uses a declarative clause to express his great anger. His behavior irritates Vladimir and he complains that Estragon is not the only one that suffers from pain. Surprisingly, Estragon shows great interests in his sufferings and asks Vladimir the same question by using the same declarative clause. This time, it's Vladimir's turn to express his strong emotion by using a declarative clause. In this example, the declarative clauses used by Vladimir and Estragon are not functioning as statements. They are used to ask questions and express strong emotions. From this example, we can see that their relationship is

III   Analysis of Four Translated Versions in the Viewpoint of Dialogue Theory

not so harmonious. This also results in the failure of their conversation.

Correspondingly, comparing the practices of four Chinese versions, we found that translator's subjectivity in drama translation activities. The four Chinese versions rearrange "the composition of the translation subject and the space of the subject's communication" (Han Jia 1).

TT1:[①]

Estragon: take off your shoes. Have you never taken off your shoes?（艾斯特岗：脱鞋子。你从来没有脱过鞋子吗？）

Vladimir: shoes have to be taken off every day. How many times have I told you, why don't you always listen?（维拉迪米尔：鞋子必须每天脱，跟你说多少次了，你为什么总是不听呢？）

Estragon: (feebly.) help.（艾斯特岗（虚弱地。）帮帮忙。）

Vladimir: Does it hurt?（维拉迪米尔：痛吗？）

Estragon: Pain! He wants to know if it hurts!（艾斯特岗：痛！他想知道我是不是会痛！）(89)

TT2:

Estragon: I'm taking off my shoes. You, have you never taken off your shoes?（爱斯特拉贡：我在脱我的鞋。你，你难道从来就没有脱过鞋？）

Vladimir: I told you a long time ago that you have to take off your shoes every day. You should have listened to me.（弗拉第米尔：我早就对你说过，鞋子是要每天都脱的。你本该好好地听我的话的。）

Estragon: (faintly) help me!（爱斯特拉贡：（微弱地）帮帮我吧！）

Vladimir: Does your foot hurt?（弗拉第米尔：你脚疼吗？）

[①] TT1 is a Chinese version of *Waiting for Godot* translated by Liao Yuru. TT2 is translated by Yu Zhongxian, TT3 is translated by Shi Xianrong and TT4 is translated by Qiu Gangjiang.

Estragon: Feet hurt! He's asking me if my feet hurt!（爱斯特拉贡：脚疼！他在问我是不是脚疼！）(254)

Yu uses a simple statement, "You should have listened to me（你本该好好听我的话的）" (254), to translate the sentence "Why don't you listen to me?" (Beckett: 13). Here, the interrogative sentence becomes a declarative sentence which implies negative emotion. It implies three transformations:

Firstly, it refers to grammatical transformation. The original sentence—"Why don't you listen to me?"—is an interrogative, questioning why the other person doesn't heed the speaker's words. Such a sentence structure often carries expectations, dissatisfaction, or even reproach.

Yu's translation, however, rephrases it into a declarative statement: "You should have listened to me." This shift implies a stronger emotional charge—perhaps disappointment, anger, or frustration.

Secondly, it refers to emotional implications. In the translated phrase, the use of "should" conveys both expectation and a sense of responsibility. It suggests that the other person has violated an expected behavioral norm, evoking feelings of discontent.

By selectively omitting the interrogative part of the original question, Yu emphasizes the speaker's stance. The transformation turns what was once a neutral inquiry into a more emotionally charged assertion.

Last is cultural and contextual considerations. In Chinese, transitions between declarative and interrogative sentences are more common. The language allows for nuanced expression of tone and emotion through different sentence structures.

Yu's translation likely aligns with the communication norms and emotional expressions familiar to Chinese readers.

In summary, Yu's choice of translation goes beyond mere grammar—it reflects an emotional decision. By transforming an interrogative into a declarative, he conveys heightened emotions, making the other person's lack of listening even more palpable.

III Analysis of Four Translated Versions in the Viewpoint of Dialogue Theory

TT3:

Estragon: Take off your boots. Have you never taken off your boots?（爱斯特拉冈：脱靴子。你难道从来没脱过靴子？）

Vladimir: I have to take off my boots every day, Do I have to tell you? Why don't you listen to me?（弗拉季米尔：靴子每天都要脱，难道还要我来告诉你？你干吗不好好听我说话？）

Estragon: (feebly) help me!（爱斯特拉冈（无力地）帮帮我！）

Vladimir: Does your foot hurt?（弗拉季米尔: 你脚疼？）

Estragon: Feet hurt! He also wants to know if my feet hurt!（爱斯特拉冈：脚疼！他还要知道我是不是脚疼！）（5）

As described, Shi's affirmative mood is the strongest. He uses two rhetorical questions "Do I have to tell you? Why don't you listen to me? (难道还要我来告诉你?你干吗不好好听我说话?)" (5) to translate the sentences "I'm tired telling you that. Why don't you listen to me?" (Beckett: 13). Rhetorical question uses interrogative sentence pattern to express affirmative views. The rhetorical question seems to be the form of question, but in fact it expresses the affirmative meaning, and the answer lies in the question. The form of rhetorical question is more intense than the general declarative sentence, which can make people to examine their own conscience to a higher degree.

Shi's translation approach wields rhetorical questions as a potent tool, amplifying the affirmative mood. By rendering the sentences "I'm tired telling you that. Why don't you listen to me?" into "Do I have to tell you? Why don't you listen to me?", Shi masterfully captures the essence of the original while infusing it with emotional intensity.

Here, the translation takes rhetorical questions as affirmative expressions. Rhetorical questions, despite their interrogative form, convey affirmation rather than seeking answers. They serve as powerful statements, implying that the answer is self-evident.

In this case, Shi's choice to transform the declarative sentences into rhetorical questions elevates the emotional impact. The implied answer lies within the question itself, leaving no room for doubt.

At the same time, it demonstrates intensity and self-examination. The rhetorical question form is more intense than straightforward declarative sentences. It compels readers to engage with their own conscience, prompting introspection.

When Shi asks, "Do I have to tell you?" and follows it with "Why don't you listen to me?"—the emotional weight is palpable. The frustration, weariness, and disappointment of the speaker resonate deeply.

Cultural nuances and translation choices also are clarified. Shi's decision aligns with cultural norms and language conventions. In Chinese, rhetorical questions are commonly used to express strong opinions or emphasize a point.

By employing this technique, Shi captures the original speaker's exasperation and emphasizes the failure of communication. The translated dialogue becomes a mirror, reflecting the listener's own actions.

In summary, Shi's skillful use of rhetorical questions transforms a mundane exchange into a charged moment. The affirmative undertones and self-reflective nature of these questions invite readers to consider their own behavior. Through translation, Shi bridges linguistic gaps while preserving emotional depth.

TT4:

Love: Take off your boots, have you never taken off?（爱：脱靴子，你从来没脱过吗？）

Buddha: Boots must be taken off every day, I'm in no mood to tell you, why don't you always listen to me?（佛：靴子必须每天脱的，我真没精神告诉你，为什么你总不听我的话？）

Love: (feebly) help!（爱：(虚弱地) 帮帮忙！）

Buddha: Does it hurt?（佛：痛吗？）

Love: (angrily) pain! He even wanted to know if it hurt!（爱：(气愤地) 痛！他竟然还想知道痛不痛！）(5)

III Analysis of Four Translated Versions in the Viewpoint of Dialogue Theory

Qiu's translation is the one with the least number of words but also the one most faithful to the original. He uses "I'm in no mood to tell you（我真没精神告诉你）" (5) to translate the sentence "I'm tired telling you that" (Beckett: 13). Their questions and answers seem so daily, but each sentence is full of complex psychological activities. Because in the dramatic dialogue, the utterance of the characters has intention, which can only be interpreted through the context. Furthermore, according to ROST EA 1.9.0.4[①], four versions of this passage all show negative emotions.

Table 3.1 Emotions

	TT1	TT2	TT3	TT4
Positive emotion [5, +∞)	0	0	0	0
Neutral emotion [-5, 5)	0	0	0	0
Negative emotion [-∞, 5)	4	3	2	1

Table 3.2 Negative Emotions

The statistical results of negative emotions are as follows	TT1	TT2	TT3	TT4
Low [-15, 5)	4	3	1	0
Medium [-35, -15)	0	0	1	1
High [-∞, -35)	0	0	0	0

Among them, there are four negative procedural words with Liao's version, three negative procedural words in Yu's version, two negative procedural words in Shi's version and one in Qiu's version. Among them, in Qiu's version the quarrel is

---

① One of the Rost series of big data computing tools for Humanities and Social Sciences Research.

far more heated than Shi's one reproducing the bitter battle between the two persons, while Shi's one is more heated than Yu's version. Liao softens her tone a little.

The above results confirm the finding that the four translators show their intention. It demonstrates different translations have the characteristics of double-voiceness. When decoding the relationship, the translator should be a careful listener, listening to the author and show their emotions. Translators could be considered as the creator of "double-voiced discourse" in the process of creative translation. Specifically speaking, they could replace the original voice with someone else's words based on the faithfulness to the source text, in an attempt to accurately convey the textual meaning.

A similar view is pointed by other scholars with the differences lie in the literature criticism. In the literature study, according to Bakhtin's Dialogic theory, restricted by various factors, the author's voice cannot be interpreted directly. The application of someone else's words with double-voiced discourse is useful to tackle such predicaments. The author creates double-voiced discourse in the course of literary creation. Bakhtin's dialogical thinking about their relationship is right on the nail: "after other's words are incorporated into our own language, we must get a new understanding, that is, our understanding and evaluation of things, that is to say, to turn them into two-voice words" (258). Furthermore, Michael Holquist et al, raise the point that "dialogue is ultimately a differential relation" (39).

Those scholar's opinions about literature criticism are consistent with this book's view that dialogic translation process bears the essence of being a relation. It convinces the translators rebuild the relations by their own translation method. The above four versions are chosen to provide a view on different reconstruction effects of sentence pattens and word choices. These translated versions show different emotional relationship between Estragon and Vladimir. The implied messages, just like voiceless invitations from the author, inspire translators to read between the lines and grope for the author's inner world.

We have verified that dialogues' translations produce "double-voiced discourse" in the dialogical translation process. The monologues translated by

III Analysis of Four Translated Versions in the Viewpoint of Dialogue Theory

the four translators also can prove this "double-voiced discourse". The following analyses intend to testify the "double-voiced discourse" in translation of the monologues. The definition of monologue by Merriam-Webster[①] is like this: "Monologue from Greek monos" alone "and" to speak "may also refer to a dramatic scene in which an actor soliloquizes, but it has other meanings as well. To a stand-up comedian, monologue denotes a comic routine"[②]. In monologues, the lyric characters are weakened and replaced by morbid characters that are tortured by split-self. They are in the state of self worship, self-compulsion and self-deception. In a broad sense, monologue mainly refers to the main characters' statements of their inner views or ideas in the process of performance. When the actor continues the monologues, monologues are focused on the stage.

The monologues are concentrated on the absurd drama. The theatre of the absurd rises in the 1950s and reaches its peak in the 1960s. Absurd drama provides a new perspective to deal with Second World War-related issues. After the Second World War, God no longer exists, old beliefs collapse, and good hopes and ideals are shattered. The world is unpredictable and society is disturbing. The survivors of the war, stroking the scars of the war, began to reflect painfully, and held a negative attitude towards the traditional values and the existing order. The spiritual support of the past has disintegrated and new beliefs have not yet been found. This spiritual emptiness is reflected on literature and art, which naturally forms a meaningless, absurd and useless theme. Being placed in this change, individuals are isolated not only from the outside world but also from themselves, so they inevitably feel a sense of loss and alienation. The book states that the nightmare of World War II has just passed. and the war has left an incurable wound to the soul of a whole generation.

---

① For more than 150 years, in print and now online, Merriam-Webster has been America's leading and most-trusted provider of language information.
② "Monologue." Merriam-Webster. com Dictionary, Merriam-Webster, https://www. merriam-webster. com/dictionary/monologue. Accessed 10 Jun. 2021.

The same opinions also can be found in other scholars' book. Life has in Adorno's words, "changed into a timeless succession of shocks, interspaced with empty, paralysed intervals" (P. Crosthwaite: 62). According to Allison and Alexander W "everything including a resurrected culture, has been destroyed without realizing it; humankind continues to vegetate, creeping along after events that even the survivors cannot really survive, on a rubbish heap that has made reflection on one's own damaged state useless" (241). All of the opinions are implied in the theatre of the absurd.

As one of the representative works of the theatre of the absurd, *waiting for Godot* is famous for its unconnected dialogues and monologues to reveal the absurdity. In monologues, the lyric characters are weakened and replaced by morbid characters who are tortured by split-self. They are in the state of self worship, self-compulsion and self-deception. In a broad sense, dramatic monologue mainly refers to the main characters' statements of their inner views or ideas in the process of performance. At that time, monologue is in the focus of the stage. In the narrow sense, soliloque refers to the monologue set up by Shakespeare for the characters in his plays. For example, in the tragedy Hamlet, there are more than ten monologues, either long or short. Shakespeare's monologue, mostly involving metaphysical philosophical discussions, is profound and enlightening. In the works of modern classical absurd dramas, dramatic monologue still plays a very important role.

Dramatic monologue refers to the words that the characters in the drama or literary works express their personal feelings and wishes alone, which can also be understood as the words expressed by the characters alone in the drama. It can fully display the characters' thoughts and characters and make readers understand the characters' thoughts, feelings and spiritual outlook. This is not only in drama, but also in various literary works. As a genre term, dramatic monologue originated from Browning's poetry and poetry theory in the Victorian period and was not widely used until the beginning of the 20th century. "Dramatic monologue" was first proposed in 1857. A poet named George W. Thornbury, who was deeply

III Analysis of Four Translated Versions in the Viewpoint of Dialogue Theory

influenced by Browning, called his series of poems collected in Songs of Cavaliers and Roundheads and Jacobite Ballads as "dramatic monologues", but did not have a wide influence (A. D. Culler, "monodrama" 366). Victorians generally refer to such poems as "spiritual monologue" and "psychological monologue" (FAAS 20), rather than "dramatic monologue"; Browning, known as the "great psychological master", although repeatedly uses "dramatic" to name his poetry collection, such as Dramatic Love Poems, Dramatic Romantic Legends and Lyric poems, Dramatic Figures and Dramatic Pastoral Poems often refer to "monologue" in their letters, but "dramatic monologue" has never been used. It was not until 1886 that Tennyson, the poet laureate, used "dramatic monologue" in his dedication to the poem Locksley Hall Six Years After. The influence of Tennyson made the term spread, and the critic Stopford Brooke used it to study Tennyson in his 1894 monograph. In 1897, Austin Dobson included "dramatic monologue" in the second edition of the Handbook of English literature, marking the formal establishment of the term (A. D. Culler, "monodrama" 366). At the beginning of the 20th century, a large number of achievements specialized in dramatic monologues were produced, such as Browning and the Dramatic Monologue (1908) by Samuel S. curry and Browning's Dramatic Monologues by Robert H. Fletcher (1908), Claude Howard's The Dramatic Monologue: Its Origin and Development (1910) and The Dramatic Monologue in Victorian period (1925) by M. W. MacCallum. It was not until 1947 that the most systematic research paper appeared, namely, The Dramatic Monologue by Ina Beth Sessions. In fact, a large number of studies have explained the obscurity of "dramatic monologue". John Stuart Mill's definition of lyric poetry vaguely contains the shadow of dramatic monologue: "eavesdropping" implies the speaker's unconscious self exposure and the silent listener (second consciousness) present (Essay on poetry 12). Abrams's definition of lyric poetry is also applicable to dramatic monologue: "a particular speaker is in a specific environment", and the speaker "speaks alone, sometimes to himself, sometimes to the outside scenery, but more often there is a human listener present or absent" (The Lyric as Poetic Form 89). In his monograph "Poetry

Of Experience: Dramatic Monologue In Modern Literary Tradition", Lampoon pointed out that the research focus shifted from objective criteria to internal reflection of readers. He pointed out that as long as the contradictory experience of readers can be aroused— "sympathy and criticism" (85), there is no doubt that Lampoon's way of examining dramatic monologue from the psychological perspective is correct. Whether it is the introspection of romantic lyric poetry in self exploration, or the social environment of Victoria, psychological attention is the dominant factor. The sharp social conflict is another reason for the rise of Victorian dramatic monologue. Victorian society is at the crossroads of history. Under the impact of industrial civilization, social structure, morality, religion, family and other authoritative value systems have been disintegrated. Mueller recognized that in this era, "human development has gone beyond the old system and the old dogma, and the new has not yet formed" (QTd. In Houghton 1). On the one hand, the speed of social development far exceeds the individual's psychological endurance. Mark Twain, an American writer, rightly commented: "Britain has a history of two thousand years, but many changes have taken place since the birth of the queen equal to the sum of its changes in 2000 years" (QTd. In Abrams and Greenblatt, 1833). Being placed in this change, individuals are isolated not only from the outside world but also from themselves (lanugbaum, Poe 12), so they will inevitably feel a sense of loss and alienation.

This situation also applies to the illogical monologue in the absurd drama. The theatre of the absurd rose in the 1950s and reached its peak in the 1960s. The nightmare of World War II has just passed. The war has left an incurable wound to the soul of a whole generation. God no longer exists, old beliefs collapse, and good hopes and ideals are shattered. The world is unpredictable and society is disturbing. The survivors of the war, stroking the scars of the war, began to reflect painfully, and held a negative attitude towards the traditional values and the existing order. The spiritual support of the past has disintegrated and new beliefs have not yet been found. This spiritual emptiness is reflected in literature and art, which naturally forms a meaningless, absurd and useless theme。

III Analysis of Four Translated Versions in the Viewpoint of Dialogue Theory

There are three monologues in this play. Pozzo's monologue expresses his feelings, but language and emotion are running in different directions. He has to build a bridge of communication language to cross the abyss. However, when he builds it in front, and the bridge collapses at the back. Pozzo has to cross the abyss just as the bridge collapses. When Pozzo crosses the bridge, he finds that his lyrical ode to the evening has turned into an elegy about extinction. In the orthodox speech, language and emotion are consistent, thus producing great appeals. In Pozzo's speech, because of the inconsistency between the two of language and emotion, the monologue becomes stiff and unnatural.

Didi also makes a monologue speech like Pozzo in the second act, and in the end, he collapses. The result of the grand plan he announced has failed. The language here tries to surpass itself and put into action, but it is trapped in the quagmire of language itself. Lucky's monologue, though not unique, has never been performed before in the history of Western Theater. There are no broken sentences in about ten minutes, and most of them are long speeches that are difficult to form sentences. It is a great test not only for the actors to perform in an increasingly urgent tone but also for the audience. When it comes to Bakhtin, dialogic thinking penetrates into all discourse. Hence, any discourse has a lineage in the life and in the context of the dialogue. No matter how it looks as a monologue, the discourse actually responds to others' words. Therefore, from this perspective, the four translators deal with such monologues with meaning. Sometimes, they transfer the meaningless sentences as epigrams. Suddenly a surprising epigram will light up the drama translation. The translators tattoo the Chinese readers with epigrams to express oneself in or as if in aphorisms. Such as: "但是，问题并不在这里。我们在这里做什么，这才是我们必须问我们自己","我们不是圣人，但我们如约而至。"有机会时，我们就做点事，不是每天都有人需要我们". This book focuses on the analysis of the most representative monologue among the three monologues-Lucky's monologue translation.

In the history of Western Theater, Lucky's monologue, though not unique, has never been performed before. There are no broken sentences in about ten minutes, and most of them are long speeches that are difficult to form sentences. It is a great test not only for the actors but also for the audience to perform in an increasingly urgent tone. "This kind of long speech, which was popular in concert hall entertainment in the early 20th century, was often a parody of pseudo professors and pseudo politicians, philosophical nonsense and scientific nonsense" (Hutchings: 33-34; Esslin, 1961: 69). Just as he used to use specious content to create more interpretation space, Beckett also deliberately blurred the seriousness of Lucky words by clown style performance. These parody languages may be difficult to understand on stage, but they succeed in creating theatrical effects in performance. Because luck, after a long silence, suddenly gushed out his words, supplemented by the exaggerated pantomime performance of the other three people, created an extremely shocking power.

Lucky's monologue is a kind of parody. "This kind of long speech, which was popular in concert hall entertainment in the early 20th century, was often a parody of pseudo professors and pseudo politicians, philosophical nonsense and scientific nonsense" (Esslin: 69). Just as he used to use specious content to create more interpretation space, Beckett also deliberately blurs the seriousness of Lucky words by clown style performance. These parody languages may be difficult to understand on stage, but they success in creating theatrical effects on performance. Because Lucky, after a long silence, suddenly gushes out his words, supplemented by the exaggerated pantomime performance of the other three people, created an extremely shocking power. This book focuses on the analysis of Lucky's monologue translation which is the most representative monologue among the three monologues.

ST:

Lucky: Given the existence as uttered forth in the public works of Puncher and Wattmann of a personal God quaquaquaqua with white beard quaquaquaqua outside time without extension who from the heights of divine apathia divine athambia divine aphasia loves us dearly with some exceptions

III Analysis of Four Translated Versions in the Viewpoint of Dialogue Theory

>for reasons unknown but time will tell and suffers like the divine Miranda ... by the Acacacacademy of Anthropopopometry of Essy-in-Possy of Testew and Cunard it is established beyond all doubt all other doubt than that which clings tennis ... the stones ... so calm ... Cunard ... unfinished ... (Beckett 60)

The specific discussion of Lucky's monologue is as follows: his monologue has 105 words, nearly half of these which are nouns. These monologues, which are often repeated words and sentences are not organized, are just the expression of Beckett's ingenuity. If we study the content carefully, we find that the Lucky monologue seems to be the epitome of the whole play. "Like vagabonds, Lucky stuttering words are also a sign of memory loss" (Gilroy, James: 25). Beckett, who personally directed the play in Berlin in 1974, told the actors that Lucky's monologue had three main themes: cold God, shrinking human beings and merciless nature. The God in the mouth of Lucky, who is holy and indifferent, at the same time, the God is always silent with a white beard, just like the Godot described by the little boy. He loves human beings, but there are exceptions with unknown reasons.

On the other hand, man's physical strength and energy are shrinking, leaving only the head; just like the waning body of a tramp, time has left traces on human beings. People's life is exhausted, and the final legacy are the cold and merciless nature. Why humans suffer from this torture is unknown, but time to give the answer. Just like a tramp waiting for an answer that has been delayed forever, Godot "will not come today, but will come tomorrow"(Beckett: 67). Lucky's parody monologue contains profound philosophical thoughts on life. Even readers find that Lucky has revealed in his speech that Didi and GoGo have been waiting for answers for a long time. As for Lucky's monologue, the four translators have their own understanding and interpretation, showing four different characteristics.

For the above Lucky's monologues, different translators make them have the characteristics of "double-voicedness". "Double-voicedness" is a term used by Bakhtin to describe the language features of the novel. The characteristics of this language are: "it immediately serves two speakers and displays two different intentions. One is the direct intention of the protagonist; the other is the author's intention reflected. There are two voices, two meanings and two modalities in this kind of discourse" (Bakhtin: 110). This term is borrowed by the book to explain the result of the dialogical translation process. Dialogic thinking penetrates into all discourse. Hence, any discourse has a lineage in the life and in the context of the dialogue. No matter how it looks as a monologue, the discourse actually responds to others' words. Translators deal with such monologues by giving meaning. That is because human is the center of translation studies. We can say this translating is a kind of "double voice" dialogue. The translation shows two different intentions: one is the intention of the original author; the other is the intention of the translator. A detailed double-voicedness examination of the four versions of Lucky's monologues is showed in the following contents.

TT1:

The work published by Boncho and Watmon expresses private gods, with white beards, with the existence beyond time and space, divine indifference, divine calmness, divine aphasia, and deep love for us. Some exceptions are unknown, but time will explain why we suffer like a holy Miranda. Unknown but time will tell.（邦喬和瓦特蒙出版的作品表現私人上帝以以以以白鬍子以以以以超越時空的存在神聖冷漠神聖冷靜神聖失語深愛我們某些例外原因不明不過時間會說明受苦如聖潔的米蘭達原因不明不過時間會說明。）(53)

When it comes to Liao's version, she makes the parody by the references from the original author. In the process of interpretation, when the translator gets the drama first, he reads it over and over to get the spirit and then he expresses the imitation of the source text with his own voice. This kind of translation lies in the fact of the footnotes. For instance: "'Fartov' means fart; 'Belcher' is an abusive word. These two words are written in capitals intentionally and they are taken as

III Analysis of Four Translated Versions in the Viewpoint of Dialogue Theory

proper nouns. Therefore, they are directly translated into 'huā tou(花头)' and 'bài chē ér(败车儿)' with a sense of banter" (54). Moreover, Liao says "Contending" has the meaning of effort, desire and planning. The translator says Beckett used that word to match with sports names, such as running, cycling, swimming, flying, floating, riding, gliding, but in fact that word is not a name of sports. It is taken just as a parody (54-55). Therefore, the translator translates it as" Try hard (考努力).

In addition, Liao notes that for the four words "Feckham", "Peckham", "Fulham" and "Clapham", the last three words are places, located in the suburb of London. The first word is just a new word that Beckett created by the homophony of the last three words (55). Just like the words mentioned in the previous two examples, these words also are translated as a parody of source text deliberately by the translator. In the source text, Lucky, as a lower-class servant, his words and deeds are appropriately in accordance with his social attributes. His monologues show his state of mind at the moment being drunk and raving. "The human being in the novel is first, foremost and always speaking human being; the novel requires speaking persons bringing with them their own ideological discourse, their own language" (Bakhtin: 332).

In the process of translation, Liao's language imitation results in such a fact that this seemingly insignificant character utters his unique voice in this capacious literary world and also contributes to the author's overall design of the play. Liao creates a profound organic bond between the most superficial elements of a character's manner of speech, the form in which he expresses himself, and the ultimate foundations of his world view. The translator imitates the monologues of Lucky and models Lucky as "the character tells the reader what they need to know, but meanwhile he plays himself" (Booth: 59). This kind of imitation expresses confused or ambiguous words as they are. It also points out the difficulties in understanding the original text and the fuzziness in expression. Such translation reflects the facts.

TT2:

Fortunately: (Shards of Monologue) Just as Powanson and Watman's recent public utilities have shown itself, a white-bearded quack-sniffing God himself. Sniffing, transcending time, transcending space, does exist in his divine numbness. Holy madness. His sacred height of aphasia loves us deeply, except for a few exceptions. We don't know why, but he will come and follow the sacred Miranda beside the people.（幸运儿：（独白碎片）恰如普万松和瓦特曼新近公共事业的存在本身所显示的那样一个白胡子的嘎嘎嗅的上帝本人嗅嗅嘎超越时间超越空间确确实实地存在在他神圣的麻木他神圣的疯狂他神圣的失语的高处深深地爱着我们除极少数的例外我们不知道这是为何但他终将会来到并遵循着神圣的米兰达的样子跟人们旁边。）（55）

Yu's translation of Lucky's monologue is performable. The lines are rhythmic and catchy. As Yu Guangzhong said, actors on the stage must be able to pronounce every word clearly. In short, stage drama is performed in front of the audience, so its lines should be heard by the audience and spoken by the actors. In a word, the translator should clearly realize that dramatic language has its own characteristics, which make drama different from other literary forms and require translators to make the translation clearly. When it comes to Yu's translation, we can see that Yu's translation has two columns in the monologue part of Lucky. On the left is the colloquial language of "White bearded quack quack sniff God himself sniff sniff quack（白胡子的嘎嘎嗅的上帝本人嗅嗅嘎）"(55), and on the right is "Vladimir and Estragon listen carefully while Pozzo is bored（弗拉第米尔和爱斯特拉贡认真地倾听；波卓则是厌烦）" (55). This shows the actions of other actors on the stage, and the overall stage effect is presented. This kind of translation reflects the translator's consideration of performability. Once the translation of stage drama is determined as the research object, the performability of drama translation is emphasized. The most obvious difference between it and other literary translation is in the recipients. Fiction, poetry, and prose are all

III Analysis of Four Translated Versions in the Viewpoint of Dialogue Theory

created for the reader to read, while drama is for the audience to watch. Bassnett's also emphasizes on the concept of performability. The performability has two important implications for the translator: "first, performability shows that the concept and performance of the text are two different aspects; second, there are some "performability" features implied in the drama text-the action of language" (Bassnett: 99). Yu 's translation takes these two implications in to account focusing on being easy to be performed. In order to ensure that the performance is natural and authentic, the lines are action oriented and catchy. Only in this way can the audience fully appreciate a play.

  TT3:

  Fortunately, as confirmed by Pench and Watman's public works, It is proved that there is a white God beyond time and beyond space/he is in the sacred indifference, holy madness and holy dumb height/deeply loves us/with few exceptions/for some unknown reason/but time will reveal him that he is like the sacred Miranda. (幸运儿如彭奇和瓦特曼的公共事业所证实的那样有一个胡子雪雪白的上帝超越时间超越空间确确实实存在他在神圣的冷漠神圣的疯狂神圣的喑哑的高处深深地爱着我们除了少数的例外不知什么原因但时间将会揭示他像神圣的密兰达。)(64)

In Shi's translation, these Lucky's drama monologues without logic are changed into fluent language. For example: "It is proved that there is a white God beyond time and beyond space/he is in the sacred indifference, holy madness and holy dumb height/deeply loves us/with few exceptions/for some unknown reason/but time will reveal him" (所证实的那样有一个胡子雪雪白的上帝超越时间超越空间确确实实存在/他在神圣的冷漠神圣的疯狂神圣的喑哑的高处/深深地爱着我们/除了少数的例外/不知什么原因/但时间将会揭示他)(79). Here Lucky's dramatic monologue makes the theme of *Waiting for Godot* to be revealed. On the whole, the translation of Lucky's monologue looks ordinary and plain on the surface, but its meaning is profound. This free translation makes the illogical monologue become a discourse that reveals the theme. It demonstrates that a character's discourse is created by the author, but it is created in such a way that it can develop to the full its inner logic and independence as someone else's discourse. The dialogic relationship between the translator and the character also calls up the reader to enter such a conversation. In understanding such kind of play, the reader should "rise to the authorial position and sense this peculiar active broadening of his consciousness" (Bakhtin 68). This kind of translation makes reader not solely in the sense of an assimilation of new objects, but primarily in the sense of a special dialogic mode of communication with the autonomous consciousnesses of others something never before experienced.

TT4:

The existence of the personal gods mentioned in the works of Pengja and Wahman has a quaquaquaqua with white beard quaquaquaqua and has no form outside of time. From the heights of the holy Abasha, the holy Ashanbe, the holy Afasi, there is nothing left to love us. Except for a few exceptions, the reasons are not known to us and time will pass. Such as the suffering of the Holy Miranda and other reasons are not known to us, but time will pass.（在彭加和瓦曼的作品里提到的个人神祇的存在呱呱呱呱有白胡子呱呱呱呱在时间之外没有形体从神圣阿巴沙神圣阿山庇神圣阿法西之高处垂爱我们一无遗漏除了少数例外其理由非我们所知而时间将有所逝并且如神圣米兰达之受苦以及其他理由非我们所知然而时间将有所逝。)（55）

Qiu adopts the translation strategy of complete foreignization[1], which makes

---

[1] According to Venuti (1995: 20) "<f>oreignizing translation signifies the difference of the foreign text, yet only by disrupting the cultural codes that prevail in the target language." Referring to Schleiermacher (1813/2004: 49) we can say that translations are foreignizing when they leave the writer in peace as much as possible and move the reader toward him.

III Analysis of Four Translated Versions in the Viewpoint of Dialogue Theory

tragedy happen in the failure of dialogue with readers. For example, "Puncher" and "Wattmann" (Beckett: 60)are translated as "Pengja（彭加）" and "Wahman（瓦曼）"(Qiu: 55) by the method of transliteration[①], "Devine apathia divine athambia Devine aphasia", are translated as "the holy Abasha, the holy Ashanbe, the holy Afasi（神圣阿巴沙神圣阿山庇神圣阿法西）" (55), "academies of antiproponometry of Essy in possy of testew and cunarda" (60) are translated as "Measurement…Measurement…Surveying(测……测……测量学) and theology（神学）"(55). Moreover, Lucky's drama monologue is constantly polished and refined by colloquialism. For example, "quaquaquaqua with white beard quaquaquaqua" (Beckett 60) are translated as "Quack quack quack with white beard quack quack quack（呱呱呱呱有白胡子呱呱呱呱）" (Qiu: 55).

This kind of hybrid by the translation method of foreignization points to a great multitude of other's speeches, which constitute the soil for the genesis of dialogicality. This translation shows an image of language which can be structured only from the point of view of another language. This book holds that discourse lives, as it were, on the boundary between its own context and another, alien context. This view also can be justified by Bakhtin's words: "On all its various routes the word encounters an alien word and it cannot help encountering it in a living, tension-filled interaction" (Bakhtin: 279).

What deserves more attention the book is that, for one thing, this double-voicedness translation, as an intrinsic linguistic phenomenon, forms a vast background for any intersubjective relationship in human communication; for another, double-voicedness translation exists in the translation process, just as in every speech, and it plays a decisive part in determining the meaning of the text. While incarnated into translated text, it may have two connotations. First

---

[①] Transliteration consists in representing the characters of a given script by the characters of another, while keeping the operation reversible. The use of diacritics or digraphs solves the problem of different number of characters between the alphabets of the two writing systems.

of all, the text itself contains voices which are of full validity and equal status, free from the original authors' predomination. Holquist et al. also agree with this book' view. They think it is "a plurality of independent and unmerged voices and consciousnesses" (69).

Secondly, the voices and consciousnesses within the text always fall in a potential tension between numerous others' discourses socially and historically formed outside the text. In this way, this kind of translation breaks with the barrier between textual world and life world. Target text becomes an aggregation of various sociocultural discourses and consciousnesses. "Human action is intentional, and determinate; self-reflexively measured against social rules and resources, the heterogeneity of which allows for the possibility of change with every self-reflexive action" (Venuti: 24). Human communication is first intersubjective and meanwhile occurs in certain social and cultural background. The separation of the two sides results in some unilateral understanding of translation phenomenon.

In translation process, the communication between the author, the character, the translator and the target reader does not occur in a vacuum space, but is surrounded from all directions by multifarious sociocultural discourses and consciousnesses inside and outside the literary text. The interaction between subjects and the relevant social communities form another dimension of the intersubjective communication, which lays a good foundation for the context analysis in translation process. Lucky monologue's translation and character construction lies in the fact that this kind of hybrid language domain is Lucky's world domain. Without a new world, there will be no new language. Only by breaking the "boundary" of the world can a "new" language be born. This view ties well with the following citation: "…a way of conceiving the world as made up of a roiling mass of languages, each of which has its own distinct formal markers. These features are never purely formal, for each has associated with it a set of distinctive values and presuppositions" (Holquist et al.: 69).

It can be seen from the above detailed examination that when the four

III Analysis of Four Translated Versions in the Viewpoint of Dialogue Theory

translators face Lucky's monologues, they come up with four different versions. All the translated versions have their own style. All the readers have different understanding of the text. All the writers have different writing style. Translator is a reader and writer. This book highlights the translator's role as a reader and writer. The dialogic model is displayed: as an observer in the utterance, the translator assumes the role to coordinate possible dialogic relations. To render the original utterances as the same as it can be in a different language system and culture, the first step is to understand. As "any true understanding is a dialogue in nature. Understanding is to utterance as one line of a dialogue is to the next... In essence, meaning belongs to a word in its position of speakers" (Maybin: 103). The first dialogic relation forms into the author and the translator as a reader, and it constructs the solid foundation for a proper translation to happen in a smooth way.

When engaged in the understanding of the original utterances, the translator already enters into a dialogic relation with the author and he ought to extract the proper meaning and value of the text. "Meaning does not reside in the word or in the soul of the speaker or in the soul of listener. Meaning is the effect of interaction between speaker and listener produced via the material of a particular sound complex" (Volosinov: 104). The central object of understanding is not language or linguistic units, but the utterance which covers both linguistic and cultural contexts. that is, meaning is realized only in the process of active, responsive understanding.

Nevertheless, literary translation will never be, and it is also not possible, to replicate exactly the same contents via a different language. Thus, outsideness is a crucial factor for a translator to experience and understand a foreign culture. Only then, the translator will be able to digest the addressed utterances and to deliver them to the target readers. The second dialogic relation, which generates between the translator as a writer and target readers, does not take place after the first phase, but almost simultaneously. The internalized utterances are delivered to the target readers who are terminal receiving end. The translator's concerns should not exclude his or her dialogic relation with the readers, for the communication between them is an indispensable part of the whole dialogic network. To ensure a complete delivery of the process less harmed, different time and space background play a key role in transferring utterances. Besides, no utterance remains the same as others even if they look identical. To the translator, the two ostensible dialogic relations require him or her connect different time and space.

Hence, translated text is such a hybrid, which neither belongs to the original author nor the translator. For the original author writes in his or her own language, and the translator relies on communication with the work. Translation, as a result, bears the name of the author and the translator. It is produced within the dialogic relation established on the utterance and the nature of translation. The invisible dialogic relationship between the reader translator and the author translator plays one of determinants for translators to make choices. The inner dialogue constructs the possibility of effective translation. The book examines the four versions from character's dialogues and arrived at a small conclusion that the discourse of the protagonist in the four versions often reflects the intention imposed by the author and the translator, thus creating a special kind of double-voice text. It is shown as serving two speakers immediately. Hence, the translated works have the characteristics of double voice. In the following part, stage description is examined in the viewpoint of dialogue theory.

3.2 The Stage Description

In the previous study, character's dialogues are checked and now is the time to examine stage description of the four versions from dialogue theory. Stage description refers to the playwright's imagination of stage rhythm (barranger 290). In fact, stage description is a kind of accompanying language guide to direct the actual performance of actors. As Suchy proposed that "the stage description should be a part of the integrity of the theater performance, they are also utterance not just the words written on the books" (72). Stage description can be divided into many different categories, including: environment description, scene description, facial expression, emotion and body movement description. The stage description is concise and formal.

In addition, Pirandello said in *Six Characters in Search of Writers*: "The stage which accepts the fantastic reality of the six characters-is no fixed. Everything is in the making…" (Pirandello: 364). There is a deep connection between Pirandello's point of view and the phenomenology of dramatic works. It is undeniable that when Pirandello imagines the dynamic characteristics of these six characters on the stage, he not only refers to his dramatic dialogue language, but also includes the natural language that describes the surrounding environment of the stage, that is, the stage description. Although many people regard the stage description as a different discourse from the drama dialogue, they can also more appropriately regard the stage description as a part of the overall conception of the script language. Stage description language also has the characteristics of utterance. Although there is no interlocutor, its form of expression is only the statement of the bystander narrator. Veltrusky's (1976a) argument that dramatic language originates from dialogue characterized by communication and interaction also applies to stage descriptions. Bakhtin's dialogism can provide more explanation for the stage explanation of discourse. "Utterance is the cornerstone of Bakhtin's concept of dialogue. Dialogue is regarded as a widespread state, which is directly based on the actual conversation between two people, but not limited to this kind of conversation. In the final analysis, dialogue refers to the communication between coexisting differences. Stage description belongs to a kind of "non two people's actual conversation dialogue". In the process of reading, readers will find that there is no speaker in the stage description of the whole play, but the dialogue is omnipresent. This is a multi-voice monologue, a combination of multiple dialogues like a silent dialogue. When the play is showed, there will be multiple listeners who are readers, a character in the drama, and a director and actors. Moreover, in these talks, the hearer is also a variety of speakers, whose words are lyric and statement, no matter what kind of words the playwright uses to express the stage description, the interactive communication contained in it always exists, even the word "pause" is also a kind of speech. The so-called "silence is better than sound", "silence is silence, but silence does not mean no communication", silence also has its profound meaning (Wang Hong, 2006: 42). Hence, the translation of different meanings of stage descriptions will also be different.

The stage description translation is vital for the play to make successful dialogues. Since stage description plays an important role in explaining the occurrence and development of drama as well as the transformation of time and space, revealing the development of characters' personalities and the formation of characters' images, enhancing drama conflicts and paving the way for the development of drama conflicts. Therefore, its non-verbal factors and stage setting can not be ignored. At the same time, as a literary text and a performing art, drama translation is mainly influenced by two aspects: the output of the script on the stage and the effect of the script on the audience. Theater performance will change due to audience reaction, actor performance, on-site environment and other factors, and stage description plays a great role. Bassnett (1991) once pointed out that performance is an interpretation, which obviously breaks the relationship between the author, the text and the reader, and produces a redundant effect that many authors do not want. The main reason for Bassnett's "interpretation interruption" is that the stage description has not been translated properly, which misleads the actors and directors and makes them unable to perform the original script accurately and completely. "How many times when the poor playwrights watched the stage rehearsals, they didn't say", no, it wasn't like that! "Pirandello commented They feel great pain and anger, because the reality of the translated version is not in accordance with the author's own ideal (Luigi Pirandello, 1987: 58-79) from the above words, we can see that if the script translation is not appropriate, the stage performance will skew the intention of the dramatists, especially the translation part of the stage description, because the stage description directly plays a guiding role for the directors and performers. Therefore, there are many playwrights, such as Bernard Shaw, who writes the stage description part at great length, even the details of the characters' appearance (Bassnett, 1991). Stage description makes stage performance unique. When translating drama, translators should pay attention to all aspects of stage description (time, performance, body language, etc.). In the corner between the literary text and the stage environment, the stage description does not need to be spoken out loudly. At least in some occasions, the stage description (some elements) requires to be performed (Suchy, 1991). As an indispensable part of the fixed language of drama text, the translator should be aware of the unique function of stage description when he is doing translation work. The successful translation of stage instructions can convey the content to performers and readers more clearly. As a kind of "operation instruction", stage instructions can guide the reading and performance process. Moreover, the stage explanation should be regarded as a part of the whole stage and enjoy the same status as the drama dialogue language text to be spoken by the performer. Therefore, the stage explanation translation should also receive the same attention as the drama dialogue translation.

This book's argument that dramatic language originates from dialogue characterized by communication and interaction also applies to stage descriptions. Bakhtin's dialogism can provide more explanation for the stage explanation of discourse. Stage description belongs to a kind of "non two people's actual conversation dialogue"(Yu Bing: 17). In the process of reading, readers find that there is no speaker in the stage description of the whole play, but the dialogue is omnipresent. Even the word pause is also a kind of speech. "Silence is silence, but silence does not mean no communication, silence also has its profound meaning" (Wang Hong: 42).

Further, the stage description translation is vital for the play to make successful dialogues. Since stage description plays an important role in explaining the occurrence and development of drama as well as the transformation of time and space, revealing the development of characters' personalities and the formation of characters' images, enhancing drama conflicts and paving the way for the development of drama conflicts. Therefore, its non-verbal factors and stage setting cannot be ignored.

At the same time, as a literary text and a performing art, drama translation is mainly influenced by two aspects: the output of the script on the stage and the effect of the script on the audience. Stage description plays a great role. As Bassnett once pointed out that "performance is an interpretation, which obviously breaks the relationship between the author, the text and the reader, and produces a redundant effect that many authors did not want" (Bassnett: 110). The main reason for Bassnett's "interpretation interruption" is that the stage description has not been translated properly, which misleads the actors and directors and makes them unable to perform the original script accurately and completely.

From the above words, we can see that if the script translation is not appropriate, the stage performance skews the intention of the dramatists, especially the translation part of the stage description, because the stage description directly plays a guiding role as the directors and performers. "There are many playwrights, such as Bernard Shaw, who writes the stage description part of great length, even the details of the characters' appearance" (Bassnett: 110). Stage description makes stage performance unique. When translating drama, translators should pay attention to all aspects of stage description which include time, performance, body language, and so on. As an indispensable part of the fixed language of drama text, the translator should be aware of the unique function of stage description when he is translating. The successful translation of stage instructions can convey the content to performers and readers more clearly. As a kind of operation instruction, stage instructions can guide the reading and performance process. Moreover, the stage explanation should be regarded as a part of the whole stage and enjoy the same status as the drama dialogue language text to be spoken by the performer. This book emphasizes on this point those translations of stage descriptions as silent dialogues in the four versions also reflect the intention imposed by the author and the translator, creating a special kind of double-voice text. The stage explanation translation should also receive the same attention as the drama dialogue translation. Take stage prompt for example.

Stage prompt, also known as stage explanation, is the explanatory text provided by the playwright to the director and actors according to the needs of the performance. According to its different contents and functions, it can be divided into four forms. It is an indispensable part of the script language and some explanatory words in the script. Stage description includes the list of characters in the play, the time, place, clothing, props, setting of the plot, as well as the expression, action, etc. These explanations play a certain role in depicting characters and promoting the development of drama plot. This part of the language needs to be concise, and clear. This part usually appears at the beginning of each scene, the ending and the middle of the conversation and it is usually enclosed in brackets (square or round brackets).

First is character description. Generally, it refers to the "character table" of drama and literature script. It mainly introduces the age, position and relationship of the characters on the stage, and briefly introduces the general situation of the characters in the play. Such as *Romeo and Juliet*:

ACT I

PROLOGUE

Two households, both alike in dignity,

In fair Verona, where we lay our scene,

SCENE I. Verona. A public place.

Enter SAMPSON and GREGORY, of the house of Capulet, armed with swords and bucklers

In the beginning of the ACT I, two households named SAMPSON and GREGORY has been introduced and they indicate the whole play was involved in many bloody and unpopular military campaigns.

There are six names of characters in *Waiting for Godot*, but in fact, there are only five characters on the stage: two vagrants—ESTRAGON and VLADIMIR, two passers-by POZZO and LUCKY, a little boy who delivers letters for Godot and a character Godot who never appears but runs through the whole play.

Samuel Beckett: (in order of appearance)
ESTRAGON
VLADIMIR
POZZO
LUCKY
ABOY

Shi's version:
登场人物：
爱斯特拉冈
弗拉季米尔
波卓
幸运儿
一个孩子

Yu's version：
等待戈多于1953年1月5日在巴黎的巴比伦剧院首演，由Roger Blin导演，出场的演员如下：

爱斯特拉贡……Pierre Latour

弗拉第米尔…Lucien Raimbourg

幸运儿……Lean Martin

波卓……Erin

一个小男孩……Serge Lecointe

Qiu's version

III Analysis of Four Translated Versions in the Viewpoint of Dialogue Theory

剧中人物表					
爱斯特拉公 Estragon	佛拉底米尔 Vladimir	乐克 Lucky	波佐 Pozzo	一男孩 A boy	

This is the first page of the play to describe the character. Literary creation always centers on the description of people and reflects the social reality through the description of characters. Therefore, the research of literature always focuses on "people". In the research of characters in literary works, the research of characters' names is very important. Because in the process of creating characters, writers often choose names carefully and cautiously for characters in order to depict their characters more deeply and predict their fate and ending according to their creative intention, rather than at will. As Nikonov said in *human name and society*, "the more famous the master is, the more he chooses the name for the protagonist of his works". And so does Samuel Beckett.

Different characters have different symbolic meanings in the play. Beckett hinted at the choice of the names of these characters. He meticulously selected the names of several characters, using different names to indicate that they belong to different races and countries. For example, Estragon is a French name for short Gogo while Vladimir is a Russian name for short Didi. It's a coincidence that the pronunciation of these two abbreviations is similar to that of elder brother and younger brother, a pair of brothers, implying the relationship between them in terms of protection and being protected, or in other words, guidance and being guided. Pozzo is an Italian, French and Spanish name while lucky is an English name, to some extent, the name has ironic significance. Judging from their names, these characters appear on the stage and they have multiple races and nationalities. Together, they represent the whole humanity. The living environment of their plays is the real reflection of the environment after World War II.

 Therefore, how to translate characters with their own name information is the most important problem for translators, because it's the first appearance for the stage description of the character at the first line. For a long time, some scholars have held the view that the name of a person or an object is independent of the existence of the language, and the name has no meaning and connotation, so it is untranslatable. According to this theory, the best way to translate people's names is the simplest transliteration. In general situations, especially in daily communication and language use, the translation of foreign names mostly adopts the method of direct transliteration, even if the words contained in people's names have other meanings. However, due to the cultural loss caused by the differences between Chinese and foreign languages, the author's communicative intention, such as transliteration, cannot be realized smoothly. However, a complete free translation often destroys the form and style of the original text. As an important part of social language, human name is also a cultural carrier, which has a long and profound history of formation and rich cultural connotation, and embodies the characteristics of national culture.

 Therefore, the research makes a comparative analysis of the stage prompt names by three visions.

 Taking cues from Buddhist philosophy, Qiu embraces contradictions, examines cause and effect, and explores spatial and temporal relationships. The six names in Qiu's translation are analyzed as follows. Qiu translates the title of *waiting for Goddot* into《等待果陀》. He adopts a combination of free translation and transliteration. "果" is "preordained fate "which comes from Buddhism 因果经曰："欲知前世因，则今生所受者是，欲知后世果，则今生所为者是。" 陀is his Buddha. The two words "果陀" are exquisite, as gentle and lovely as the Mandarin in Taiwan accent. In fact, "果陀" a perfect illustration of the god. It also adds warmth to the so-called obscure theme. As for "waiting", this is also a proposition in western literature and Christian belief: only waiting, Whether the god comes or not, people wait. This wait is a pessimistic optimism and this anxiety is the distance between living and living goal. It's like looking for the Buddha in the East. At the same time, this translation version takes the vertical layout, that means when the readers turn over every page, he will see "爱"and "佛", just like waiting in the process of looking at Buddhist scriptures. So He translates ESTRAGON and VLADIMIR with "爱斯特拉公"and"佛拉底米尔". The transliteration method is adopted. Lucky was translated into"乐克". The combination of free translation and transliteration is adopted.""乐", which Buddhism pursues, is not the desire for happiness stimulated by the senses, but the happiness formed by extinguishing the desire for love. "克" is a surname, which means restraint. So the two words "乐克" together make the image clearly that the person is a sad character. Obviously in the play lucky is not the real lucky child, hence, the ironical meaning is manifested incisively and vividly. Pozzo is also translated by the combination of transliteration and free transliteration. The name is translated as "波佐". "佐" refers to an official in an auxiliary position. For example, "有赵孟以为大夫，有伯瑕以为佐。——《左传》"some Zhao Meng think he is a doctor, while others Bo Xia think he is a assistant.". —— *Legend of Spring and Autumn Century by Zuo Qiuming*. In China, there are some other examples like: 佐杂 (assistant official of local government); 佐吏 (assistant official of local government in Han Dynasty); 佐将 (general name of military commander and local administrative name in the early days of Taiping Heavenly Kingdom), so it embodies the characteristics of Pozzo as the lord. A boy is directly translated into a boy. The six names are all translated by the domestication translation strategy, with both form and spirit, revealing Beckett's mind.

Shi's translation and Yu's translation adopt the strategy of foreignization. All four names were transliterated, including Godot, Esteragon, Vladimir and Pozzo. Transliteration is a good choice when there is no exact corresponding expression in the source context. Both of them take a literal translation to introduce the original meaning for "Lucky "and "a little boy". Shi's translation is different from Yu's translation in that he uses a child to translate one boy, which make the child more common, while Yu's translation is from a spectator's perspective to introduce the name of the characters and actors into by "*Waiting for Godot*'s premiere at the Babylon theatre in Paris on January 5, 1953, directed by Roger blin, the following actors appeared".

In fact, the characters names and images in the three versions are abstract. They have no social and historical background, no specific name, only the first name and no family name. Therefore, the audience don't know any specific information about them, such as family, faith, etc. in fact, the names specially arranged by the author symbolize the whole human being, so the tragic experience of the characters in the play has certain representatives. That's why the three translators have adopted the same method in their translations, and there are no specific information about these names in China. Therefore, in the process of translation, the three translators have made a dialogue with the original work and completed the transformation of stage information.

To specify this statement, the research compares time, place, props, as well as characters' on-site and off-site actions. These explanations play a certain role in depicting characters and promoting the development of drama plot. The scene of traditional drama provides people's living environment and social environment, and the scene is close to real life. However, in *Waiting for Godot*, the scene does not introduce the living environment and social environment of the characters. Moreover, the connection between people and the scene is illogical. The scene of *Waiting for Godot* is very simple, just a path in the wilderness and a bare tree. The road is the stage. Estragon and Vladimir had no idea where they would meet with Godot, and the baldness of the trees was suggestive of suicide. This kind of disconnection between people and their living environment causes people to feel that they have lost themselves and have a sense of being out of place and meaningless to society and others. Life is meaningless and life becomes absurd, which is what Beckett wants to express. To illustrate this, we compare time and space between the source text and the four Chinese versions.

ST: A country road. A tree. Evening. (Beckett 2)

III Analysis of Four Translated Versions in the Viewpoint of Dialogue Theory

TT1: A tree in the country road in the evening.（乡村小路。一棵树。傍晚。）(5)

TT2: There is a tree on a road in the country in the evening.（乡间一条路，有一棵树。傍晚。）(235)

TT3: A road and a tree in the country at dusk.（乡间的一条路。一棵树。黄昏。）(3)

TT4: One township road, one tree, dusk.（乡道一条。树一株。黄昏。）(3)

Waiting for Godot is composed of two scenes. When the first scene starts, the audience can only see the whole scene of "A country road. A tree. Evening" (Beckett: 2). This scene presents the most basic time and space elements of the living environment. "*Godot* unfolds in a haunting and barren setting. Yet *Godot* tempts the audience with a Promethean glint of anticipation." (Anya M. Cronin: 2). A road to the country implies that it is a place where people come and go, but the whole place seemed barren and desolate. What the audience can see is only a tree. They don't see anything else with life. Liang Benbin points that Beckett once said: "'when I wrote *Watt*, I felt it is necessary to create a smaller space. In this space, I can control the position of the characters and the scope of their activities, especially from a certain angle. So, I wrote *Waiting for Godot*'"(97). Therefore, Beckett uses "A country road. A tree. Evening" (Beckett: 2) to set up a narrow space, and expresses its spatial sense with simple nouns.

When it comes to the Chinese versions, Shi, Qiu and Liao adopt literal translation to translate nouns directly into the of numeral-classifier-noun structures to describe the scene. They create an impression of space. That is because "the thing represented by the noun in the numeral-classifier-noun structures is the concept formed by brain. it is the subjective projection of the objective world in language" (Wang Hongbin 36). In addition, "the things represented by nouns are 3-dimensional images of length, width and height in the objective world. Therefore, spatiality is a characteristic of nouns". (Chen Ping: 6).

Yu's translation is composed of a noun phrase and a you（有）sentence. Numeral-classifier-noun can act as object of you（有）sentence. The translation uses a you（有）sentence "there is a tree（有一棵树）"(235), which takes the numeral-classifier-noun as the object of the existential sentence. Semantically, "nouns show its spatiality"(Wang Hongbin: 36). Moreover，"in terms of the relationship between things represented by nouns and actions represented by verbs, verbs have different spatial adaptability, and the verb 'you（有）' is one of the verbs with the strongest spatial adaptability"(Chu Zexiang: 17). At the same time, because of the strongest spatial adaptability of "you（有）", its semantic representation of the existence of objects is vague. That lies in the fact that "the stronger the spatial adaptability is, the less obvious the existence of things is" (Wang Hongbin: 39). Therefore, a noun phrase and a "you（有）" sentence create not only the sense of space in the text, but also the sense of uncertainty of space. This uncertainty sent an invitation to the reader to have a dialogue. "It stimulates answers, guesses answers, and organizes itself by taking into account replies" (Bakhtin: 59). Iser also puts forward that "a literary text is something like an arena which the reader and the author participate in a game of imagination" (Iser: 190).

In literary translation activity, the game of imagination between the translator and the original author can be better carried out with the participation of stage description. Since "discourse is formed into the atmosphere of what has been said, and at the same time, it is determined by the unanticipated reply. This is true of all realistic dialogues" (Bakhtin: 59). The characters of *Waiting for Godot* are trapped in where they are, living in a world of motionless, cold and depressing stagnation. In the act One, there is only one line of stage direction: "A country road. A tree. Evening" (Beckett: 2). The whole story, if there is a story happening at all, takes place on a terrifying empty road near a tree. "The lone tree on Godot's country road blooms leaves between acts. Vladimir sees the surfacing of the wasteland's buried transformative capabilities" (Anya M. Cronin: 2). The writer sets his story on the road in order to give his characters a chance or even hope. The road symbolizes hope or at least it provides people with an opportunity. A road is the metaphor for a movement, a development, a progress which takes someone from one place to the other. One can make full use of the road according to its purpose. Only on the way one can have the chance to change their miserable condition. The employment of the road suggests the total breakaway from the present situation and getting the probability toward the distant, vague and uncertain future, a new life. Road is the place that possible changes might happen. Therefore, Yu's translation focuses on the unreal feeling of *Waiting for Godot*, emphasizing the despair and hope of waiting. In this sense, four versions adopt different semiotic expressions. "In interpreting a stage direction, whether on page or stage, semioticians most often want to attribute authorial force to either the playwright or the production" (Suchy: 72).

In fact, any expression emphasis is on the event itself. It seems to be a mini dialogue, in which the translator's interpretation of "what has been said", the translator's new intention, and the reader's "reply" in speculation all exist in this expression. To understand the translation is to understand the translator's expression. These views are in line with "a better way of describing the execution of the stage direction is suggested by Bakhtin's dialogism, in which both voices author and are authored simultaneously, and the emphasis is on the event itself, rather than any abstract system" (Suchy: 72).

The time of stage description shares the same quality of space scene. The source text just shows the stage time by using one-word "evening". The definition of "evening" in Merriam webster dictionary is like this: the latter part and close of the day and early part of the night. In the four versions, "evening" is translated as "evening（傍晚）" and "dusk（黄昏）". Although both of these two words refer to the time of sunset to the time when the sky is not completely dark. But "dusk（黄昏）" is better than "evening（傍晚）". This can be proved by the following citation. "The image of dusk（黄昏）is one of the most frequently used archetypal images of the image group of classical literature. It has gone far beyond the scope of time and space in the expression of literati and has been emotionalized and spiritualized by the subject"(Zheng Haitao and Zhao Xin: 5). In Fu Daobin's words, "the sadness of time and the warmth of space constitute the symbolic meaning of the image of dusk（黄昏）in Chinese literature" (82). "Evening", translated by "dusk（黄昏）", can show readers archetypal cultural images. In China, if people emphasize time, they often use "傍晚", if they blend sentiment with scenes, they often use "黄昏". For example, 傍晚时分，先是电闪雷鸣，然后就下起了大雨。In the evening, the lightning first, and then it rained heavily. 驿外断桥边，寂寞开无主。已是黄昏独自愁，更著风和雨。Outside the post-house, beside the broken bridge, Alone, deserted, a flower blooms. Saddened by her solitude in the falling dusk, She is assailed by wind and rain.

In *Waiting for Godot*, people can't see the light in the dark, while they can't disperse the shadow of the dark in the light. It can be seen that time seems to have become a powerful alien force of human beings. In its passing, we can neither find the glory of Western civilization in the past nor foresee its glory in the future. The only clear and unmistakable thing is the approaching of death. In the book of *philosophy of symbolic form*, German philosopher Cassirer pointed out that "it is the opposition between light and darkness, the opposition between the East and the west, and the resulting primitive feelings about space that form the driving force of human culture, and thus derive the opposition between life and death, which has become the eternal theme of all religions and philosophies." (Cassirer, 1990: 128). Based on this, *evening* is the critical point of light and darkness. When people in ancient times feel the evening, they give this image the original feelings of light and darkness which signifies life and death, so that *evening* becomes a prototype image that condenses the ancient life consciousness. In Chu IX Huaisha's:《九章·怀沙》"迷路北次兮，日昧昧其将暮。舒忧娱哀兮，限之以大数。"lost in the north, the day will be dark. When it comes to comfort, sorrow and sorrow, it is limited to a large number." "黄昏" is also a symbol of confusion and hopelessness, which reflects the author's state of mind of loss. Moreover, in 黄昏独立佛堂前，满地槐花满树蝉。大抵四时心总苦，就中肠断是秋天。——白居易《暮立》白马逐朱车，黄昏入狭斜。狭斜柳树乌争宿，争枝未得飞上屋。东房少妇婿从军，每听乌啼知夜分。——李端《乌

栖曲》摇落秋天酒易醒,凄凄长似别离情。黄昏倚柱不归去,肠断绿荷风雨声。——韦庄《摇落》. According to Baker, "Selecting a particular text and embedding it in a temporal and spatial context that accentuates the narratives that touch our lives, even though the events of the source narrative may be set within a very different temporal and spatial framework" (Baker, 2006: 112). As a result, *evening*, translated by "黄昏", can show more silence, suffocation and fear, and deeply reflect the absurdity and despair of the real society.

According to Baker, "Selecting a particular text and embedding it in a temporal and spatial context that accentuates the narratives that touch our lives, even though the events of the source narrative may be set within a very different temporal and spatial framework" (Baker: 112).

Besides, there's a penetrating statement in *Discourse in the Novel*: "form and content in discourse is one, once we understand that verbal discourse is a social phenomenon-social throughout its entire range and in each and every of its factors, from the image to the furthest reaches of abstract meaning" (Bakhtin: 259). The familiar symbolic meaning of the image of dusk can make the target readers involved in the play and have a strong connection with it. In fact, translation as a discourse, it is a real and concrete existence of social thought, at the same time, it is taken as the opinion of miscellaneous language, which is of great significance of individual consciousness. It is at the juncture between self and others. This book holds that drama translation is influenced by both the source culture and the target culture, and assimilation is inevitable because translation is not carried out in a vacuum, and the context in which translation takes place inevitably affects translation practice, just as "the norms and restrictions of the source culture play a role in the source text, the norms and restrictions of the target culture must play a role in translation"(Bassnett: 93).

In the end of the comparative analysis of nonverbal dialogue factors of the stage description, we take an example of lighting effect and props application to examine the four Chinese versions. These stage descriptions manifest a simultaneous attraction for their actability. If speakability is the manifestation of verbal language, then actability is the revelation of the hidden signal of these stage descriptions. When the translator translates the hidden information about these stage descriptions, he should take stage into consideration to promote plot development, to help the actors to perform on the stage and to help the audience to understand the deep relationship hidden in the stage. Besides, if the translation can help the actor to express his emotions and psychological status, and then we can say the translation is full of actability. They are examined by the following citations.

ST:

The light suddenly fails. In a moment it is night. The moon rises at back, mounts in the sky, stands still, shedding a pale light on the scene. (Beckett: 72)

TT1:

The lights suddenly dimmed, and it was night when the moon rose from behind and stopped quietly in the air, with a weak and pale light shining on the scene.（灯光突然变暗，须臾间已是夜晚时分。月亮自后方升起，静静地停在空中，微弱苍白的光照耀场景。）(67)

TT2:

When the lights suddenly turned dark, the sky turned dark and the moon rose at the end of the stage. It climbed to the top of the sky and stood still, leaving a silver light on the stage.（灯光突然转暗。一时间里，天色变黑。月亮升起在舞台尽头，爬上了高天，一动不动，在舞台上撒下了银色的光芒。）(309)

TT3:

The light is suddenly dim, and the night has come. The moon rises behind it, hanging in the sky, motionless, and shedding its gray-white glory on the stage.（光线突然暗淡。夜已降临。月亮在后面上升，挂在天空，一动不动，将灰白色的光辉泻在舞台上。）(54)

TT4:

The lights are dim for a while, and then it is night. The moon rises from

Ⅲ Analysis of Four Translated Versions in the Viewpoint of Dialogue Theory

behind, stays in the air, hangs still, and shoots White and slightly bluish light on the stage.（灯光忽暗。一会儿工夫之后就是夜晚。月亮自背后升起，停留在空中，悬着不动，射出苍白的光线在舞台上。）(69)

The above scene depicts the moon rising after nightfall. By literal translation, Shi, Qiu, and Liao simply translated this scene as a static description of the moon rising from behind and resting quietly in the air. However, by additional translation Yu translated the sentence as "the moon rose at the end of the stage. It climbed to the top of the sky.（月亮升起在舞台尽头，爬上了高天）" (309). Here, "climb（爬）" vividly points in the movement of the props, while "end of stage（舞台尽头）" and "high sky（高天）" point out the position of the props. This kind of translation is dynamic. Hence, this is a good translation of situational context. Through the ingenious stage layout, the original silent background on the script becomes a living language. That lies in the fact that dramatic information may be conveyed by any or all of the systems involved, being translatable from one kind of message into another irrespective of the physical qualities of the signs or signals involved: "the information 'night falls', for instance, can be conveyed by means of a lighting change" (Keir Elam: 35). Readers usually expect to receive a more or less coherent set of information about the world they represent and are interested in the events narrated. A good translation of situational context can construct specific pictures in the original text and assemble imagery information, thus activating the reader's understanding of the information in the target language.

Besides, for the word "pale", it shows the colour which creates the stage light environment. Color is the most straightforward information at first sight. Different colors bring us different emotions. Color has a great impact on people's psychology. When the color in people's mind has been positioned as a symbol of things, whenever you see this kind of color, you instinctively think of the things or events represented by this kind of color, and then psychologically have some feelings. when we observe the four translation words "silvery（银色）", "gray white（灰白色）", "White and slightly bluish（苍白）"and"pale and weak

（微弱苍白）", the book finds that as the color is getting darker and darker, the emotion is getting stronger and stronger. Liao's translation of "pale and weak（微弱苍白）" is one of the most infectious expressions of emotion. The addition of "weak（微弱）" shows there is no exuberant vitality. Most important of all, this supplement indicates the translator's female identity to transfer the waiting meaning. Liao shows her concerns on desolation.

As "female translators choose more-specific color terms; and female translators are more explicit. It is that translations by women reflect a greater concern for the transfer of meaning" (Miriam Shlesinger: 187). Under such circumstance, translators convey the sense of desolation to readers, and express the helplessness of waiting. Just like this sentence "I see myself as conceive others might see it" (Holquist: 27). Waiting in hopeless situation is the torturing and suffering of human beings, but it also contains hope in the despair, holding the belief and strength. Because there is no definite answer to the present situation, waiting seems to be the best action they should take.

Becketts characters face with helplessness, terrible loneliness, the cruelty of man and the absence of God. But meanwhile, they give their corresponding reactions. they persevere, endure, wait and hope, refusing to give in to the temptation of despair. This perseverance remains constant throughout *Waiting for Godot*. They do not move from the place and have already decided to stay there unless Godot comes, this waiting can be regarded as a quest which is totally fearless dedicated and uncompromising. The translator plays the role of communication bridge between the source text and the target readers. She transfers the concern and the emotion by inserting situation. Snell-hornby offers a perspective that similarly encompasses such event by the sentence "for the translator, the text is not purely a linguistic phenomenon, but must also be seen in terms of its communicative function, as a unit embedded in a given situation" (69).

This part compares the four versions from the aspects of stage description. These translations have an impact on the visual effects and emotional tone and even they determine the reader's perception of the roles in the work. An excellent

III Analysis of Four Translated Versions in the Viewpoint of Dialogue Theory

translation of stage description activates imagery information. These translations of stage descriptions play a role in dialogue with readers accompanying with the translator as a shadow to influence each selection made by the translator in the whole translation process. The four versions show the intention imposed by the author and the translator, thus creating a special kind of double-voice text. In this chapter, the book examines the four versions by Bakhtin's dialogic theory which focuses on the translator subjectivity in drama translation process and translation's double voice. it is with this internal cause that the book explores the detailed analysis of four Chinese versions. In the next chapter, the same four versions are examined in the viewpoint of rewriting theory.

IV Analysis of Four Translated Versions in the Viewpoint of Rewriting Theory

In the above chapter four Chinese versions are checked by Bakhtin's dialogic theory in view of the internal cause and in this chapter the book aims to place the four versions into the norms and constraints of the target culture, which represents the external influence on translation process. How are *Waiting for Godot* registered and changed in these four versions? Whether implicitly or explicitly, this question is central to the book. *Waiting for Godot* in China has been studied for nearly fifty years, from Shi Xianrong's first Chinese translation in 1965 to the world's first *The Complete Works of Beckett* released by Hunan Literature and Art Publishing House in August 2016. During this period, many translators have participated in this translation process. This chapter examines four representative translated versions to check the influence of ideology, poetics and patronage on *Waiting for Godot* in different historical periods from the perspective of Lefevere's rewriting theory.

What is rewriting theory? Theo Hermans, a British contemporary translation theorist, first applies "manipulation" to the study of translation theory. In 1985, Theo Hermans uses the introduction of *The Manipulation of Literature: Studies in Literary Translation* to write up the development of the operational school and clarify the common assumptions of this group of scholars in the preface.

IV Analysis of Four Translated Versions in the Viewpoint of Rewriting Theory

A view of literature as a complex and dynamic system; a conviction that there should be a continual interplay between theoretical models and practical case studies; an approach to literary translation which is descriptive, target-oriented, functional and systematic; and an interest in the norms and constraints that govern the production and reception of translations, in the relation between translation and other types of text processing, and in the place and role of translation both within a given literature and in the interaction between literatures (Hermans, 1985: 10-11).

It points out that from the perspective of target literature, all translation means to manipulate the original text to some extent for a certain purpose. As a target text, it is constrained by the target culture and ideology. It is "an interest in the norms and constraints that govern the production and reception of translations" (Hermans: 10). This is regarded as the embryonic form of the manipulation school of translation theory. The cultural turn of translation studies, makes the translation studies being researched from the perspective of manipulation school possible. Literature has been more generally taken as "a differentiated and dynamic conglomerate of systems characterized by internal oppositions and continual shifts" (Hermans: 11).

Later, Andre Lefevere (1985), a well-known American comparative literature expert and translation theorist born in Belgium, proposes that translation studies should be included in a variety of "rewriting" and "refraction". Within this period, he later develops this view. In the published book *Translation, Rewriting and the Manipulation of Literary Fame* (1992), he combines translation studies with power, ideology, patronage and literary views. In this book, it points out that translation must be dominated by the ideology and literary view of the translator or the authority. Translation, editing, compilation of anthologies, literary history and reference books are all called "rewriting". Translation is a form of rewriting the literature text. In other words, translation creates the literary and cultural images of the source text.

Rewriting is manipulation. Translation is the manipulated result by the translator. Subsequently, Lefeverer systematically discusses the manipulation of translation, which has an important impact on translation studies in the cultural context, marking the formal formation of "Manipulation School". Following are some main viewpoints of translation manipulation school. (1) Translation is a kind of "Rewriting", and rewriting is manipulation, which is a means of serving power. (2 What kind of image translation establishes for literary works mainly depends on two factors: one is the ideology recognized by the translator or imposed by the patron; the other is the dominant Poetics (literary view) in the target literature at that time. (3) Rewriting (translation) is restricted by the ideological norms of Poetics (literary concepts) of the target culture, within which the translator operates. (4) "Faithfulness" translation is only one of many translation strategies, not the only possible or correct one. (5) Translation is not only a force to shape literature, but also a principled means of text manipulation.

In order to better analyze the influence of factors outside the text on literature, Andre Lefevere provided a set of new terms. There are three key words in this set of terms: ideology, poetics and patronage.

Ideology is a collection of ideas. In 1796 the term "ideology" was first put forward by French philosopher and statesman Distuttde Taryc (1754—1836) in his book *the Elements of Ideology*. It tried to provide a real scientific philosophical basis for the generation of all ideas and gave it the meaning of science of ideas. Since then, ideology has been widely used by other philosophers and politicians in many fields, such as social science, social psychology and political science. Ideology is a variety of ideas rooted in the human brain, and these concepts are dominated by the social right structure and right relations. As an activity of understanding, interpreting and recreating, translation is dominated by the translator. However, as a person living in the society, the translator is bound to be influenced or even dominated by the social ideology. Behind the translation act, as "the conscious form of the thought and interpretation system is always playing a role". As ideology is determined by social existence, the social ideology in different historical periods is different. Therefore, the social ideology in different historical periods has different influence on translation. Lefevere defines ideology as what the society has or is allowed to have. He believes that ideology is all kinds of socially acceptable concepts and attitudes in a particular society in a specific period of time, through which translators and readers can accept and understand translation works.

Further elaboration are as follows. Translation must be carried out in a specific political, social, historical and cultural environment. Firstly, the translator is, to a certain extent, the product of the above factors. Secondly, when he is engaged in translation, the environment has both influence and restriction on him. The filtering function of translation lies in intervening in power, which leads to the secondary distribution of power. The distribution power possessed by the translator is a kind of restriction mechanism and can make him engage in the manipulation of ideology quietly. At the same time, translation is a kind of cultural behavior. Any cultural form and practice may provide opportunities for ideological criticism, because cultural interpretation itself has many connections with ideology. In addition, the re-contextualization caused by translation also erodes the original text. The effects sound mostly negative, but erosion promotes change, and the change is often positive. This can be proved by Benjamin who pointed out that the regeneration of the original text must undergo changes. In fact, it is a targeted manipulation of the instability of the original work (rather than too obvious "violence") to eliminate the historical, political and ideological forces of the source language (Jay, 19: 7, 412). The new representation of translation presents the mode of usurpation, transformation and substitution. The cultural turn of translation pays attention to the characteristics of translation activities and its transformation function in political and historical sense. In other words, the task of translation is to transform the local cultural products into cross-cultural products. The product structure of culture is different, and the ecological environment of culture is also different. Therefore, to a certain extent, the cultural localization of cross-cultural products is also the process of cross-cultural communication. It is not easy to introduce foreign culture into local culture, and it is not easy to introduce foreign culture into local culture. The pressure of ideology forces us to look for some "relevant" content. Although there are great differences in living conditions, cultural psychology, aesthetic fashion and other aspects, generally speaking, it seems not difficult to find what you want in the text, and it seems not difficult to add something to the translation At the same time, "smuggling" into the translation, so it involves a certain degree of hybridity. Therefore, it is inevitable that local cultural traditions and foreign cultural elements mix together. First of all, translation leads to language hybridity, because complete foreignization and domestication are impossible, and the mutual penetration of the two languages is inevitable. It should be pointed out that although ideology cannot be separated from language as a carrier, not all languages can be separated from ideology, such as mathematical language. However, any language related to culture is more or less related to ideology. In the process of recombining different cultural symbols, translation is inevitably carrying out cultural hybridization in order to achieve a certain balance. The decline of foreign culture, including strong culture, which has been packaged by local culture, may be due to ideology. How to hybridize and to what extent should be considered from the effect of cross-cultural communication, and not be free from the influence of ideology. Hence, the ideology of translation involves discourse power. The advanced and powerful western civilization has created a strong discourse, while the reception politics of local culture, supported by ideology, also has the power of discourse resistance, which is reflected in the operation of translation through the translator, which is mainly reflected in rewriting, deleting, selecting and omitting and so on.

Sometimes translators actively participate in the process, while sometimes passively drift with the tide. Whether it is caused by subjective consciousness or forced by objective environment, translators can not help but misappropriate and transform the original culture. The problem of cultural connotation and denotation can not be ignored in translation, and the transmission of cultural information is indispensable. Otherwise, the translation will be incomplete, although the integrity in the strict sense is unattainable. Due to the different forms (denotation) of

IV Analysis of Four Translated Versions in the Viewpoint of Rewriting Theory

culture (in addition to different connotations), the cultural transformation in form is generally carried out within the scope of expectation. If we have the tolerance to absorb and accommodate foreign cultures, then the cultural transformation will be mild and limited, although it will intentionally or unintentionally eliminate or weaken the unacceptable ideological discourse elements. To a certain extent, the text is tailor-made for readers in a specific historical and cultural context. Although translation inevitably changes the nature of the original text, it should not ignore the target language readers. That means the translation also should be taken into account in terms of acceptance. Translation is the replacement of sound. In other words, the translator uses different sounds to convey the information of the original text. How to transmit information seems to be mainly related to the competition and control of the survival space of the representation of culture, and to further explore the connotation, it also involves the power of ideological discourse. Generally speaking, the translator has no direct right to speak, but the misappropriation of voice gives the translator the opportunity to manipulate the text. In addition, cultural survival in cross domain communication is an unavoidable problem. Foreign voice will be expressed, but not fully. That is because translation always pays attention to the problem of sufficiency. Due to ideology and other reasons, the inadequacy of translation lies in the operational level on the basis of subjective considerations, caused by various concerns: the results of filtration may result in the reduce of the composition. However, objectively, translation is subject to different cultural, social and historical conditions, and it is difficult to fully convey the meaning of the original text, especially the cultural information of the source language when it is in the face of the change of cultural value on the operational level. Sometimes translation can be decoded, while sometimes it cannot be decoded, or between the two, so it leads to inadequacy. Furthermore, if ideology is in harmony or can be used, it is natural to change the uncertain meaning into the definite meaning, otherwise, it will change the definite meaning into the uncertain meaning. Ideological interpretation is a common decoding method. SuarHall emphasized that although encoding and decoding are relatively autonomous, they are "decisive moments" (1993: 91). The so-called decisive nature refers to meaning, that is, whether encoding or decoding, can directly affect meaning. As a kind of double coding, translation naturally has the opportunity to influence the formation of meaning. It can achieve some ideological or aesthetic purpose by manipulating the symbols in the semantic group chain of discourse. This is the fact the translator is to intentionally ignore or ignore author's coding intention.

Ideology focuses on what society should or can be, while poetics focuses on what literature should or can be (Lefevere, 1992: 14) . poetics will be studied in the following paragraphs.

The concept of poetics comes from Aristotle's *Poetics*. "Poetics" in Aristotle's *poetics* is in the same position as ethics, rhetoric and metaphysics. It mainly studies the general theoretical problems of literature. For example, what is literature, the components of literature, the means and purpose of literature, the similarities and differences between literature and other arts, and the relationship between literature and reality. Although the author does not directly discuss these issues, but through the study of Greek tragedy to achieve the purpose of discussing the general theory of literature. In poetics, Aristotle not only discusses the types, functions and properties of poetry, but also discusses other artistic theories, such as tragedy and imitation. In fact, Aristotle uses "Poetics" in a general sense, that is, Poetics is art. While discussing the structure, content and influence of tragedy and epic, he especially pointed out that poetry should be recreated or imitated human life and behavior. A basic idea throughout the whole poetics is that "poetics" is closer to philosophy and more serious than history. In the sixth chapter of *Poetics*, it discusses the key points of his poetics and his aesthetic theory.

Aristotle's poetics is not only the first work of western historiography, but also provides a direction for the study of Western poetics in the future. Since then, the western classical literary theory works have been used to call it "Poetics". For example, the most important literary theory work in Rome is Horace's *Ars Poetica*. In the middle ages, Aristotle's poetics was submerged. At that time, the poetic theory had little relationship with Aristotle's. During the Renaissance, a large number of literary theory monographs named after "Poetics" were produced. Until the 17th century, the French classical theorist Boileau Despréaux, Nicolas made *L'art Poetique* his theoretical classic. These works are not simply theoretical works of poetry, but general literary theoretical works. Most of the classical theorists established poetics to make laws and regulations for their creation, which, to a certain extent, restricted the writers' freedom of creation. Under the impact of romanticism, classical poetics began to lose its reputation, and there were not so many works like poetics published since then. At least they don't have much authority.

Then, the rising poetics theories are mainly aesthetics based on Baumgarton and literary criticism starting from Blankenbu. In the 19th century, poetics evolved into two parts: philosophical aesthetics and literary criticism using historical methods. The former is a poetic theory established by the transcendental aesthetic system, which tends to strengthen the theoretical color of poetics and replace the rules. The main tasks of the former are Baumgarton, Hegel, Schopenhauer, Croce, etc.; the latter deals with poetics from the perspective of historicism, which is known as literary theory.

In the 20th century, it has become a foregone conclusion to use poetics to refer to general literary theory in western literary theory. This is due to the redefinition of the purpose and object of poetics by Russian formalist theorists. In the view of formalist theorists, the main purpose of poetics is to answer what factors make language materials into works of art. That is what makes literature become literature.

In the late 20th century, Impressionist poetics tended to return to the traditional concept of poetics, such as the poetics of Eliot and pound. Other contemporary concepts of poetics are based on linguistic, sociological, anthropological or psychological theories, such as structuralist poetics. Poetics sometimes interacts with literary theory. Wellek suggested that "Poetics" should be replaced by literary theory in his *poetics*, but now critics often use this term to emphasize the nature of "internal research".

After the Second World War, new criticism, structuralism, psychoanalysis, archetypal criticism and semiotics emerged one after another, becoming the main body of modern western poetics, and paid more attention to the analysis of the internal language characteristics and deep structure of literature. Modern poetics is also different from traditional poetics. The answer of modern historiography to the core question of what is literature is quite different from that of traditional poetics. But they all use the concept of poetics in the general theory of literature. At present, the extension of the concept of poetics has a tendency to expand. In the works of some scholars, poetics has become a synonym of theory. For example, Canadian scholar Linda Harqin called his work on postmodernism as *Postmodern Poetics*. The meaning of the poetic concept she used here is theoretical expression. In addition, the anthologies of Harold Bloom, an American theorist, have also been named "Poetics of influence" by the editors; there have also been vilis Barnes's *History of Translation,* Crossman Weimas's *Reading Poetics,* and Richard Halpen's *Poetics of Primitive Accumulation*.

There are many definitions of modern poetics and when it comes to the definition on the literature, they are as follows:

Tomashevsky said in *the Definition of Poetics*: "the task of poetics is to study the structure of literary works. Literature with artistic value is the object of poetics. The research method is to describe, classify and explain the phenomenon"Rhetoric is the discipline that studies the structure of non artistic works; poetics is the discipline that studies the structure of artistic works."

Shklovsky said: "the establishment of scientific poetics should start with the recognition of the existence of "prose" and "poetic"languages on the basis of a large number of facts (the two languages have different ways to return), and should start with the analysis of these differences." (*Poetics*)

Zhirmonsky divides poetry into theoretical poetics and historical poetics. "It is the task of theoretical poetics to explain the artistic significance of these poetic techniques, the relationship between them and their essential aesthetic function.

IV Analysis of Four Translated Versions in the Viewpoint of Rewriting Theory

As for historical poetics, it should clarify the origin of various poetic techniques in the style of the times, and clarify their relationship with different periods of the history of poetry development." (*the Task of Poetics*)

Todorov said: "poetics, contrary to the interpretation of individual works, aims not to reveal the meaning of a work, but to identify the general rules on which each work is based. It is different from psychology, sociology and so on. It is devoted to exploring these principles from the inside of literature. Therefore, poetics is a kind of "abstract" and "internal" understanding and mastering of literature. The object of poetics is not the literary works themselves, but the attributes of a special language literary discourse. As a result, any work is considered to be an exhibition of an abstract structure, which is the embodiment of a possibility in the process of concrete spreading of this structure. Therefore, what this discipline focuses on is not the real literature but the possible literature. In other words, it focuses on the abstract attribute of literature, that is, literariness." (*Structuralist Poetics*)

Todorov and Duclow wrote in the "Poetics" entry in the Encyclopedia of language science: "the first question poetics has to answer is: what is literature? ... In other words, it should try to direct the social phenomenon of 'Literature' to an internal theoretical entity; or it should also define literary discourse by comparing it with other discourses. Therefore, it needs to assign itself a cognitive object, the product of theoretical research. It originates from the observed facts and keeps a certain distance from it." "Secondly, poetics should provide tools for the description of literary works: distinguishing different levels of meaning, identifying the units that constitute the works, and describing the relationship between the participating units. With the help of these basic classifications, one may study some of its relatively stable forms. In other words, the study of types and genres also involves the study of inheritance rules, that is, the study of literary history."

"Poetics, according to traditional concepts, first refers to theories involving literature; secondly, it also refers to a writer's choice and application of literary principles (theme, conception, style, etc.), such as 'Hugo's Poetics'; finally, referring to the claims of a literary school, it refers to all the rules that the school must follow." "In the west, people used to regard ancient Greece as the beginning of poetics. In fact, at the same time, or even earlier, this kind of thinking about literature began in China".

Israeli critic Khrushowski believes that poetics is to study literature as a system of literature. It aims to solve the problem of "what is literature" and all other possible problems caused by this problem, such as: what is the art of language? What are the forms and types of literature? What is the essence of a certain literary school or trend of thought? What is the "art" or "language" system of a particular poet? How is the story made up? What are the specific aspects of literary works? How are these aspects made up? How to express the "non literary phenomenon" in the text of literary works and so on.

When it comes to the definition on the translation, they are as follows:

Itamar Even-Zohar, the first editor in chief of *poetics today*, an International Journal of literary communication theory and analysis, said that today's poetics is constantly expanding its territory. It has stepped out of the vacuum of literary discourse research, taking all cultural discourses as its research object, thus penetrating into all fields of humanities, Such as literary theory, literary criticism and interpretation, literary and cultural history, cultural semiotics, linguistics, rhetoric, communication, cultural anthropology, cognitive science, translation theory, etc. He said that these different fields share the same poetic aspiration, that is, to understand the literary and cultural discourse in the context of local cultural system and the context transfer of cultural system, develop advanced theories and research methods of literature, communication and culture, and put literary research in the grand background of humanities and even the whole scientific field.

In the *Encyclopedia of Translation Studies* compiled by a British scholar Mona Baker, Genzler thinks that translation poetics includes two aspects: one is the sum of the genre, theme and literary methods that constitute any literary system; the other is that in translation studies, translatology represents the role of a literary system in a larger social system, It also shows how this literary system interacts with other (foreign) literary systems or symbolic systems. At the same time, translational poetics also studies the poetical comparison between the source text in its own literary system and the target text in different systems. according to Lefevere, poetics in translation has two components: "one is a list of literary techniques, genres, themes, typical characters and situations, and symbols; the other is the concept of what role literature has or should play in the whole social system". The latter "is obviously closely related to ideological influences outside the scope of poetics, and it is produced by various ideological forces in the environment of the literary system"(Lefevere, 1992: 26-27). In other words, in translation, poetics refers to its role in the field of literature and even the whole society from a macro perspective; from a micro perspective, poetics refers to the specific creative techniques, themes, characters and so on used in literary creation or translation.

Patron refers to the person or institution that "promotes or hinders the reading, writing and rewriting of literature". (Lefevere, 1992: 15). In Andre Lefevere's three factor theory, patronage is regarded as the most important factor. In his opinion, patrons play an important role in the whole process of translation, and they always control the whole process of translation activities. Translation itself is not an isolated act, but closely related to political, social and economic factors. Most translators translate well and safely within the space allowed by the social and political authority of their time. As "any force that may contribute to the production and dissemination of literary works, but may also hinder, prohibit and destroy literary works" (Chen Dehong, Zhang Nanfeng, 2000: 176), the sponsorship system can play a role in three aspects: ideology, economic interests and social status. Specifically speaking, the first is ideology, that is, literature must keep pace with other systems in a specific social context; the second is economic interests, that is, sponsors need to ensure translators' economic needs; the third is status guarantee, that is, translators can obtain certain social status through literary creation. If the three elements are concentrated on the same sponsor, it will form a non-differentiated sponsor, otherwise, it will become a differentiated sponsor.

Generally speaking, patronage plays an important role in the trend of translation activities, the future of translation literature and the social status of translators. Andre Lefevere (1992: 14) pointed out that "ideology is often strengthened and implemented by patrons, i. e. the person or institution entrusted with the translation or publication of translation works." If a translator wants to translate a work, he needs the support of necessary material conditions, and some publishers are willing to publish the translation, that is to say, the translator must contact with the patron and the publishing house, especially in the contemporary society. If the patron agrees to provide the necessary funds to help publishing the work, he will inevitably put forward various demands on the translator. These requirements involve all aspects. Once they conflict with the translator's translation view, translators often have to sacrifice or adapt their own principles. Mr. Lin Yutang, another famous translator in China, enjoys a high reputation in the United States because of his high level, and on the other hand, he has a lot to do with his patrons, Pearl S. Buck and his wife. Pearl S. Buck's husband is Lin Yutang's editor, publisher, literary agent, news agent and public relations consultant (Shi Jianwei, 1999: 351). Lin Yutang's abridged translation or a series of translated works are inseparable from Pearl S. Buck's request and suggestion. In addition, government departments, religious groups and other patrons may directly determine the rise and fall of translation activities. This type of patronage is often powerful, exerting pressure on the translator himself by using power and ideology under his control to influence and guide the spread and development of translation ideas (Gentzler, 1993). Patronage influences the selection of translators, and translators are more passive in cooperation and obedience under various privileges and pressures. As a translator and thinker, Yan Fu has his own clear purpose and idea in the selection of translation materials, but he is also an official appointed by the Qing government, so his selection of translation materials is also controlled by the ideology of the patrons.

In order to better analyze the influence of factors outside the text on literature, Andre Lefevere provides a set of new terms. There are three key words in this set of terms: ideology, poetics and patronage. They are adopted by this book. By comparing the four Chinese versions of *Waiting for Godot*, it is not difficult to find that the translator is manipulated by ideology, poetics, and patronage in the process of translation. In the following contents, this book probes into the four versions by these three aspects.

4.1 Manipulation of Ideology

In 1796, the term "ideology" is first put forward by French philosopher and statesman Antoine Louis Claude Destutt, comte de Tracy (1754—1836) in his book *the Elements of Ideology*. It provides a real scientific philosophical basis for the generation of all ideas and gave it the meaning of science of ideas. Since then, ideology has been widely used by other philosophers and politicians in many fields, such as social science, social psychology and political science. Ideology is a collection of ideas. "Ideology is an organic ideological system composed of various forms of consciousness political thought, legal thought, economic thought, social thought, culture, education, ethics, art, religion and philosophy" (Yu Wujin: 131). Various forms of consciousness influence and restrict each other, forming an ideology with dynamic structure. In ideology, the status and the role of various forms of consciousness are different. Any ideology has a philosophy or religious thought as its core, and on this basis, it forms the most straightforward ideological expression of political thought, legal thought and economic thought. All the forms of consciousness influence each other and maintain the unified idea together.

Translation is a special form of consciousness. Translators are often influenced by local ideology to rewrite the source text, but at the same time, it is subversive because it is the platform for the direct confrontation between local ideology and foreign ideology. Under the influence of local ideology, the rewritten version can still convey foreign ideology and subvert local ideology in some periods. In this part, the book examines rewriting of sex-related descriptions and adding annotation to prove the influence of ideology on different Chinese versions of *Waiting for Godot*.

Beginning by rewriting of sex-related descriptions, the book observes the fact that material determines consciousness. Each nation's different material and cultural life shapes its distinctive ideology. The ideology of the source language countries is not necessarily applicable to the target language countries, and may even be excluded. Translators share an acute awareness of the close interrelationship between ideology and translation strategies. Accordingly, they rewrite the play appropriately. This can be checked by the following citations.

ST:

Estragon: What about hanging ourselves?

Vladimir: Hmm. It'd give us an erection

Estragon: (highly excited). An erection! (Beckett: 27)

TT1:

Estragon: How about we hang ourselves?（艾斯特岗：我们来上吊怎么样？）

Vladimir: Mmm! This will make us erect!（维拉迪米尔：嗯!这样会使我们勃起！）

Estragon: (very excited) get an erection!（艾斯特岗：（非常兴奋。）勃起！）（17）

TT2:

Estragon: How about hanging ourselves?（爱斯特拉贡：咱们上吊怎么样？）

Vladimir: That can be regarded as a method of tightening.（弗拉第米尔：那可以算是一种拉紧的方法。）

Estragon: (Being teased) How about we tighten it?（（被挑逗起来）

IV Analysis of Four Translated Versions in the Viewpoint of Rewriting Theory

咱们拉紧一下怎么样？）（13）

TT3:

Estragon: Let's try hanging ourselves?（爱斯特拉冈：咱们上吊试试怎么样？）

Vladimir whispered to Estragon. Estragon is very excited.（弗拉季米尔向爱斯特拉网耳语。爱斯特拉大为兴奋。）（13）

TT4:

Love: How about we hang ourselves?（愛：我們上吊如何？）

Buddha: Mmm! Hanging can make our penis erect.（佛：嗯!上吊可以使我們的陰莖勃起。）

Love: (greatly excited) penis erection!（愛：（大为兴奋）陰莖勃起！）（14）

The above four versions show different attitudes to the sex-related descriptions. Shi Xianrong's version published by people's Literature Publishing House in 1965 and Yu Zhongxian's version of 2006 are the authoritative versions in mainland China. The purposes of these two versions are to enhance readability and recommend more world-famous works to readers at all levels, while the purpose of the Taiwan translators is that readers can see this work in the eyes of modern people with the author's accusation of the whole human society. Different purpose of translation makes different translation strategies. China's cultural tradition holds a repressive attitude towards sex, and even regards it as a moral taboo. The dominant ideology of Confucianism advocates controlling individual's biological desire, regarding the restraint of sexual desire as an important part of "cultivating one's moral character and cultivating one's nature（修身养性）". Even discussing this issue openly is not polite.

After 1949, under the dual pressure of culture and ethics, the sexual field became the forbidden area of Chinese society before the reform and opening up. In China before the reform and opening up, sex industry and homosexuality were regarded as extremely immoral and illegal behaviors, and they were completely prohibited. Under the ideological background of the 1960s, Shi Xianrong, graduated from the Department of western languages of Peking University in 1953, worked as an editor for 28 years in the people's Literature Publishing House. He translated many political works. He wanted to encourage people spiritually and guide people to look at foreign countries and their cultures positively. We can learn his translation purpose from his answer for *The Catcher in the Rye*. he says, "translating is just like building bridges between China and the West. I translated the book for the purpose that the Chinese readers see the social phenomena critically." (Tu Zhen: 34). The translator's ideology aims at transferring the contents positively. Since the translation process is directly controlled by the mainstream ideology of the target culture, the translator's translation purpose makes the translator delete the content that contradicts it.

Therefore, in Shi's version, the words related to sex are deleted and hidden. In this case, "Vladimir: Hmm. It'd give us an erection. Estragon: (highly excited). An erection!" (Beckett: 27). "Erection" has been omitted and replaced with "Vladimir whispered to Estragon. Estragon is very excited（弗拉季米尔向爱斯特拉贡耳语。爱斯特拉大为兴奋）" (Shi Xianrong: 13). It can be seen that Shi Xianrong adopts the translation method of deletion. He follows the ideology which means the world view of a certain society at that certain moment. This lies in the fact that "these rewriters will much more frequently adapt works of literature until they can be claimed to correspond to the poetics and the ideology of their age" (Daniel weissbort and Astradur eysteinsson: 437). Ideology is a variety of ideas rooted in the human brain, and these concepts are dominated by the social right structure and right relations. As an activity of understanding, interpreting and recreating, translation is dominated by the translator. However, as a person living in the society, the translator is bound to be influenced or even dominated by the social ideology. Behind the translation act, the conscious form of the thought and interpretation system is always playing a role. As ideology is determined by social existence, the social ideology in different historical periods is different. It has different influence on translation. Just as Lefevere defines ideology as what the society has or is allowed to have, this book believes that ideology is all kinds of socially acceptable concepts and attitudes in a particular society in a specific period of time, through which translators and readers can accept and understand translation works.

When it comes to Yu Zhongxian's version, which is also a Chinese version, is published in 2006, "Erection" is not removed, but translated as "tightening (拉紧)" (Yu Zhongxian: 13), We can interpret it in English as stretching and tensing as much as possible, euphemistically conveying a sexual action. In other words, Yu adopts euphemism, which expresses some facts or ideas in a tactful or gentle way to reduce the degree of vulgarity. In addition, footnotes are added in translation, which is interpreted as a word game. Because the reference is the original French translation, the translator explains his translation idea like this: in French, "Se Pendant" and "bander" are similar in form and pronunciation. In addition, the word "bander" also has the meaning of "Erection" in slang. In the following conversation, the word "bander" has the double meaning.

From the comparison of the two mainland versions, we can see the change of Chinese ideology. At the turn of the 1970s and 1980s, China launched a discussion on the standard of truth. In addition to "emancipate the mind (解放思想)", another direct result of reform and opening up is that China has a new understanding of the world through opening up. Freud, Foucault, Marcuse, Fromm and others' philosophy and psychology about sexual love are widely spread in Chinese university campuses and intellectual circles. Their works, together with the works of other scholars such as Nietzsche and Sartre, which emphasize rebellion and freedom, constitute an important ideological source of enlightenment for Chinese people in the reform and opening up era.

In the influx of western thoughts, feminism and sexual emancipation as the most mysterious and innovative part is watched. These views are so far away from the traditional ideas of Chinese people that they are gradually spread in the shock of Chinese people. The 1980s is a turning point. In the last 30 years, the atmosphere becomes relaxed. Neutral reports and theoretical discussions on sexual issues have appeared in newspapers. The society has also experienced a process from strictness to leniency in terms of the norms of sexual description and expression in literature and art: from being neither able to write about love nor sex, to being able to only write about love but not sex and finally to be able to write both love and sex.

As a result of the socio-economic and political situation of the special, translations greatly transform the environment. Translation must be carried out in a specific political, social, historical and cultural environment. Firstly, the translator is the product of the above factors. Secondly, when he is engaged in translation, the environment has both influence and restriction on him. The filtering function of translation lies in intervening in power, which leads to the secondary distribution of power.

The distribution power possessed by the translator is a kind of restriction mechanism and can make him engage in the manipulation of ideology quietly. At the same time, translation is a kind of cultural behavior. Any cultural form and practice may provide opportunities for ideological criticism, because cultural interpretation itself has many connections with ideology. In addition, the re-contextualization caused by translation also erodes the original text. The effects sound mostly negative, but erosion promotes change, and the change is often positive. This can be proved by Benjamin who pointed out that the regeneration of the original text must undergo changes. In fact, it is a targeted manipulation of the instability of the original work to eliminate the historical, political and ideological forces of the source language.

After analyzing the two mainland versions, we analyze the two Taiwan versions. Wen Jun（文军）says that Qiu Gangjian's plays are pioneering, and his thinking and scripts are often ahead of the trend. Qiu Gangjian's version of Beckett's masterpiece *Waiting for Godot* is the most experimental work. To some extent, it also determines the modernity of Qiu's creation, and his ideology determines the boldness of translation. His wife Zhao Xiangyang（赵向阳）said that "Qiu Gangjian once said He can express his feelings, thoughts and ideals at will. His poems, like his film and TV plays, are inseparable from the description of women, death and sex, which is probably due to his personality"(2014).

Therefore, we can see the bold description of sex in Qiu's version. In this case, "erection" is directly translated as "penile erection". The sentences "the land where the semen falls will grow out of the flower. That's why they shriek when you pull them up." are translated as a direct description of sexual behavior on the land where semen drips. Although it is translated in 1968 when it is a conservative era, the translator's ideology influences the translation. In Xu Anhua's（许鞍华）words, Qiu is a man who has never experienced political turmoil. In fact, he is a completely naive person who describes and constructs the script from the perspective of human nature.

Another version is published by Liao Yuru in 2008, and her version has almost no abridgement. In the translation of this plot, she adopts the method of literal translation. At the same time, she added a footnote which can be interpreted in English as: "Datura[①] is a plant mentioned in the song of the Bible for flirting, which is related to the erection mentioned above" (Liao 17). In 2008, people's minds are relatively open, and it is easy to accept such literal translation. At the same time, the footnotes introduce foreign cultures and point out the connections in the text. These two translated versions can also be proved by the sentence: "ideology focuses on what society should or can be" (Lefevere 14).

After examining the sex related words, annotations are checked in the following contents. What is annotation? In 1997, Genette put forward the concept of "sub-text", trying to achieve functional equivalence with the original text by adding content to the translation. The "sub-text" here includes the annotation we refer to. As far as word meaning is concerned, annotation "is also known as explanation note. The explanation of vocabulary, content and citation source in an article is generally printed in a smaller font than that of the text"（Genette: 37）.

---

① Solanum lyratum

All the four versions of *Waiting for Godot* have one printed in the foot of the page which is called the footnote. The translators believe that a country's works not only reflect the country's unique social reality, customs and habits, laws and regulations, utensils and costumes, but also involve the country's unique cultural connotation, such as narrative mode, antithesis rhythm, literary image, historical allusions, aesthetic psychology, etc., which are the hidden information shared between the original author and the reader. When these contents are transmitted across cultures and arrive at a brand-new cultural environment, they become obstacles for readers to understand. Translators make these contents annotated for explanation. The reason for the translator to make such choices in the process of translation lies in the translator's pre understanding and the translator's ideology choice. The translator's pre understanding includes innate factors and acquired factors. The innate factors are psychological factors such as personality and temperament. These specific factors that constitute the pre understanding of the translator are inexhaustible, so it is not convenient to do the most research. The acquired factors are indirect experience such as historical and cultural knowledge, direct life experience and aesthetic taste.

This book selects culture ideology of acquire factors to research translators' annotations translation compensation for culture. This is because they repress certain works of literature and these works are rewriting by these rewriters for their culture ideology. The culture ideology makes literary translation is not only a process of how to follow or use rules, but also a process in which translators make decisions. "Rewriters much more frequently adapt works of literature until they can be claimed to correspond to the ideology of their age" (Daniel weissbort and Astradur eysteinsson: 435). For example, there are some dialogues to discuss the beard of Godot in *Waiting for Godot* between Vladimir and a boy.

Vladimir: Has he a beard, Mr. Godot?
Boy: Yes Sir.
Vladimir: Fair or … (he hesitates) … or black?

IV Analysis of Four Translated Versions in the Viewpoint of Rewriting Theory

Boy: I think it's white, Sir. (Beckett: 131)

This is to explore the image of Godot in *Waiting for Godot*. Before this discussion, Lucky has a long speech in the play also implies this image and at the beginning of the speech he says: "Given the existence as uttered forth in the public works of Puncher and Wattmann of a personal God quaquaquaqua with white beard quaquaquaqua outside time without extension who from the heights of divine apathia divine athambia..."(Beckett: 60). The image of God depicted by the Lucky man clearly comes from the Bible. John put it in the *Resurrected Savior*, "clothed in robes, straight down to the feet, and girded with gold bands between his breasts. His head and hair are white as white wool, as snow; his eyes are like fire; his feet are like copper in a furnace to exercise light; his voice is like the sound of many waters"(15). In this conversation, two tramps also ask the boy about the color of Godot's beard. When it is confirmed that it is white, Vladimir says "Jesus bless us" (Beckett 131). Obviously, the white bearded "Godot" that vagrants have been waiting for is exactly what Lucky calls "white bearded" God. Their description of Godot is strikingly similar to the Christian description of God, which is connected with the attribute of God. They say that they know Godot, but they hardly recognize him and can't recognize him when they see him.

Compared with the four translated versions, the other three translate "fair"into "gold". We find that Liao's version translates "fair"into "white", and then the version writes clearly why it is translated into "white" in the annotation. If "fair" describes the mane, it should be translated as gold, but considering the general saying, it is still translated as white beard, which can echo the image of God in Lucky's monologue. This kind of annotation indicates the translator's choice is similar to the Christian description of God. That can be explained by one sentence that is "translation annotation are compared to the translator's 'footprints' and 'the second voice'" (Paloposki: 91). When two different ideologies collide, translators adopt appropriate translation strategies to promote the transformation of source culture to target culture. In order to better serve the interests of the leading ideology, the translator uses the rewriting strategies such as adding footnotes. it can help readers understand the implied meaning of the original text, and thus understand the implied meaning of the original author.

In order to further explain the phenomenon that the translator's culture ideology chooses to annotate translation compensation for culture, this book makes a comparative table of annotations.

Table 4.1 Annotations in Four Versions

TT1: 47 annotations	TT2: 16 annotations	TT3: 16 annotations	TT4: 9 annotations
4) Vera demir refers to hope, but Beckett doesn't make it clear in this sentence, so the translation is also deliberately omitted. (維拉迪米爾指的是希望，但是貝克特在此句裡不刻意說明，因此譯文也故意省略。)	4)Atlas Zhu's son (Greek mythology) （阿特拉斯·朱的儿子（希腊神话））	4) All four of the characters are wearing top hats （四个登场人物都戴着礼帽）	4) Pan,The Faun of half man and half sheep in Greek mythology （潘·希腊神话中半人半羊之牧神）
10) There is a sense of participation （有参与之意）	10) Miranda is the heroine of Shakespeare's The Tempest. （米兰达是莎士比亚暴风雨的女主人公）	10) Miranda, the heroine of Shakespeare （密兰达，莎士比亚的女主人公）	
…	…	…	…

Ⅳ Analysis of Four Translated Versions in the Viewpoint of Rewriting Theory

续表

TT1: 47 annotations	TT2: 16 annotations	TT3: 16 annotations	TT4: 9 annotations
16) Pan is the son of Zeus, sheep horn, leg, sheep, leaving animal traces, with greed, desire, lust and other features. (Pan牧神是宙斯之子，羊犄角、羊腿、羊，留獸的痕，帶著貪婪.欲望.情欲等官能的特征)	16)Laplansh, it's a stage (拉普郎什，有舞台的意思)	16) Latin; Reminiscence of happy times in the past (拉丁文；回忆过去的快乐时光)	
Miranda is the daughter of Prospero, the Duke of Milan, the hero of Shakespeare's play *The Tempest*. (Miranda是莎剧《暴风雨》的男主角米蘭公爵普洛士丕之女。)			

From the above table, we can see that there are annotations in the four versions. There are sixteen for Shi's version, sixteen for Yu's version, nine for Qiu's version and forty-seven for Liao's version. The number and the content of the annotation are different. As translation explanatory notes, they play the role of different cultural functions. The cultural functions are explained as following three functions.

Firstly, the annotation plays the role of the compensatory function of cultural ideology. The western culture in *Waiting for Godot* is different from the contemporary Chinese culture in terms of times, regions, nationalities. In addition, the absurdity of the dialogues makes it possible for the original readers to flinch from the obscure *Waiting for Godot* at that time. Hence, it is tougher for Chinese

· 109 ·

ordinary readers to understand the contents. Cultural defects are inevitable in literary translation.

The translator should give full play to the role of imagination and creativity, and make up for the loss within the text and supplement outside the text. By means of annotation outside the text, the loss of translation can be reduced to the minimum. Translation compensation is an important topic in translation studies, which plays an important role in making up for the defects of language and culture. The names of gods, people, place names, plants and scenery in myths and legends appear vacancy and non-correspondence between Chinese and English.

Annotation is an effective way to solve this cultural gap. In the above table, "Atlas" is translated into "阿特拉斯" by the method of transliteration and then it has a footnote which can be explained as in Greek mythology, a god is holding the sky in both hands. "Pan" is translated as "潘" by the method of transliteration and also has an explanatory note of the Faun of half man and half sheep in Greek mythology and "Cain" is translated as "该隐" with an annotation of *Genesis*.

Mythology and history are precious spiritual heritages of human beings. The historical origins of all nations in the world are always entangled with myths. The legendary characters in ancient history have gone through the long-term evolution process and most of the annotations of this kind focus on the historical figures, allusions and gods of myth. The inheritance of vernacular culture in translation needs the help of annotation. After all, the translation cannot be crammed with too many explanations. Annotation has become the best way for translators to transfer foreign cultures. In the process of translation, how to retain and inherit these mythical thoughts becomes the responsibility of translators.

Secondly, it plays a role in the extension function of text's humanistic information. Intertextuality is one of the important features of translation, which not only permeates the translated text, but also embodies in the annotation. Translators are limited by time and space, that leads to the relevant information has to be generated in the annotation. Annotation intertextuality is the solution to the extension of culture. This book holds the view that translation is a process of adjustment and balance with various factors. Luo Xuanmin (罗选民) also believes that "Even if the translator has mastered the intertextual references of the original text, these references only work in the original text and are unique to the original text. Therefore, the translator can not find the same intertextual references in the target language" (142). We can say the translator needs to construct annotations so that the aesthetic taste and cultural elements of the translation can be expanded and extended in the notes.

Contents and annotations in the target text constitute a typical humanistic interaction. Wang Hongyin (王宏印) holds the same opinion as the book. "In the process of reading, the target readers actually see a melancholy figure at the intersection of the dual literary history, that is, the translator, who is a dual identity cultural disseminator" (164). It is the intertextuality that makes the translated works drag the long shadow of the literary history of the source language when they enter the literary history of the target language. For example, In the annotation Miranda is the daughter of Prospero, the Duke of Milan, the hero of Shakespeare's *The Tempest*, and the first sentence "art thou pale for weariness" of the poem *To the Moon* which is written by Percy B. Shelley, an English Romantic poet. Both annotations carefully reinterpreting traces that overlapping each other between the source text and the target text, which means to pay close attention to the intertextuality.

Thirdly, it has the communication function. The translator appears directly and explains to the readers the inadequacies of his translation or his feelings in translation. Take these annotations for instance, "weeping has the meaning of weeping and drooping branches and leaves: Here we can see the clever meaning of Beckett's words, but it is a great challenge for translators"(Liao: 13), and "Vladimir refers to hope, but Beckett doesn't mean to explain it in this sentence, so the translation is also intentionally omitted" (Liao: 8). The translator explains what are the difficulties and why she chooses the method of omission for the readers getting closer the distance between the target readers and the source text. Accordingly, the annotations of the four Chinese versions of *Waiting for Got* have different functions which can be showed in the following table.

Table 4.2　Annotation Function

Functions	The Four Chinese Versions			
	TT1	TT2	TT3	TT4
Function of compensatory cultural ideology	12	8	12	7
Function of extending text's humanistic information	2	1	1	0
Function of communicating with readers	33	7	3	2

After the contrastive study of the four versions, we can find that Liao's version is with the most annotations of forty-seven and most of them are focused on the function of communicating with readers. While Qiu's version is with the least nine annotations and most of them are focused on the function of the compensatory function of cultural ideology. Yu's version and Shi's version are transferred with 16 annotations while Yu's version focuses on both the function of the compensatory function of cultural ideology and the function of communicating with readers, Shi's version focuses on the function of the compensatory function of cultural ideology. It can be seen from this table, under the culture ideology of the 1960s, when translator introduces foreign culture into China, the translator takes such a kind of act of seeking common ground to dialogue with the source culture actively and make cultural compensation. In the early 21st century in the process of introducing foreign culture into China, translators have paid more attention to the dialogue with readers and tend to communicate with readers. In other words, target readers are becoming more and more important.

From the previous analysis, annotation is an important part in translation process. The cultural turn of translation pays attention to the characteristics of translation process and its transformation function in political and historical sense. That enables translator to make use of someone else's discourse for his own purposes "by inserting a new semantic intention into a discourse which already has, and which retains, an intention of its own" (Bakhtin: 189). Target readers don't read or understand the original text, and naturally they don't understand the mystery. Translation is the main means to construct the image of literature. Through the translator, "self" and "other", "native" and "exotic" can construct interactive relations. "'I' pays attention to 'the other', and the image of 'the other' also conveys a certain image of 'I', who is the watcher, speaker and writer" (Meng Hua: 4). In order to pay attention to "the other" from the "self" and convey the "exotic sentiment", it is wise for translators to recognize the foreign literature image by contrasting the differences between Chinese and Western cultures from the observer, that is, juxtaposing the distance of space poetics with the help of annotation platform, which highlights the foreign literature image and achieves the goal of cultural utilization and cultural transmission.

In the book's view, the task of translation is to smoothly transfer the culture information, aesthetics and plots contained in the original text from one language to another language. Moreover, as a bridge between the original author and the target readers, the translator is not only responsible for the translation, but also responsible for the readers of the translation. Through the effective way of annotation, the translator can not only help the author expand the field of ideological communication, but also retain the original language and cultural characteristics to the maximum extent. It is necessary to add appropriate, reasonable and sufficient annotation for a translation. With the help of necessary annotation, the reader can deeply and smoothly understand the original theme and artistic conception.

This part examines the four versions from the perspective of manipulation of ideology. It begins by locating the sex related description in four versions within the context of the Chinese ideology. In the process of rewriting, translation is inevitably carrying out cultural hybridization in order to achieve a certain balance. The decline of foreign culture, including strong culture, which has been packaged by local culture, may be due to ideology. How to hybridize and to what extent should be considered from the effect of cross-cultural communication, and not be free from the influence of ideology.

Hence, the ideology of translation involves discourse power. The advanced and powerful western civilization has created a strong discourse, while the reception politics of local culture, supported by ideology, also has the power of discourse resistance, which is reflected in the operation of translation through the translator, which is mainly reflected on rewriting, deleting, selecting and omitting and so on.

In the later part, the book focuses on annotations in four versions within the context of the Chinese culture ideology. The problem of cultural connotation and denotation cannot be ignored in translation, and the transmission of cultural information is indispensable.

Otherwise, the translation is incomplete, although the integrity in the strict sense is unattainable. If we have the tolerance to absorb and accommodate foreign cultures, then the cultural transformation is mild and limited, although it intentionally or unintentionally eliminates or weaken the unacceptable ideological discourse elements. The text is tailor-made for readers in a specific historical and cultural context. Although translation inevitably changes the nature of the original text, it should not ignore the target readers. That means the translation also should be taken into account in terms of acceptance. How to transmit information seems to be mainly related to the control of the representation of culture, and how to further explore the connotation, it also involves the power of ideological discourse.

Due to ideology, the inadequacy of translation lies in the operational level on the basis of subjective considerations caused by various concerns. It is difficult to fully convey the meaning of the original text, especially the cultural information of the source language when it is in the face of the change of cultural value on the operational level. Ideological interpretation is a common decoding method. Translation operates first of all under the constraint of the original, itself the product of constraints belonging to a certain time. "In translation, however, they need to be resuscitated, though nobody is quite sure in what form: loan translation, calque, footnote, a combination of the three" (Wang Hongyin: 164)? Translation is a complete transferring process from the source text to the target text by using the translator's own knowledge. As a kind of double coding, it can achieve some ideological or aesthetic purpose by manipulating the symbols. In the following four versions of *Waiting for Godot* are examined in the view point of manipulation of poetics.

4.2 Manipulation of Poetics

In the above part four versions of *Waiting for Godot* are checked from the perspective of manipulation of ideology. This part emphasizes the rewriting symbols by poetics. What's poetics? In the *Encyclopedia of Translation Studies* compiled by a British scholar Mona Baker, translation poetics includes two aspects: "one is the sum of the genre, theme and literary methods that constitute any literary system; the other is that in translation studies, translatology represents the role of a literary system in a larger social system" (Mona Baker: 183). It shows how this literary system interacts with other literary systems or symbolic systems.

At the same time, "translational poetics also studies the poetical comparison between the source text in its own literary system and the target text in different systems" (Baker: 183). According to Lefevere, poetics in translation has two components: "one is a list of literary techniques, genres, themes, typical characters and situations, and symbols; the other is the concept of what role literature has or should play in the whole social system"(Lefevere 26). The latter "is obviously closely related to ideological influences on the scope of poetics, and it is produced by various ideological forces in the environment of the literary system"(Lefevere 27).

In translation, poetics refers to its role in the field of literature and even the whole society from a macro perspective; from a micro perspective, poetics refers to the specific creative techniques, themes, characters and so on used in literary creation or translation. Poetics evolves with the change of mainstream ideology. When translating literature, it is generally necessary to make the translation conform to the mainstream poetics of the target culture. Manipulation school holds that "from the perspective of target linguistics, all translation means a certain degree of manipulation of the source language in order to achieve a certain purpose" (Lefevere 29). Manipulation is not only self-conscious, but also self-directed. No matter whether self-conscious or self-controlled, it must be shown in translation only through the translator. In this part, four Chinese versions of *Waiting for Godot* are researched from the perspective of how the translators apply writing literature techniques in their poetic systems so as to attract target readers.

As for the writing literature techniques, logical differences are involved when from the perspective of target linguistics. When it comes to logical differences, nothing is more obvious than hypotaxis[①] and parataxis[②]. Nida, a famous contemporary American translator, also believes that the difference between Chinese and English is parataxis and hypotaxis. Hypotaxis is a term "used to describe elaborate systems of grammatical subordination" (210). Parataxis is used for "combinations of clauses which are closely related semantically, but which have no formal markers" (210).

Due to the differences in thinking between Chinese and English, English emphasizes hypotaxis, and a large number of related words are used to express the logical relationship between clauses clearly through strict language structure.

---

① Parartaxis: The arranging of clauses one after the other without connectives showing the relation between them. Example: The rain fell; the river flooded; the house was washed away. (The World Book Dictionary)

② Hypotaxis: The dependent or subordinate relationship of clauses with connectives; for example, I shall despair if you don't come. (The American Heritage Dictionary of the English Language)

IV　Analysis of Four Translated Versions in the Viewpoint of Rewriting Theory

Subject-predicate structure is the main line, which is expanded by non-finite verb structure, noun, preposition or clause, and it becomes a tree structure vividly. However, Chinese attaches great importance to parataxis. It pays little attention to the rigor of language form structure, but hides its semantics in a seemingly complicated and disorganized language structure. The internal structure of sentences is extremely loose, and it seldom uses related words. The relationship between clauses is not expressed through obvious language structure, and its semantic expression usually depends on the order of time or things, which is called "bamboo structure" in image.

In the oral expression of Chinese, this kind of phenomenon is particularly obvious, especially in the instant speech. The speaker fails to go through strict language organization. Dialogues even appear multiple subjects and multiple topics jumping in the same sentence, which we call flowing sentences.

The concept of flowing sentence is first put forward by Lv Shuxiang（吕淑湘）, who thinks that "there are many flowing sentences in spoken Chinese, one small sentence after another, and many places can be broken and connected" (27). In the four versions of *Waiting for Godot*, flowing sentence is an important feature of sentence construction. For example: "He glanced at his boots, reached in and touched them, tipped them upside down, and looked up to see if anything had fallen out of them, but he saw nothing. touched them again, staring forward in a trance（他往靴内瞧了瞧，伸进手去摸了摸，把靴子口朝下倒了倒，往地上望了望，看看有没有什么东西从靴里掉出来，但什么也没看见，又往靴内摸了摸，两眼出神地朝前面瞪着）" (Shi 5).

Sentences take meaning as the boundary, and the information capacity of sentences is not limited by grammatical form, which is very flexible. It describes the action one sentence after another, just like flowing water, showing "linear flow" pursuing flowing rhythm, not staying in shape. Compared with English, the subject-predicate structure of Chinese running-water sentences is much more complicated, and its subject is changeable, which can express the agent, the time and place. The same is true of predicates in running water sentences: they can be verbs, nouns or adjectives; It can be one verb, multiple verbs, or no verbs; It can be a single word or multiple phrases. We cite examples to examine the differences between the source text and the target text.

  ST: Vladimir breaks into a hearty laugh which he immediately stifles. (Beckett 131)

  Qiu: Vladimir suddenly laughed happily, but immediately stopped. (弗拉迪米尔突然开心大笑，但立刻就刹住双手)(7)

  Yu: Vladimir suddenly burst out laughing, but immediately stopped. (弗拉迪米尔突然开怀大笑起来，但立即就止住了笑。)(240)

  Shi: Vladimir laughed loudly, suddenly stopped laughing (弗拉基米尔纵声大笑，突然止住笑。)(6)

  Liao: Vladimir suddenly burst into laughter, almost lost breath (维拉迪米尔突然爆笑，差点岔气。)(9)

  As shown above, the original English sentences uses "which" as the antecedent of the attributive clause, and in the following actions, it uses three "his" to indicate his actions clearly. It lies in the fact that English has the dominant feature of hypotaxis. Relation words are required to demonstrate how things are connected. These relation words must use with cohesive and coherent functions to show the logical relationship between English sentences. such as prepositions, prepositional phrases, non-finite verbs and relation conjunctions, etc.

  In Chinese, there is no attributive clause in Chinese and "his" is omitted in all four translations. Only by sentence order Chinese readers can understand the logical relationship of a series of actions. This is determined by the characteristics of parataxis in Chinese. In the process of translation, the translators adopt the translation method of omission in the four versions. From the linguistic features of Chinese and English, Chinese pays attention to the interaction between scenery and people, pays attention to the theme consciousness, and is usually "subject-oriented". Parataxis is an extremely important mechanism for emphasizing ideas and making sentences unfold with ideas as the main axis, thus making syntax implicit. This is a typical literary means in Chinese poetics.

On the contrary, English is concise, and translators adopt rational and intuitive expressions, which also accords with the contemporary aesthetic habits of western readers. Besides, the logical relations between clauses in Chinese lie in flowing sentences which can be clearly expressed by time, order of events and even by mood. When it comes to translation, translators transfer this difference by making use of poetic rules. "Most writing on translation have elevated what are, basically, simple and inescapable facts rooted in the very difference between languages and in the dictates of translation poetics" (Lefevere 101).

Therefore, the English translation of Chinese running-water sentences should externalize the implied logical relations in the original text and transform the parataxis in Chinese into hypotaxis in English. When it comes to translate English into Chinese, the logical relationship in the original text must be hidden.

The differences in sentence patterns of English and Chinese can be divided into two types: tree type and bamboo type (Chen: 6). It is pointed out by Chen Anding（陈安定）in his *English and Chinese-A Comparative Study* published in 1985. in English, the main structure is prominent, that is, the structure of subject, predicate and object is prominent, just like the trunk of a tree. When English is used to express complicated ideas, it often comes to the point. First, the subject and the main verb of the sentence are put up, and then the attributive clause and other phrases are linked to the two buildings with various relative words. People compare English sentences to a towering tree with luxuriant branches and leaves. In Chinese, verbs are often used. According to the order of action or logical order, semantic connected verbs give people a relaxed and bright feeling. Its sentence structure is like a bamboo, one after another.

More specific, English sentences have a rigorous subject-predicate structure, in which the subject is indispensable, the predicate verb is the center of the sentence, and other sentence components are spread around the subject and predicate. They have distinct priorities, clear levels and tree structure. According to the types of subject-predicate structure, English sentences can be divided into five sentence patterns, namely SV, SVP, SVO, SVOO and SVOC.

By contrast, Chinese is not restricted by form. it has no strict subject-predicate structure, and has a "bamboo-knot" structure. For instance: "Vladimir breaks into a hearty laugh/(A) which he immediately stifles(B)/ his hand pressed to his pubis, his face contorted(C)" (Beckett 131). "Vladimir suddenly burst into laughter /(A), almost lost his breath /(B), pressed his hand, twisted his face(C) [维拉迪米尔突然爆笑/(A),差点岔气/(B),手按沁骨，脸部扭曲(C)。]"(Liao 9) .

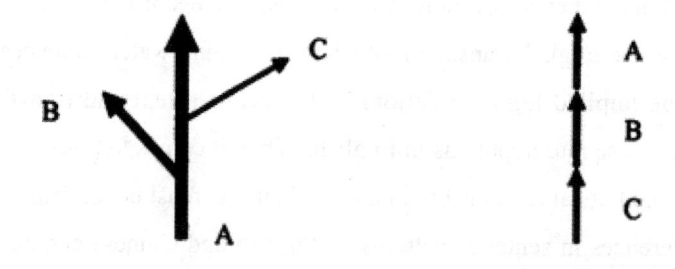

Chart 4.1   Tree Type and Bamboo Type

The diversity of Chinese sentence patterns is also reflected in a large number of loose sentences and zero sentences. That is, the whole sentence has a subject-predicate structure, while the zero sentence has no subject-predicate structure and is composed of words or phrases. For example: "There was a terrible cry, very close to them. They were in a daze, stood still（一阵恐怖的喊声，离他们很近。他们发愣了，站着不动）"（Shi Xianrong: 18）. Zero sentence is a basic sentence pattern of Chinese. The whole sentence is composed of zero sentences, which are mixed and interlaced to form a flowing sentence. Therefore, translators should pay attention to explicit cohesion and implicit semantic coherence in the process of pursuing cohesion transformation, pragmatic equivalence and natural expressive way.

Moreover, one of the literary techniques of parataxis in Chinese is the

IV Analysis of Four Translated Versions in the Viewpoint of Rewriting Theory

four-character structure. It is defined in the *Dictionary of Modern Chinese*. The Chinese four-character structure referred to in this book mainly refers to a Chinese expression in the form of four characters, which can be literally understood as a language format composed of four characters. Strictly speaking, Chinese four-character structure should belong to a fixed language in the form of four characters, which excludes many uncured four-character phrases from the scope of four-character lattices.

Chinese four-character structure has its own independence, which forms two important characteristics of four-character structure: first, four-character structure cannot be expanded syntactically; Secondly, the four-character structure adopts the rhythm type of two plus two and it has a fixed stress pattern. Chinese four-character structure can be roughly divided into four categories.

The first are proper nouns, including proper names and place names, such as Shakespeare（莎士比亚）、and Australia（澳大利亚）; The second is newspapers and periodicals, organization names, place names and brand trademarks in proper names, such as People's Daily（《人民日报》）, Peking University（北京大学）, and Alpes（阿尔卑斯）; The third is the word four-character reduplication, such as: high and low（高高低低）, more than enough（绰绰有余）, fixed（板上钉钉）and so on; The fourth is four-character idioms, which are one of the most typical language expressions in Chinese. They are indispensable and important components in Chinese which are used frequently, such as play the lute to a cow — to have the wrong audience（对牛弹琴）, perspiration came down like raindrops（挥汗如雨）and so on. Chinese four-character structure has a long history, which is concise in content, neat in form, harmonious and pleasing in melody.

Table 4.3 Examples of Poetic Style of Four Versions

ST: (Beckett 86)	TT1：(85)		TT2: (326)		TT3：(65)		TT4: (83)	
Estragon: All the dead voices.	Estegang: These sounds of death.	艾斯特岗：這些死亡的聲音。	Estragon: A dead voice.	爱斯特拉贡：死了的嗓音。	Estragon: All the dead voices.	爱斯特拉冈：所有死掉了的声音。	Love: It's all the sound of death	爱：都是死的声音
Vladimir: They make a noise like wings	Vladimir: They make a noise like wings.	維拉迪米爾：他們發出的噪音彷彿翅膀。	Vladimir: The sound of a kind of wings.	弗拉第米尔：构成一种翅膀的声音。	Vladimir: They make a sound like wings.	弗拉季米尔：它们发出翅膀一样的声音。	Buddha: They make noises like wings	佛：它们发出像翅膀的噪声
Estragon: Like leaves.	Estegang: is like a leaf.	艾斯特岗：彷彿葉子。	Estragon: leaves'.	爱斯特拉贡：树叶的。	Estragon: the same as leaves	爱斯特拉冈：树叶一样	Love: like leaves	爱：像叶子
Vladimir: Like sand.	Viladimir: is like sand.	維拉迪米爾：彷彿沙子。	Vladimir: Shashi's.	弗拉第米尔：沙石的。	Vladimir: the same as sand	弗拉季米尔：沙一样。	Buddha: like sand	佛：像沙
Estragon: Like leaves.	Estegang: is like a leaf.	艾斯特岗：彷彿葉子。	Estragon: leaves'.	爱斯特拉贡：树叶的。	Estragon: The same as leaves.	爱斯特拉冈：树叶一样。	Love: like leaves	爱：像叶子
Silence	(silence.)	(沉默。)	silence.	沉默。	(silence)	(沉默)	(Silent)	(静默)

For this reason, in translation of English to Chinese, many translators like to use the four-character structure flexibly, which makes the translation not only accurately and vividly convey the content and theme of the original text, but also enrich the vocabulary of the translation. For this reason, poetic style is transferred by four-character structure in the four Chinese versions of *Waiting for Godot*. The following examples can justify this transfer.

Poetic style deserves enough attention. Like the poetic drama in English in the late 1940s and early 1950s in which the dominant form of expression was "a lyrical, poeticised, often purely decorative form of language" (Knowlson 105), many impressive dialogues in Beckett's plays can be described as poetic. *Waiting for Godot* is also featured by this poetic language. It is undeniable that the language of the play is unbelievably simple and colloquial. More often than not, the simple dialogues appear to be arranged in artless fashion.

However, the seemingly meaningless cross-talk includes melodious wording and repetition, which features the characteristics of poetry. As McDonald claims, "the one-or two-word utterances, carefully shaped into repetition and variation, give them a poetic, estranging quality that unsettles the colloquial banality" (McDonald 151). Shu Xiaomei, a Chinese scholar, also supports this book's view. She argues that when dealing with the dialogues, Beckett often deliberately simplifies sentence structure in order to obtain poetic features (56).

It deserves attention to study the poetic characteristics and figure out the author's intention for comparative study the four versions. A very typical example is the one that the two tramps try to shut out the haunting "dead voices" by means of conversation. In this long dialogue, Vladimir's repeated words and the repeated silences have little to do with poetry. However, they are essential parts of a lyrical pattern.

This repetition develops into the concept of poetic style. According to Paul Lawley, "the passage has even been extracted and reprinted in an anthology of modern Irish poetry" (49). Moreover, Lawrence Graver also claims the dialogue is "recognizably more poetic and musical than any of the routines that have occurred in the play until now" (56). In this conversation, the poetic feature is mainly embodied in rhyme. Alliteration, assonance and consonance are the typical rhyming schemes in the passage. "L" is the alliteration between "Like" and "leaves". "Sand" and "ashes" share the same /æ/, so they have assonance. With the same /ə/ in the last syllable, "whisper" and "murmur" have consonance.

All these rhyming schemes enable the dialogue to possess lyrical quality. As for rhythm, Beckett employs onomatopoeic words and silences to create a slow-down atmosphere. When Vladimir and Estragon talk, the onomatopoeic words "whisper", "rustle", and "murmur" imitate the sounds of "wings", "sands", "leaves", "feathers", and "ashes", which together obtain "a soothing susurration" (McDonald 151).

In addition, with repeated pauses separating the two tramp's conversations, the melodious words mimic the sounds of the dead (Worth 15). Therefore, when reading, the readers may feel time is slowed down to a crawl in the intervals of the brisk little conversational "canters" which Vladimir and Estragon devise. However, behind the poetic language is the two friends' dilemma. "The blending of rhythm, repetition, and variation express a kind of disharmony embodied in the characters' language and their torment" (McDonald 151).

That is to say, the poetic content and form suggest Vladimir and Estragon's torture. They are waiting for Godot for so long. The two tramps deem time as crawling and silence as suffering. They invent a conversation to break silence and accelerate the passing of time. However, the two tramps, with no great passion, just generate talk for talk's sake, which are more than "wedded like alternations of a pendulum" (Mays 160).

Furthermore, what Vladimir and Estragon utter are the onomatopoeic words which imitate the "phantom voices" (Graver 57). Afraid of death or the apparition, they choose to keep silent in order to avoid the dead voices. The silence in turn traps them in the suffering of waiting again. It is noteworthy that Beckett presents their bitterness through poetic language in an indirect way.

What the readers listen to is the poetry, but what Vladimir and Estragon listen to are the dead voices. By means of the poetic features, the passage expresses lyricism with a slow-down rhythm. However, the dead voices they hear remind them of their tortures. That's why they want to keep the conversation moving on to block out the sound of the dead voices. Nevertheless, all their struggles turn

IV Analysis of Four Translated Versions in the Viewpoint of Rewriting Theory

out to be in vain. It seems that they employ the duet-like dialogues to dispel a terrifying silence. However, the poetic conversations do not save them from the "static time", but suggest the hopelessness in life.

According to the analysis mentioned above, there is no doubt that the poetic language in this part possesses thematic implication as well as musical characteristics. In this case, when it comes to translation, the translator should attach much importance to it to achieve functional equivalence for the target readers. Therefore, in *Waiting for Godot*, the comparison of the four Chinese versions should highlight the treatments of the poetic style of language.

First, it's necessary to look at the four translations: with rhyming schemes and rhythm of poetic language distinctive in this part, the four Chinese versions should also obtain attention on the two aspects. As Nida puts it, "if a translator makes a translation of a poem into something which is not a poem, this translation is not a functionally equivalent translation" (228). Owing to different linguistic characteristics between English and Chinese, it is hard to reproduce alliteration, assonance and consonance in Chinese versions.

There is a need for adaptation in translation if necessary. Since alliteration and assonance do not exist in Chinese, the four translators choose parallel structures respectively to imitate the pattern "Like..." with the patten "… same(一样)","like（像）…", "…'s（的）" and "be alike（仿佛）…". In Shi's version, compared with four characters "It's the same as a leaf（树叶一样）", the three characters in "It's the same as sand（沙一样）" does not fully express the parallel structure. In contrast, the three four-character structure in Liao's version reproduces its poetic style, which reveals a keen sense of Gogo and Didi's inflexibility. Furthermore, we can justify the same opinions that translators are influenced by the translation poetics of their day by the following table.

Table 4.4 Four-character Structure of Four Versions

ST: (Beckett 86)	TT1:（85）		TT2:（326）		TT3:（65）		TT4:（83）	
Vladimir: Rather they whisper.	Vladimir: It's better to say they were whispering.	維拉迪米爾：不如說他們在低喃。	Vladimir: It's better to say, they are murmuring.	弗拉第米爾：还不如说，它们在喃喃出声。	Vladimir: It's better to say they are whispering.	弗拉季米尔：不如说它们窃窃私语。	Buddha: They would rather speak softly.	佛：他们宁可微声细语。
Estragon: They rustle.	Estegan: they murmured.	艾斯特崗：他們嘰咕。	Estragon: They whispered.	爱斯特拉贡：它们窃窃私语。	Estragon: They rustle.	爱斯特拉冈：它们沙沙地响。	Love: They rustle.	爱：他们飒飒作响。
Vladimir: They murmur.	Vladimir: They mumbled.	維拉迪米爾：他們嘟囔。	Vladimir: they rustle	弗拉第米爾：它们沙沙作响	Vladimir: They whispered softly.	弗拉季米尔：它们轻声细语。	Buddha: They muttered endlessly.	佛：他们喃喃不休。
Estragon: They rustle.	Estegan: they murmured.	艾斯特崗：他們嘰咕。	Estragon: they whisper	爱斯特拉贡：它们窃窃私语	Estragon: They rustle.	爱斯特拉冈：它们沙沙地响。	Love: They rustle.	爱：他们飒飒作响。
Silence. (Beckett 86)	(Silence.)	（沉默。）	silence.	沉默。	(silence)	（沉默）	(Silence)	（静默）

As for consonance in "whisper" and "murmur" with onomatopoeic feature, this part becomes more complicated. In Shi's translation, the onomatopoeic words "whisper" and "murmur" are translated into "whisper to one another（窃窃私语）" and "say in a soft tone（轻声细语）" respectively, emphasizing the rhyming feature. In Qiu's translation, the words are translated into "rustle（飒飒作响）" and "endless speeches（喃喃不休）", focusing the reduplication which is not a simple repetition. It emphasizes rhythm of the language and is full of musical beauty.

In Yu's translation, the words are translated into "whisper to one another（窃窃私语）" and "rustle（沙沙作响）",focusing the reduplication while Liao translates them into "mumbling（低喃）" and "mutter（嘟囔）", focusing on the onomatopoeic feature. On account of the differences in English and Chinese languages, it is unlikely to blindly follow the English features in translating poetry or poetic style of language. Instead, the translator has to make some adaptations to achieve functional equivalence for the target readers. As Nida puts it, since there are no fully exact translations in two different languages, a translation can be close to the source text in readers' responses, but not limited in detail language (Nida 126).

In this aspect, compared with Liao's version, three versions of four-character structure are more acceptable for better reproducing the rhyming schemes by means of functionally equivalent translation. However, Liao's treatment of the onomatopoeic words better expresses the musical feature and slow-down rhythm which imitate the dead voices. As for Liao's version, it indeed pays attention to the parallel structure and the onomatopoeic words. The translation is more colloquial than musical. In addition, there is no essentially slow rhythm in her version, thus failing to suggest the stillness of time and man's sufferings.

Compared with Liao's version, Shi's version is better in reproducing the implied theme as well as the poetic style of language. All the translators change the meter and rhyme for Chinese poetics. Lefevere shares the same view with the book, The need to rhyme, therefore, by no means comes out of the "structure" of the original. It is imposed on translators by the "translation poetics" of their day, held that acceptable poetry translations should make use of the illocutionary strategies of meter and rhyme (100).

Furthermore, cultural poetics emphasizes finding the significance of literature works through the language of texts. Although in daily language communication, the most important function of language is the referential function, in literature, the poetic function is the dominant and decisive function. This poetic function is very enlightening and alarming for literary translation. Jacobson also agrees with this view, he points out "the subject of literary studies is not literature, but "literariness", that is, what makes a specific work become a literary work(62). "What kind of expression has poetic function?" The main problems to be studied in poetics are: "What turns a language message into a work of art? Because the theme of poetics is the differentia specifica between language art and other language behaviors" (Jakobson 350).

First, poetics is literary research, and vice versa; Second, the puzzling "differentia specifica" in the is literariness; Third, the theme of literary research or poetics research is not literature, but literariness, and literariness is the expression of "turning a language message into a work of art"; In other words, it is the things that make literature become literature, which is the "difference" between language art and other language behaviors; Fourthly, poetics is a leading knowledge in literary studies.

The third point deserves our attentions, which actually tells us that literariness is the expression of "turning a language message into a work of art". *Waiting for Godot* expresses the literariness of absurd play by its absurd dialogues. The absurd dialogues in *Waiting for Godot* are mysteries set by Beckett for readers. It is the translator's task to convey the author's language features accurately and skillfully, and let readers appreciate the style of the original work as much as possible. It's the translator's goal to turn the translated text into a work of art.

The four versions have made corresponding adaptation choices of conveying the language arts of the original and interpreting the author's intentions. Both English and Chinese have their own unique meanings. The more abundant this meaning is, the more difficult it is for each other to replace each other. Slangs have expressive power and strong appeal, which can better highlight characters and produce special effects expressed in specific languages. Slangs are used in the four versions of *Waiting for Godot*. This choice of language with regional characteristics is the translator's efforts to adapt to transfer the absurd effect of the source text and reflect this effect on the translated text.

In consist with the art of the original language, the translator creatively uses slangs mixed with dialects to convey the colloquialism style of the source language,

IV Analysis of Four Translated Versions in the Viewpoint of Rewriting Theory

so that the protagonists and language characteristics are fully reflected on the target language. "Translator training can alert translators both to the relativity of translation poetics and to strategies that may be used not to "overcome" the differences between languages, which may be influenced by not just of poetics but also of the intended audience of the translation" (Lefevere 100). In comparison, Qiu's translation is more casual in the use of slangs. On the one hand, it may be Qiu's writing habit as a writer. For example, he uses slangs many times in his memoirs. On the other hand, this is Qiu's deliberate pursuit, because he likes to translate humorous things. In the preface to the translation, he clearly states that he hopes to "make the translation as smooth and colloquial as possible", for example:"not to shed a tear until one sees the coffin(不见棺材不流泪)" (Qiu 5) and "to spend a tremendous amount of labor or money(费尽九牛二虎之力)"(Qiu 5).

It can find the similar translation method in Liao's "really nerve-wracking (真伤脑经)" (Liao 23), and Yu's "the leopard cannot change its spots(江山易改，本性难移)"(Yu 258) and "It's better to strike iron while it's hot(打铁最好还是要趁热)"(Yu 251) and Shi also uses dialects, especially when Vladimir and Estragon start yelling at each other. What the author wants to show is the chaos presented by absurd dialogue. Shi uses many dialects to express this promiscuity of language, such as, "a fake polite monkey"(假客气的猴儿) and "A prude pig (假正经的猪)"(Shi 81). These language in source text passage is confusing. In order to preserve the form of the original text and make readers feel the meaning of the original text, Shi chooses to use two kinds of address with cultural characteristics in the translation to imply their absurdity. Among them, "loser(窝囊废)" (Shi 81)and "opium ghost(鸦片鬼)" (Shi 82)are swearing words in China, while "priest(牧师)" (Shi 82)and "critic(批评)" (Shi 82) are normal address in English. This mixed language also shows the confusion of this person's thinking.

Dialects and slangs are expressive. They can be used to express protagonists' characters. The translator follows the characteristics of the original text and he creatively uses dialects and slangs to convey the style of the original text, thus

· 129 ·

embodying the protagonists and language characteristics in the target language. This translation method of adopting slangs, dialects and official language mixed languages of different classes is the same as the carnival theory, which originates from Bakhtin's cultural poetics. Emphasis is placed on finding resources from folk festivals, which completely abandon the usual hierarchy.

The four versions of *Waiting for Godot* are different from the source text, and this fact lies in the difference of poetic value. Translation is a series of optimal choices, and the translation is the result of the translator's choice to adapt to the target poetic environment. The four translators adapt to poetic function different degrees when using dialects and slangs, presenting readers with different styles.

With regard to poetic function, Jakobson also points "poetic function is to project the equivalence principle from the axis of selection to the axis of combination" (71). This sentence means that the expression with poetic function is selected by the author from a series of symbols with equivalent relationship, and then this choice is put into the combination sequence of sentences. Why does this choice have literary and poetic functions?

This is because only the sender of discourse needs to construct literary and poetic functions, he makes choices on the axis of choice. Jacobson's theory of "axis of choice" and "axis of combination" is initiated by Ferdinand de Saussure's semiotic thought. Saussure holds that "in the language state, everything is based on relations" (Saussure 122). Therefore, he distinguished two kinds of relations, one is called "syntagmatic relation" and the other is called "associative relation", which is equivalent to the combination relation and choice relation that Jacobson said. In the face of cultural poetic intention, translators should consider the imbalance of cognition, and then adopt active and flexible translation strategies and methods to make it as balanced as possible. Only in this way can the translation adapt to the target poetic environment of the target language and have more vitality. Lefevere holds the same view that "the translation poetics of a given period in a given culture often forces translators to privilege one or two illocutionary strategies at the expense of others" (100).

It can be seen from the above content that influence of poetics puts forward higher requirements for translators. The occurrence of literariness is the result of selection, which means that there is more than one equivalent option on the selection axis, and literariness is the option that deviates from the most conventional expression. When we use language in daily life, there are few such absurd language repetitions, which is abnormal. In literary works, this is literariness. Poetic translation is to translate this literariness. This is the goal of poetic translation. In the following part, the influence of patronage on the four versions is examined.

4.3 Manipulation of Patronage

In the above part four Chinese versions are rewritten in the viewpoint of poetics and now is the time to check the influence of patronage. What is Patronage? Patron refers to the person or institution that "promotes or hinders the reading, writing and rewriting of literature". (Lefevere 15). Patronage is regarded as the most important factor of Andre Lefevere's rewriting theory.

In this book, patrons play an important role in the whole process of translation, and they always control the whole translation process. Translation itself is not an isolated act, but closely related to political, social and economic factors. Most translators translate well and safely within the space allowed by the social and political authority of their time. As "any force that may contribute to the production and dissemination of literary works, but may also hinder, prohibit and destroy literary works" (Zhang Nanfeng 176), the sponsorship system can play a role in three aspects: ideology, economic interests and social status. Specifically speaking, the first is ideology, that is, literature must keep pace with other systems in a specific social context; the second is economic interests, that is, sponsors need to ensure translators' economic needs; the third is status guarantee, that is, translators can obtain certain social status through literary creation. If the three elements are concentrated on the same sponsor, it forms a non-differentiated sponsor, otherwise, it becomes a differentiated sponsor. Patronage plays an important role in the trend of translation process, the future of translation literature and the social status of translators.

Andre Lefevere also points out that "ideology is often strengthened and implemented by patrons, i. e., the person or institution entrusted with the translation or publication of translation works" (14). If a translator wants to translate a work, he needs the support of necessary material conditions. Some publishers are willing to publish the translation, that is to say, the translator must contact with the patron and the publishing house, especially in the contemporary society. If the patron agrees to provide the necessary funds to help publishing the work, he will inevitably put forward various demands on the translator. These requirements involve all aspects. Once they conflict with the translator's translation view, translators often have to sacrifice or adapt their own principles. Fox example: Lin Yutang, a famous translator in China, enjoys a high reputation in the United States because of his high level, and on the other hand, he has a lot to do with his patrons, Pearl S. Buck and his wife. Pearl S. Buck's husband is Lin Yutang's editor, publisher, literary agent, news agent and public relations consultant. Lin Yutang's abridged translation or a series of translated works are inseparable from Pearl S. Buck's request and suggestion.

In addition, government departments, religious groups and other patrons directly are involved in the translation process. This type of patronage is powerful, exerting pressure on the translator himself by using power and ideology under his control to influence and guide the spread and development of translation ideas. Patronage influences the selection of translators, and translators are more passive in cooperation and obedience under various privileges and pressures.

IV Analysis of Four Translated Versions in the Viewpoint of Rewriting Theory

As a translator and thinker, Yan Fu[①] has his own clear purpose and idea in the selection of translation materials, but he is also an official appointed by the Qing government, so his selection of translation materials is also controlled by the ideology of the patrons. As a professional in the literary system, the patrons outside the literary system are the main characters to rewrite the text.

First Chinese version of *Waiting for Godot* by Shi Xianrong is published by the People's Literature Publishing House. The People's Daily reported on August 17, 1951 that the People's Literature Publishing House was founded in Beijing in March 1951. The publishing house is state-owned under the joint leadership of the Ministry of Culture of the Central People's Government and the General Administration of Publication of the Central People's Government. In 1950 the national report on cultural and artistic work and the key points of the plan of 1951 of the Ministry of culture put that year was a time when the General Administration of publication and publication had deployed a division of labor, and a number of professional publishing houses should be established. In order to establish a unified management and strengthen the planning for publishing industry, China has set up a series of professional publishing houses, through which the publishing authorities assist the publishing management departments to adjust the relevant publishing tasks and plans.

People's Literature Publishing House is the first, largest and most influential national literature professional press in China. Since the beginning of the construction of the society, China has always regarded the cultural construction of the country as its own foundation. The first president and editor in chief, Feng Xuefeng, 1951 put forward the policy of "improving at home and abroad（古今中外，提为主）", and "improving" is relative to popularization, that is to say,

---

① Yan Fu (January 8, 1854—October 27, 1921) was a famous Chinese translator. Yan Fu's translation standard of "faithfulness, expressiveness and elegance" has a far-reaching influence on later translation work.

the books we publish cannot stay on the general level, but should be higher in order to make readers gain from it. In 1950 the national report on cultural and artistic work and the key points of the plan of 1951 of the Ministry of culture put that our requirement for publishing house is to realize the unity of social and economic benefits on the premise of putting social benefits first. At that time, the first task of publishing house is to serve the overall situation of national cultural construction and promote the development of social civilization. It is publishing houses' common goal to build a cultural country, to build a scholarly society and to promote reading for all.

At the same time, to build a cultural country, it is inseparable from the support of cultural industry; and the development of cultural industry cannot be separated from the prosperity of cultural market, especially the publishing market. From these two aspects, we can see that the existence and development of the publishing house can make reading more dramatic. Publishing professionals express the professional ideas of editors and publishers through published books, periodicals supplement and internal exchange of editing and publishing documents of topic report, review comments, editing letters, etc. Taking the review comments as an example, in the review opinions of the "17 years" of the People's Literature Publishing House, it first affirms that the works have certain progress significance of antifeudalism, and points out the ideological problems focusing on the criticism mode of the inappropriate "human nature" contents such as "abstract human nature", "human sex", "love" and so on.

In the comments on the review of the Indian novel *Chandar Novel Collection* by Wang Shoupeng, the reviewer points out that "most of the ideas are healthy and the artistic skills are also at a certain level", but "some of them also have the tendency of sex description"(Zhang Guogong and Gao Junkai: 28), so nine novels of the collection are deleted. The editor He Qizhi's final judgment is like this: "it is necessary to approve such description should be controlled, or the explicit sexual description should be turned into virtual writing and desalinated." (Zhang Guogong and Gao Junkai: 28). Do not think that sexual description is

IV Analysis of Four Translated Versions in the Viewpoint of Rewriting Theory

optional or even ugly, pornographic. The key is: it should be necessary for the plot development, and it should be beneficial to the characterization of characters and the civilized level of the characters. Naturally, it should be avoided vulgar and direct. They are not against the general description of gender relations with regard to sexual description. The description of the relationship between the two sexes which can be highlighted and can express the relationship between the characters, the character and the plot development should be preserved.

Zhu Shengchang（朱盛昌）, who presided over the work of *Contemporary*, writes: "the detailed description of direct sexual acts and sexual actions is not the focus of publicity, and should be resolutely deleted. Obscene, stimulating and vulgar sexual descriptions should be deleted and should not be preserved" (Zhang Guogong, Gao Junkai: 28). These normal opinions and modifications based on the professional spirit of literature and editorial rationality play an important role in ensuring the quality of literary publishing. In reading the applied literature editing, we should not ignore it.

We can see that the mainland versions of *Waiting for Godot* to take the deletion of sex related content. In addition, the following citations also demonstrate the function of the publishing house. "What makes power hold good, what makes it accepted, is simply the fact that it doesn't only weigh on us as a force that says no, but that it traverses and produces things, it induces pleasure, forms knowledge, produces discourse" (Lefevere 15). The publishing house or editor may modify or delete some sentences with the consent of the translator. For example, in the 1950s, *The Gadfly*, which was translated and introduced by Li Liangmin（李良民）, was first published by China Youth Publishing House in 1953 after adopting the strict selection criteria for translation by the mainstream ideology at that time. However, the complete translation presented to readers in fact is not complete, because "the publishing house carries out the translation of Li's translation according to the Russian version of the Publishing Bureau of the Soviet youth guard army" (Ni Xiuhua: 116).

In addition to influencing the specific process of translation, the incompatibility with ideology is also detrimental to the spread of the translation. When Lin Shu translates the *Biography of Kayin*, he faithfully translates the love between the hero and heroine and the unmarried pregnancy of the heroine. Some people complain about this: the heroine in the previous version was a pure girl like an angel, but his version turned her into a dirty and dissolute prostitute. Under the mainstream ideology of mainland China, when publishing and editing literary works, the mainstream ideology of mainland determines the theme and presentation of translated literary works, which is mainly realized through the activities of translators and publishers

The background of Taiwan publishing company is as follows: Linking Publishing Co., Ltd. is founded on May 4, 1974 and is a comprehensive publishing company. Over the past 30 years, more than thousands of books have been accumulated, including academic books on humanities, society, economy, science and technology, as well as novels, art, biographies, industrial and commercial enterprises, reference books, health care, tourism, children's books, etc. Since Linking Publishing has always maintained a high-quality publishing level, it has won the Golden Tripod Award, which represents the highest honor in publishing, and ranks first among all publishing houses in Taiwan. Liao Yuru's *Waiting for Godot* published by Linking Publishing is a version of the National Science Council plan. We can see from the Humanities and Social Sciences Newsletter Quarterly[①] that Liao's translation purpose is to translate and annotate the foundational foreign works that must be read in the development of traditional or modern schools. Therefore, her translation aims to spread Beckett's thoughts and introduce foreign characteristics. Hence, this version has critical introduction, introduction of the author, the era of the work, the classic version, and important related documents from the age and so on. Therefore, Liao's version is of the most annotations in the four versions.

---

① National Science Council Plan (ac731b41-2749-4252-b1cb-ecbfb0dd4692 (most. gov. tw))

Furthermore, publishing professionals express the professional thoughts of editors and publishers through published auxiliary articles and internal communication official documents such as topic selection report, peer review opinions, editor letters, etc. Taking the official website of Linking Publishing house as an example, it states the original intention of giving back to the society with academic publishing, and puts forward the purpose of integrating Chinese and Western cultures and breed a breadth of vision and understanding to readers. In the 1970s, Taiwan's economy took off. Wang Tiewu, founder of Linking Publishing daily, and Liu Changping, President of Linking Publishing daily, "felt that Taiwan ignored cultural construction at that time, and decided to set up a publishing company to support the publication of academic works" (Wang Fuming: 408) . It can be proved by Linking Publishing has invested in academic publishing and complete works of scholars for many years. Linking Publishing chooses May 4th as its birthday also shows that Linking Publishing inherits the spirit of the May 4th movement[①] (Wang: 408) . The core content of the May 4th spirit is patriotism, progress, democracy and science.

From the previous analysis, the patron's manipulation, what Lefevere said mainly includes external forces such as investors or institutions, among which the most important is the influence of publishing houses. The readers who have just entered the new era are full of curiosity about the excellent foreign literary works, and are eager to feel the exotic taste and appreciate the unique style of other countries' literary works. Therefore, based on the strong reading expectation of readers, publishers vigorously promote the translation of excellent works of foreign outstanding writers to meet the needs of readers. the publishers should not only pay attention to the language transformation of the source language,

---

[①] The May Fourth Movement was a Chinese anti-imperialist, cultural, and political movement which grew out of student protests in Beijing on 4 May 1919. https://en. wikipedia. org/wiki/May_Fourth_Movement

but also adapt to the whole cultural system to which the language belongs, and pay attention to the transmission of bilingual cultural connotation in translation process. Publishers affect the transmission of meaning, artistic conception and representation of characters.

Given the above three parts of manipulation of ideology, poetics, patronage, this chapter analyses the rewriting reproduction in four Chinese versions of *Waiting for Godot* from the perspective of rewriting theory. It has been found that shifts occur in the four versions and consequently result in variation in the images of *Waiting for Godot*. The shifts are made by translators in accordance with specific conditions. Translator is like a bridge connecting two cultures. He should take the different ideologies, poetic styles and patronages these external factors into consideration, catering to the reading habits of the target readers and making corresponding rewriting, so that the translation can better promote the communication between the two cultures. In the next chapter, two theoretical versions for performance are examined from the perspective of narratology theory. These two versions are given typically thoughtful productions translated focusing on performance with stage effects.

V Analysis of Two Theater versions in the Viewpoint of Narratology Theory

    In the above chapter, four versions for reading are examined from the perspective of rewriting theory. In this chapter two theatrical variation of *Waiting for Godot* by Yi Liming and Wu Xingguo are focused for their stage in the view of narrative theory. As one of the representative works of the absurd drama, the particularity of *Waiting for Godot* makes it necessary to take its stage into comprehensive consideration to achieve interaction between the source text, the performers and audience with expressive forms in translation process. Translation is a conscious narrative. To explore how the translator constructs the narrative in the target stage, this book analyzes two Chinese theatrical versions from the perspective of narrative framing methods which are put forward by Mona Baker. He advocates four framing methods, including temporal and spatial framing, selective appropriation, labelling and repositioning of participants (Baker: 105).

    What is narrative? Narratology, a theory about narrative behavior and narrative text, intends to "analyze what is typical of narrative as a macro genre or text type in contrast to description, instruction, argumentation, or in contrast to drama type or the lyric in literature studies" (Fludernik & Pirlet: 727). It mainly involves the empirical expression of narrative, and analyzes the form and structure of narrative behavior and its relationship.

Originating from the ancient Greek times, Narratology has been mentioned by Aristotle in *Poetics*, but it is generally believed that modern narratives originated in Russian formalists. In the 1960s, influenced by the analysis of Russian Prop folktales and French structuralism, a new theory and critical method of studying narrative art is gradually formed. This new theory is called narratology. Its research objects are no longer limited to content elements, but take the narrative style of the story, the voice characteristics of the narrator, the relationship between the narrator and the recipient of the narration, and so on as the new research focus.

In 1969 the word "narratologie" first appears in Tzvetan Todorov's book called *Grammaire du Décaméron* (Todorov: 72). It refers to the question of what is narrative, with answers ranging from suggestions to fuzzy concept solutions and constructivist frameworks. In the 1990s of the 20th centuries, narrative research borrows from feminism, deconstructionism, psychoanalysis, historicism, film theory, computer science, and many other theories and methods, expanding research thinking and vision, and it is called "small-scale narratology revival". In the book of *Western Narratology: Classical and Postclassical*, rhetorical narratology, feminist narratology, cognitive narratology, and non-literary narratology, these four schools are introduced. Rhetorical narratology is a narrative theory in which narrative research draws on rhetorical theory to study narrative works.

This kind of research began in 1983 when Wayne Booth published his book *Fictional Rhetoric*. Booth is a member of the "Chicago School", which is a school that studies "new Aristotelianism" rhetoric. Then feminist narratology combines the feminist review and classical structural narratology to study the literature. Susan Lancer, the representative of feminist narratology. She focuses on the gender of the narrator and extends the narrator's characteristics to the gender field. The specific naming, description or behavior of characters should be regarded as an implicit process of sexualization through clothing codes, behavior patterns and cultural programs.

In the 1990s, with the integration of narratology and cognitive science, another interdisciplinary school of cognitive narratology emerged. The term "Cognitive Narratology" is first used in the paper *Frame, Reference and Third Person Narrative Reading: Towards Cognitive Narratology* (Jahn: 450) and the representative of cognitive narratology is David Herman. This school advocates cognitive linguistics is a way to study the structure of language determined by human cognition. The school's goal is to explore the relationship between narrative and mind or psychology with a focus on how cognitive processes function in narrative understanding and how readers such as audience as listener reconfigure the narrative world. There are two aspects in the study of narrative, namely, cognitive structure and action theory. After the join of feminist review, rhetoric, and cognitive science, narratology has earned an abundant theoretical foundation since the 1980s.

Except for the literary field, narratology also intervenes non-literary circle like painting, film, television, drama and other digital areas. Christian Metz advocates applying structural linguistics to analyze film works in his book *Language and Cinema*. After the combination of feminist criticism, rhetoric and cognitive science, narratology have gained a rich theoretical foundation since the 1980s. In addition to literature, narratology is widely used in many social sciences, such as jurisprudence, psychology, medicine and economics. Occupancy of non-literary subjects may weaken the basis of narrative, but narrative theory should allow the exposition of non-narrative contexts on the concept of narrative. These non-literary narratives are based on narration and they are aimed at revealing common features in the unfolding process of the story. According to the above contents, we know that narrative is an international trend of literary research, divided into classical structural narrative and postclassical narrative. The focus of classical narrative research is on the content of the text to explore the structure of narrative work and the correlation between various elements. The post-classical narrative was born in the 1980s in response to readers' criticism and cultural research, and focused on readers and contexts. Notably, beginning with the International Symposium on Narrative Studies at Hamburg University in Germany in November 2003, scholars begin to explore how to apply traditional narrative concepts to non-literary texts.

Among them, Mona Baker creatively unifies narrative theory and translation, and points out that through different construction methods, translators can establish different narratives and records to clarify the narration in the translator's point of view. Therefore, this book aims at studying the drama translation narrative by Mona Baker's narrative theory. There is such a wonder: Why did the early translation tends to focus on the source text while the later translation tends to be reader oriented. This is because, at the beginning, a culture is often reluctant to accept a text, which is external. According to the above contents, we know that narrative is an international trend of literary research, divided into classical structural narrative and postclassical narrative. The focus of classical narrative research is on the content of the text to explore the structure of narrative work and the correlation between various elements (Shindan: 2005). The postclassical narrative was born in the 1980s in response to readers' criticism and cultural research, and focused on readers and contexts (Shen Dan, 2006: 727). Notably, beginning with the International Symposium on Narrative Studies at Hamburg University in Germany in November 2003, scholars began to explore how to apply traditional narrative concepts to non-literary texts. It can be noticed that over the past 20 years, there has been a kind of "extensive narration view" which regards all kinds of activities and fields as narration. This kind of thinking is actually an interdisciplinary application of narration, "from the narrative point of view, a cultural product, a daily phenomenon, a social activity, etc. may gain a new understanding of culture, history, life, etc." (Jiao Guqiang, 2005) Mona Baker is a Western scholar who successfully combined narrative theory with translation research. Unlike the narratives used in literary research, the narratives she used in her research mainly came from social and social theories and explored ways in which translators participated (Baker, 2006: 3). In this sense, Baker (2006)

V Analysis of Two Theater versions in the Viewpoint of Narratology Theory

argues, "everyday stories we live by". The narratives in her narrative theory contain various genres and modes, not only representing social reality, but also constructing social reality. The narrative is also a dynamic entity, which is an important feature of the narrative. These features of the narrative make it possible to combine it with translation studies. In the process of combining narrative theory with translation research, Baker (2006, 2007) adopted four types of narration, namely ontological narrative, public narrative, conceptual/disciplinary narrative and mete or master narrative as proposed by Somers (1992, 1997). Among them ontological narrative refers to personal narratives of personal history and our own situation. Although it is "nature (about oneself) narration", it also has the nature of human relations and society and is the construction and understanding of our life. Since individuals must live and narrate in society, the most individualized narratives cannot be separated from group narratives. In translating from one language into another, because of the interdependence of individual narratives and group narratives, the translation is subject to the constraints of common language and narrative resources in the new environment. According to the Somers (1992, 1997) and the Summers & Gibson (1994) model (see Baker, 2006, 2007), public narratives are narratives that spread outside the personal sphere, i. e. between families, religions, and educational institutions, political or activist groups, media, and countries. The advertising words are also public narratives. In the process of translating public narratives, it is usually an abridgment of content that is profane and taboo. Interpreters play a vital role in the dissemination of public narratives. When it comes to conceptual/disciplinary narrative, Baker tends to define it as the narratives and explanations of their subjects for themselves and others by scholars in any field. Historical and other academic works are conceptual and disciplinary narratives. Like public narratives, the translator can choose to accept, advertise, or question a particular concept narration. Baker exemplified this by Sir George Staunton's Qing-dynasty criminal code, translated in 1810. Staunton's translation seeks to present understandable, reasonable, and just Chinese law, refuting some of James Barrow's accusations against the Chinese in his 1806 Travels to

China (Baker, 2006: 43). We can say Barrow's Travels to China is a conceptual narration, and Staunton's translation of the Qing Dynasty's criminal law is a similar narrative, as shown by Baker's example. Somers & Gibson (1994) defined the "meta narrative" as a narrative embedded in our history as a contemporary participant. According to the sociological theory and concept, history refers to major events: development, decadence, industrialization and enlightenment. Somers (1992) further interpreted the meta narrative as "our contemporary epic events," such as capitalism versus communism, individual versus society, and barbarism/natural versus civilization (Baker, 2006: 44). According to Somers, the Cold War is a meta-narrative, and the war on terror is also a meta-statement. Baker (2006: 48) believes that without the direct involvement of translators, narratives cannot cross the boundaries of language and culture and develop into global meta-narratives.

Therefore, in order to be accepted in the field of new culture, it is necessary to adapt to the target language. Hence, translation itself is a process of re-narration. Later, translation begins to be more reader oriented. These can be proved by Mona Baker's narrative theory. Therefore, this book tries to study the drama translation narrative by Mona Baker's narrative theory. There is such a wonder: Why did the early translation tends to focus on the source text while the later translation tends to be reader oriented. This is because, at the beginning, a culture is often reluctant to accept a text, which is external. Therefore, in order to be accepted in the field of new culture, it is necessary to adapt to the target language. Hence, translation itself is a process of re-narration. Later, translation began to be more reader oriented. These can be proved by Mona Baker's frame theory. In the process of translation, translators, editors and other participants work together to weaken, implement or change some narrative meanings in the original text or discourse. She (2006: 106) believes that "translation may be seen as a frame in its own right, whether in its liberal or metaphorical sense". She discusses four main strategies employed by translators in dealing with narratives in source language texts: temporal and spatial framing, framing through selective application, framing by labeling, and repositioning of participants (Baker, 2006: 112-139). Baker believes that translators will consciously use various framework setting strategies to choose the translated text, choose a certain angle, focus on certain content, and adopt certain translation strategies to "interpret" and "rewrite" the source text in order to achieve their political purposes. Translators themselves have embedded all kinds of narratives. Whether they are translators or scholars, their work is neither to build bridges nor to eliminate barriers. They are promoting and disseminating various narratives and discourses in a decisive way (Baker, 2005). George Steiner, in his book after Babel (1975), wrote that the translator's personal life experience, values, culture and historical background infiltrated into the translation process, making the translation "re-creation". Maria Tymoczko and Edwin Gentzler (2002) hold that "translation is not a simple and faithful reproduction, but an intentional and conscious act of selection, act of assemblage, act of structuration, act of fabrication, and even in some cases, act of falsification, refusal of information, counterfeiting, and creation of secret codes (2002: i-xixii.). Through these methods, the translator participates in the process of narrative communication. Some of these narratives and discourses have promoted peace, while others have aroused conflicts. In this sense, the translator influences the relationship among politics, power, peace and conflict through narration and discourse. Mona Baker creatively unifies narrative theory and translation, and points out that through different construction methods, translators can establish different narratives and records to clarify the narration in the translator's point of view.

Hence, as the core role of communication, the nature of translation refers to the narration of another language. Drama, as a complex and unique literary type, needs to consider many unstable factors in the process of translation, such as rhythm, translation, publishing house, characteristic drama text, the balance between text and playability, and the relationship between dialogue and language. These can also be proved by Susan Bassnett's words. He points out "dramatic text cannot be translated in the same way as the propse text". Because the dramatic text is read differently as "something incomplete", instead of "a fully rounded unit" (Bassnett, 2010: 119-120), This is true. Because if translation only focuses on drama rather than performance, without director, stage and audience, then the real drama and dramatic narration will be meaningless (Li Yunfeng, 2000: 28). In dramatic narratology, it is true that stage narration is far more important than dramatic text. Translation is a conscious narrative. Mona Baker advocated four framing methods, including temporal and spatial framing, selective appropriation, labelling and repositioning of participants (2006: 105). In this section, this book will analyze two Chinese theater versions of *Waiting for Godot* from the perspective of narrative framing methods.

5.1 Temporal and Spatial Framing

When it comes to temporal and spatial framing, it refers to transfer the temporal and spatial framing in original text into a relative familiar framing in the target language. This can be proved by the citation of the following sentences: "Selecting a particular text and embedding it in a temporal and spatial context that accentuates the narratives that touch our lives, even though the events of the source narrative may be set within a very different temporal and spatial framework" (Baker, 2006: 112).

Beckett once explains the dramatic space of *Waiting for Godot*: "when I was writing *Watt*, I felt the need to create a smaller space in which I could control the position of the characters or the range of their activities, especially from a certain angle. So, I wrote *Waiting for Godot.*" (Liang Benbin: 97). The images of characters or scenery in the script are compressed to the minimum, and only the limited amount of information is provided. The spatial scene is characterized by minimalism. That stage of *Waiting for Godot* is an open three-dimensional

V Analysis of Two Theater versions in the Viewpoint of Narratology Theory

space composed of dry straight trees and horizontal ground. In the two-act play, which starts with waiting and ends with waiting, Beckett constantly mentions the existence of tree and intentionally reminds them of its existence.

Furthermore, according to the interpretation of Frye, the famous critic, in the anatomy of criticism, "tree" has been a meaningful literary prototype since ancient times. In ancient literature, trees often held sacred significance. For example, in Norse mythology, Yggdrasil, the world tree, is central to its cosmology. In the Bible, the Tree of Knowledge and the Tree of Life are pivotal to the narrative of Genesis. These examples illustrate how trees were revered and attributed with profound meaning in ancient times. Trees have been used to symbolize various concepts. For instance, in literature, a tree can symbolize life and growth, as seen in Oscar Wilde's "The Selfish Giant" where the blooming of the garden represents the Giant's character development. Conversely, a withered tree might symbolize death or loss, as seen in T. S. Eliot's "The Waste Land". In modern literature, the symbolism of trees has evolved to reflect contemporary issues. For example, in Barbara Kingsolver's "The Bean Trees", the protagonist's journey is paralleled with her growing a wisteria, a type of flowering vine, reflecting themes of nurturing and resilience. The tree has been a versatile symbol in both poetry and prose. In Robert Frost's poem "The Sound of the Trees", trees are used to explore themes of nature and introspection. In prose, such as Harper Lee's "To Kill a Mockingbird", the Radley oak tree serves as a symbol of communication and understanding. The symbolism of trees can be a powerful teaching tool. For example, analyzing the use of tree symbolism in literature can help students understand how symbols can convey complex themes. This approach can foster critical thinking skills and deepen students' appreciation of literature. This book focuses on the tree on the stage of *Waiting for Godot* as geographical coordinates to compare the spatial framing of the two versions. Tree's first appearance is in the first act. The first act is concise and clear with a sentence "a country road, a tree"(Beckett 2). In the conversation that followed, Estragon and Vladimir are waiting for Godot to arrive, at the same time, they begin to strongly doubt the accuracy of the waiting place like these dialogues: "Estragon: (despairingly). Ah! (Pause.) You're sure it was here? Vladimir: He said by the tree. (They look at the tree.) Do you see any others" (Beckett: 17)? They also discussed whether the dead tree is a willow or a shrub, and the tree became more eye-catching. Vladimir's answer shows the role of trees as place markers "All the same … that tree … (turning towards auditorium) that bog…" (Beckett: 18) In this way, the two protagonists decide where to wait.

As for the stage space, the tree image provides the necessary place and background for a series of events in the script. It enriches the space and it makes the plot appear authentic. Image is a combination of subjective emotion and objective image presented by the writer with specific emotion and moral, which can arouse readers' psychological resonance and cultural memory. The images blending of the subjective and objective is the writer's inner life experience, which concentrates on the words. The same things, under the operation of different writers, different texts and different contexts, show different situations. It's the same the other way round. Images affect the situation of narrative, set off the scene atmosphere, create rich imagination space, and point to a more profound world. Wang Guowei, a famous scholar in China, once says that "all scenery words are emotion words（一切景语皆情语也）" (Wang Guowei: 10). If the scenery is endowed with emotion, the scenery will bring people's will, and the viewer will be moved; if you put your feelings on the scenery, the feelings and scenery will blend together. Although the scenery has no words, it is like thousands of words. Scenery words have the power to transport readers to different places and times, creating vivid mental images. For example, in Charles Dickens' "A Tale of Two Cities", the opening lines paint a vivid picture of the era: "It was the best of times, it was the worst of times…". Scenery words often carry emotional weight. For instance, "storm" might evoke feelings of turmoil or conflict, while "sunrise" might symbolize hope or new beginnings. In Emily Bronte's "Wuthering Heights", the desolate moors reflect the tumultuous relationship between the characters. In poetry, scenery words can create a powerful emotional response. Consider Robert

Frost's "Stopping by Woods on a Snowy Evening". The quiet woods, the falling snow, the darkest evening of the year—all these scenery words work together to evoke a sense of peace, solitude, and introspection. In prose, scenery words can set the mood of a scene or reflect a character's emotional state. In F. Scott Fitzgerald's "The Great Gatsby", the description of the "valley of ashes" not only sets a bleak and desolate scene but also mirrors the moral decay of the characters. Scenery words can also play a role in character development. In Harper Lee's "To Kill a Mockingbird", the town of Maycomb is described in great detail, reflecting its influence on the characters and their worldview.

The use of imagery is an important means to enhance the poeticization of narrative works. "It is a contribution made by the Chinese to the marriage of narrative and poetics, and its existence in narrative works has often become a prominent symbol of the poetic richness and roundness of the lines"(Yang Yi: 37). The generation of images is always realized by certain characters, things, backgrounds, etc. In the process of literature creation, the author's choice of image depends on the writer's overall grasp and conception of a certain life form, which implies the writer's inner picture.

Hence, the image of the literature works is neither a simple external description nor a direct expression of the feelings bursts out. It is based on the feelings and the intended meaning implied in the image. As an ancient image with great vitality, trees exist in the myths and religions of all nations in the world, and they are closely related to beliefs and gods. There are many myths and legends about trees in many national cultures. Therefore, some archetypal meanings of trees have become the accumulation layer of primitive culture and exist in the collective unconsciousness of all mankind. In the archetypal system of Bible, the joy of softness and the sadness of fallen leaves embody the human emotion pattern. The prosperity and withering of trees represent the life and death of human beings, and the trees without leaves represent the sinner and death. In the Bible, trees are created on the third day before humans and animals. They are the pillars of the whole system of life.

In the long river of human history, trees have always been the important coordinates of culture, religion, symbolism. Gaspar sums up this phenomenon in his essay *The Tree's Meditation*: "they are often amazed at the need to create human being's feelings, to create such a sense of love. The image of the tree we present to us by the senses and the brain: the root whiskers, the leaves lost in the night" (Gaspar: 292). In literary works, the first important image of trees is "home". Trees represent the life of nature and the universe, and are the symbol of inexhaustible vigor and vitality. Because trees are flourishing and multiply, they provide food, rest and shelter for human beings, and they become a green home with a sense of security and belonging. The earliest images of trees come from the records in Genesis. God created the garden of Eden for Adam and Eve. The tree images interpreted by orchard, grove or tree of life often symbolize heaven, innocence, flawless beauty and abundance.

However, in the play of *Waiting for Godot*, the tree which should have been flourishing on July 19 doesn't show the archetypal image consistent with the collective unconsciousness of human beings. Contrary to this, it is neither green nor vigorous. The tree begins to look decadent and bleak. The image of "tree" is undoubtedly shaped as a kind of inverted image. The concept of "home" and "residence" represented by trees lacking in vigorous life hides destructive disaster. In the classic American literary works, the images of "trees" described in Frost's *Stopping by Woods on A Snowy Evening*, Whitman's *Leaves of Grass*, Hawthorne's *The Scarlet Letter* and Toni Morrison's *Beloved* all show the reflection and transcendence of human beings to the predicament. In fact, stories about trees are often retelling people's experiences as well. In *Waiting for Godot*, it becomes the embodiment of the distorted life of the generation in abnormal political times as the spiritual symbol of the existence of the ill-fated dream. This is a kind of symbol, at the same time, it also produces a kind of image in the reader's mind, which is a kind of poetic principle that uses vivid and dramatic images to indicate the subtle spiritual world.

After analyzing the stage space of the tree in the original work, we explore

V Analysis of Two Theater versions in the Viewpoint of Narratology Theory

the two Chinese theater versions of *Waiting for Godot*. The stage narration of *Waiting for Godot* in Yi Liming's edition is quite interesting: the steel cross replaces the dead trees on the wasteland, forming the spiritual cemetery intention of modern industry, and with the hanging cross light box it emphasizes the status of lofty belief without substance. Juxtaposed with the intention of the cross is the effect of glass specular reflection. The audience is absorbed into the play. It is strange that such an important image of the tree has disappeared and why the stage space narrative is replaced by the cross?

As we noticed that over the past 20 years, there has been a kind of "extensive narration view" which regards all kinds of activities and fields as narration. This kind of thinking is an interdisciplinary application of narration. From the narrative point of view, a cultural product, a daily phenomenon, a social activity, etc. may gain a new understanding of culture, history, life, etc. The answer can also be drawn from the interview. Yi says he uses the stage to re-narrate the story. In *Waiting for Godot* all over the world, there is a tree on the stage, but there is no tree on Yi's stage. "We only have a cross and a mirror on the stage. They are actually talking in a cemetery. The so-called 'willow' is actually a cross in a cemetery"(Zhang Yanyan, 2019). Stage space narrative is a new understanding of storytelling. The sentence one day it was bare, but the next day it grew leaves refers to the wreath that Westerners used to put on the cemetery in memory of the dead.

In this version of *Waiting for Godot*, the relationship between it and Godot is almost completed by the stage narration. On the sand pile full of gullies, there are broken glass mirrors, and the Cross stands in the forest, with skeletons and white bones scattered. Especially the large cross hanging in the sky screen of the stage, the audience can understand it as soon as they enter the arena. "Even though I speak the northeast dialect, it's about the religion of God" (Zhang Yanyan, 2019). At the same time, the light hits the mirror, glass and wall, forming multiple images. The audience can see the shadow from the wall, and can see themselves or other audiences from the mirror. In the second act, Gogo shouts

"They are coming" and runs around, but seems to be surrounded on all sides and has no place to escape. The audience watches each other through the mirror and the actors. The two tramps also view Pozzo and Lucky boy as a play. Later, they play them, including the declaration that we are all human beings, breaking the traditional relationship between watching and acting. We are all audience of life. On the stage, the cross replaced the hanging tree. "Everyone has to carry his cross on his back until he dies, until he is forgotten, before he can unload it" (Zhang Yanyan, 2019). This kind of temporal and spatial framing can also be supported by Ricoeur , '[t]he game of telling' is itself 'included in the reality told'. It is characterized by 'rich ambiguity of designating both the course of recounted events and the narrative that we construct' "(Baker: 294). Symbolism and metaphor are often used in drama to convey deeper meanings. For example, in Tennessee Williams's "The Glass Menagerie", the glass animals represent Laura's fragility and isolation. Similarly, the motif of the "American Dream" in "Death of a Salesman" symbolizes the protagonist's pursuit of success and the disillusionment that follows.

As the citation proved, drama is an art of storytelling. The story narrated not only has the level of story time, but also has the level of story space. The main unit of the story is the duration of the events. In the art of drama, story space is generally constructed by playwrights. The media used by playwrights is the same as that of novelists. Therefore, story space needs imagination in essence. When the drama narrates something in the stage, the materiality of the media requires not only the story space created by the playwright, but also the stage narrative space constructed by the theatrical performer headed by the director. Therefore, in the story space, only those scenes presented in the stage narrative space can be directly felt by the audience, and then lead to imagination. Such a scene is the place where the characters act, the place where the dramatic events occur, and also the main component of the drama scene. Since it is presented by the stage narrative space, it has a certain degree of intuition. Therefore, the scene presented is a special part of the story space and has independent value. Here, "temporality also means that everything we perceive, our narratives of the world, are 'history laden' and that history, in turn, is a function of narrativity. 'We are members of the field of historicity as storytellers'" (Baker: 294). This is conducive to the pluralism of the narrative structure of the drama, and it also puts forward higher requirements for the presentation of narrative space.

For the other version, the stage narration of *Waiting for Godot* in Wu Xingguo's edition is simple with an indistinct upside-down tree, forming the subject scene, the connected scene and the associated scene. For the structure and presentation of a dramatic scene, the scene itself can be divided into the subject scene, the connected scene and the associated scene. The scene as the main activity place of the character in the drama is the main scene. In general, this scene must be presented in the narrative space. Otherwise, the action cannot happen. The scene that extends around the subject scene is the drama scene. The relationship between the connected scene and the main scene forms some kind of relationship, which is beneficial to the scheduling of the characters in the drama, so as to make the relationship between the characters in the main scene change correspondingly and enhance the drama. It can be presented directly or unseen, and it can be imagined by the audience by hinting that the associated scene is more distant from the main scene, and it opens a wider world where events occur.

When it comes to temporal and spatial framing, it refers to transfer the temporal and spatial framing in original text into a relative familiar framing in the target language. This can be proved by the citation of the following sentences: "Selecting a particular text and embedding it in a temporal and spatial context that accentuates the narratives that touch our lives, even though the events of the source narrative may be set within a very different temporal and spatial framework" (Baker: 112). In this version, an indistinct upside-down tree makes the three scenes as one narrative space. As the material basis of drama narrative, the intuition is its essential attribute. In highly realistic drama, the intuition of narrative space is equivalent to the life verisimilitude of visual effect. At this time, the imagination of the scene presented is highly integrated with the intuitive and visual reality of the narrative space, which is difficult to distinguish.

The two Chinese theater versions present different narrative spaces. Translators consciously use various framework setting strategies to choose a certain angle for focusing on certain content. They adopt certain translation strategies to "interpret" and to "rewrite" the source text in order to achieve their translation purposes. Translators themselves have embedded all kinds of narratives. "Whether they are translators or scholars, their work is neither to build bridges nor to eliminate barriers. They are promoting and disseminating various narratives and discourses in a decisive way" (Baker: 2).

This also can find similar views from scholars. For instance, George Steiner, in his book *After Babel*, writes that the translator's personal life experience, values, culture and historical background infiltrated into the translation process, making the translation "re-creation". Castelán, Anabel holds that "translation is not a simple and faithful reproduction, but an intentional and conscious act of selection, act of assemblage, act of structuration, act of fabrication, and even in some cases, act of falsification, refusal of information, counterfeiting, and creation of secret codes" (7). Through these methods, the translator participates in the process of narrative communication. Some of these narratives and discourses have promoted peace, while others have aroused conflicts.

In this sense, the translator influences the relationship among politics, power, peace and conflict through narration and discourse. Zola, a famous French writer, once points out that every literary form has its specific conditions. A novel can be read at home and on the sofa. The creation of a novel is different from that of a play to be performed in front of 2000 audiences. The novelist is not limited by time and space; the plot can be written in an easy way, and it can take a hundred pages to analyze a character as long as he is happy; the description of the environment can be presented as it likes, and the narration can be compressed if it needs to be compressed; what has been written can be repeated and the place can be changed constantly. In a word, the novelist is the absolute master in dealing with the subject matter. The playwright is different. His creation is strictly restricted and must follow various rules. The playwright must consider that the play is not a single reader, but a group of audiences, and that the appreciation of the play has its specific time and space constraints.

The book holds that the translation of the play for performance shares the same quality. A written literary text is just a text. Images and actions are implied in the script, which cannot be interpreted by different actors in different narrative space and time. Although audio text also contains images and actions, it cannot bring real-time communication, because the information of audio text is not "received" while it is "sent". For the translation of *Waiting for Godot*, as a second creation of drama retranslation, there are two directions: one is stage installation art, the other is performance, or taken together, it can be called theatricality. That is, the absurd drama must be translated as a performance script.

5.2 Selective Appropriation

Selective appropriation means some translation choices like omission and addition, foregrounding, cumulative interventions of the translator that a translator makes (Baker: 71). It means the fact that the translator omits or adds textual materials to weaken or strengthen certain specific narratives in the original text. Different translators often adopt different narrative translation strategies due to their different translation purposes and readers' reception. In the Chinese version of *Waiting for Godot*, Yi Liming and Wu Xingguo adopt different narrative translation methods, either abandoning or retaining all kinds of information in the source language.

Beginning with Yi Liming's work, this book finds that Yi specifically uses several examples to illustrate selective appropriation existing in his drama text.

For example, Estragon's first line of the play, "Nothing to be done (Beckett: 10)" is translated by Shi and Yu into "There's nothing you can do about it（毫无办法）" (Shi: 3) and in Yi's work "Nothing to be done" is translated into "it's all in vain（一切都是徒劳）" (Yi: 1). Why is this change made in the script? The answer can be found in an interview with Yi Liming. He said this when the reporter interviewed him "And if you've read *Waiting for Godot*, you'll find that this sentence is the most important sentence and Becket is skillfully picking up Faust's problem, that we can't solve the problems we're facing with all the knowledge we've created since the birth of man" (Zhang Yanyan: B1). Hence, in his version "Nothing to be done" is translated into "it's all in vain（一切都是徒劳）" (Yi: 1). That would be a good match for Vladimir's next quote "I've never wanted to believe it in my life" (Yi: 10). The "it" here refers to the sentence "Nothing to be done", Vladimir means that "I don't want to believe everything is in vain, because there are so many things I haven't tried. Why should I believe that, so I'm going to continue the struggle" (Zhang Yanyan: B1).

Another example cited by Yi Liming also illustrates his selective appropriation. In the conversation between Lucky and Pozzo, after Pozzo said that the lucky guy had calculated him with a sentence "You count me", he immediately said "Atlas, the son of Jupiter". In the existing Chinese text, the annotation for this sentence at first sight is that "Atlas is a character of Greek mythology. After he failed to resist Zeus, he was punished to hold the sky with his head and hands. He was not the son of Jupiter". He points out that "such annotation is completely caused by the lack of knowledge of Greek cultural background, and if readers and audiences have no relevant cultural background, naturally they cannot understand the meaning of this sentence" (Zhang Yanyan: B1). He didn't know that until later. It turns out that this sentence tells a story in three words. This is actually a plot in the story of the golden apple of Hesperides in ancient Greek mythology. Hercules, the eldest son of Jupiter, is asked to pick the golden apple from the holy garden guarded by a hundred dragons. After a difficult time, Hercules comes to the place where Atlas carried the blue sky, and nearby the holy garden of the golden apples.

V Analysis of Two Theater versions in the Viewpoint of Narratology Theory

At Prometheus' suggestion, Hercules decides to ask Atlas to help him pick the golden apples and take over for a while. But when Atlas picked the golden apples, he says he doesn't want to carry the blue sky anymore, and then Hercules tricked Atlas out of it again with another trick, and he quickly took the golden apples. "That's why in the first half of the sentence, Beckett writes "you count me（你算计我）" (Zhang Yanyan: B1).

In addition to the interview with director Yi, his selective appropriation can also be examined by the Mona Baker's explanations. Mona Baker is a western scholar who successfully combines narrative theory with translation research. Unlike the narratives used in literary research, the narratives she used in her research mainly come from social theories and she explores ways in which translators participated. In this sense, Baker argues, "everyday stories we live by" (6). The translation narratives in her narrative theory contain various genres and modes, not only representing social reality, but also constructing social reality.

When it comes to translation narrative, the translator can choose to accept, advertise, or question a particular concept narration. The narrative is also a dynamic entity, which is an important feature of the narrative. These features of the narrative make it possible to combine it with translation study. We take this to examine Yi's version which questions a particular concept narration. Yi says "He even questions Shakespeare's" to be or not to be "in the script" (Zhang Yanyan: B1). For example, Beckett's writing method is very delicate. In the monologue that the Lucky guy is going to save Pozzo in the pit, there is such sentences "The tiger bounds to the help of his congeners without the least hesitation, or else he slinks away into the depths of the thickets. But that is not the question. What are we doing here, that is the question" (Beckett: 112)? These thoughts are then brought into Yi Liming's concept of drama translation narration. He finally tells the interviewer that after finishing the *Waiting for Godot*, "he has a richer understanding of drama, and he hopes that this performance version can become a bridge to help everyone out of Beckett's darkness of reason"(Zhang Yanyan: B1). The narrative version for performance can make people wake up from the inherent knowledge and experience, then to find more possibilities for drama, so that drama can bring people more courage to face difficulties. It can be further proved that the reason for this selective appropriation made by the performance version can be found from the following quotations: "To elaborate a coherent narrative, it is inevitable that some elements of experience are excluded and others privileged. But what guides this process of selection? Somers suggests that this process is thematically driven" (Baker: 602).

From the above content, Yi Liming's stage version exists in the omniscient view of the drama narrative translator. Although the narrator has nothing to do with the characters and events in the work, he knows everything about what has happened, is happening and what will happen. The translators in stage performances are often omniscient. Such narrators have a broad perspective and are almost unrestricted. Therefore, the performance version can not only freely display the concepts and emotions of the characters in the text, but also freely express his thoughts and feelings. Emotions can even make all kinds of comments directly to the public.

In Wu Xingguo's version, he also adopts selective appropriation to make it performable. Wu Xingguo's selective appropriation lies in the use of Buddhism and Peking Opera. Wu Xingguo's Peking Opera version returns to *Waiting for Godot* itself. As a contemporary legendary theater work in Taiwan led by Wu Xingguo, it has made a radical adaptation of the original work with traditional Peking Opera techniques. Both the recitation and the moving are full of drama charm. According to statistics, there are more than 100 western classic dramas adapted from traditional Chinese opera. This kind *Waiting for Godot* obviously has its own unique characteristics and value. *Waiting for Godot* has the philosophical foundation of existentialism. In the book, *Existential Thought & Fictional Technique*, Edith Kern offers parallels between Beckett and existentialism. She defines "the [existential] paradox that has permeated Beckett's entire work [which] has made it an affirmation and a negation of individuality" (Kern: 240). Human beings live in a meaningless universe, and human existence itself has no meaning.

V Analysis of Two Theater versions in the Viewpoint of Narratology Theory

However, people can shape themselves and achieve self on the basis of their original existence, so as to obtain meaning.

For Wu Xingguo, this edition uses drama elements, but needs to solve the philosophical and religious problems in cross-cultural adaptation. That is because *Waiting for Godot* is the product of the western post-war ideological trend. Human beings have lost God and become exile. They bid farewell to their last home. In the process of localization and adaptation, they need to find the corresponding contrast in this cultural background. In China, Buddhism has a natural affinity with existentialism. Therefore, we can see many shadows of Buddhism in *Waiting for Godot*. Even Beckett copyright center's "prohibition of any form of music" has been "ignored", and "Buddhist music has been added, which also provides a philosophical basis for the landing of classic works" (lv Xueping, 2019). That selective appropriation can find explanation by the following narrative quotations: "issue with selectivity is whether it introduces new information in terms of unfamiliar dilemmas, puzzles, and contradictions of the sort that promote critical thought and a self-consciousness of problem-solving behavior" (Bennett, W. Lance, and Murray Edelman: 164). The translator immerses into the philosophical thought and replace it with self-fulfilling ideas and habituated action imperatives.

As can be seen from above citation, when the translated text is used for performance, it enters the dramatic narrative situation. In view of the uniqueness of dramatic art, the prerequisite of drama translation for performance is that the translator must be familiar with the medium of theatre. For a translator of drama works, in addition to mastering language skills and measuring what is familiar to the audience and what is not, he must also have a sense of drama. The most important thing is the translator's selective appropriation. This book points out that when translating drama works, translators should direct their ow translation in mind while translating. This remark highlights the close relationship between the task of the translator and that of the director and actor.

5.3 Labelling

Labelling refers to the words that identify the key elements in the narrative. The definition can be found in the book of *Translation and Conflict: A Narrative Account*. Baker writes "by labelling I refer to any discursive process that involves using a lexical item, term or phrase to identify a person, place, group, event or any other key element in a narrative" (Baker: 137). Therefore, the naming system and title are the main ways for the translator to construct narrative. The naming of characters and places is not only a matter of address, but also a matter of standing, which is often due to translators' narrative attitude. The differences in translation methods reflect the different narrative positions of translators. The two versions of *Waiting for Godot* reflect that Yi and Wu have different labelling systems for different things.

Yi Liming's version of *Waiting for Godot* is more coherent and almost qualified in terms of performance visibility. Originally, the experimental text of *Waiting for Godot*, which was "like a psychopath fixed in a hospital bed for reflection" (Zhang Yanyan: B1) is extremely difficult to enter the theater. It dispelled the dialogue between logic and conventional meaning. The plot without progress and purpose almost tormented the ordinary audience. Therefore, Yi Liming first adapts the original script in this aspect by reintroducing logic and conventional meaning into the dialogue, and even trying to arrange the plot. All these play a good theatrical effect. He uses the means of re-empowerment, which means renaming by free translation, for example: the name of Pozzo is ridiculed with the passage of "Bobo fleeing to the United States", while "Lucky boy" is renamed as "pig head". According to a pioneer that discusses film arts from narrative semiology, Albert Laffay, who takes "narrative as a core concept to explain the relation structure" (Shen Dan: 249). By using the word narrative as a reference, these non-literary narratives also intend to reveal the common

V Analysis of Two Theater versions in the Viewpoint of Narratology Theory

features during the process of unfolding the story. Hence, his version existence is extremely weakened, hoping that the audience completely forget the translator's criticism. That is consistent with Baker's point of view. It can be proved by the following quotation "Names and titles are particularly powerful means of framing in the sense elaborated here" (Baker: 138).

Furthermore, for the source text, Beckett establishes the destruction of the basic discourse in *Waiting for Godot*, and draws a clear line between the absurd drama and the traditional drama. it is no longer able to show a world that has been broken up and absurd by the traditional language expression. "The Theatre of the Absurd[...] tends toward a radical devaluation of language, toward a poetry that is to emerge from the concrete and objectified images of the stage itself" (Esslin 7). Only by using a language which has its own absurd characteristics and has been disintegrated, can the irrationality of the world be fully revealed. Therefore, he uses meaningless dialogues in his drama creation, but conversation continues. For the target text, Yi Liming extends every incident that is immediately interrupted and forgotten, such as the discussion about taking off his shoes and going to travel in his stage performance He tries to refine and integrate the original fragmented dialogues and thoughts, so as to make it seem meaningful and to make it back and forth. For example, he adds the current catchwords like sketches in the Spring Festival Gala. These words greatly devolve the power of colloquial lines to actors. As a result, vulgar slangs can be found everywhere on the stage. Every time, it is like a cross-talk, and the audience always laughs with laughter.

Hence, it can be seen from above analysis, through the determination to break away from the original work, Yi's version reconstructs a world of simile with strange language with labelling skills while the source text expresses the connotation and theme of the drama through meaningless language. Wayne Booth, a member of the "narrative Chicago School", studies "new Aristotelianism" rhetoric in his book *Fictional Rhetoric*. He holds that the object of rhetorical narratology research is the rhetorical relationship between the author, the text and the reader. Yi applies a series of rhetorical strategies to the target text, and achieves a certain rhetorical effect through labeling, completing the purpose of rhetorical communication between source and audiences. In the form of analogy, it expresses the original absurd world and expresses Yi's own understanding of the drama, which makes it radiate a unique drama narrative beauty.

For Wu Xingguo's version, it continues Beckett's style and performs absurdity with absurdity. Peking opera aria is used in the stage, and derogatory language has become an important feature of the work. The performance version is full of a large number of meaningless dialogues but not divorced from the text, emphasizing direct access to people's hearts. Characters talk to each other without communication. Its real purpose is to doubt rational thinking, dispel the external cover of shielding the truth of the world, pry into its essence, and make an abstract understanding of the world. In this context, reason and logic have no way of doing something, only "clear your heart, and see the Buddha". At the same time, the source text which is almost "boring" is injected with vitality by the Peking opera. The laughter from time to time during the performance also shows the joy of the tragicomedy, although a considerable part of the "laughing effect" is achieved by the "black humor" and "Satire" outside the performance or the drama. We can see that the author uses transliteration and free translation to mark the name again. After the first day of waiting, the old tree sprouts a new bud in the next day, "破梭" (the name of Pozzo who is a master)and "垃圾"(the name of Lucky who is a servant), one blind and the other dumb, their life is getting worse and worse. "垃圾" is carrying boxes full of sand in both hands with the master "破梭" and he do not know where to go. He forgets seeing "Gege（哭哭）"and "Didi（啼啼）"(the names of Estragon and Vladimir)before. We can explain the Chinese name meaning in the following chart.

V Analysis of Two Theater versions in the Viewpoint of Narratology Theory

Table 5.1　Charcters' names in Wu Xingguo's Version

Beckett	Wu Xingguo	Chinese interpretation
Pozzo	破梭[pò suō]	Broken shuttle. There is an allegorical saying in China, Broken shuttle-Take advantage of available opportunities.
Lucky	垃圾[lā jī]	It means waste products that have lost use value and cannot be used
Estragon(Gege)	哭哭[kū kū]	weep and wail endlessly
Vladimir(Didi)	啼啼[tí tí]	weep and wail endlessly

　　From the chart, we can see Wu Xingguo uses his labelling systems to rename the characters' names. This translation frame method means "any type of label used for pointing to or identifying a key element or participant in a narrative, then, provides an interpretive frame that guides and constrains our response to the narrative in question. This explains the motivation for the use of euphemisms in many contexts" (Baker: 137). In this case, labelling is totally taken as a kind of game, which reveals the absurdity of the world mercilessly and at the same time it vividly embodies the incompetence of human beings and the authority of language. No matter what questions the characters put forward, they can't get accurate answers, or they don't answer the questions correctly.

　　Such labelling also implies that it is completely impossible to communicate between the smallest interpersonal units in modern society. Through the deconstruction of language communication function, Wu Xingguo uses this "discourse without ending" to echo the "behavior without ending" of "waiting" in Beckett's play. This lies in the fact that "translators and interpreters, then, may want to consider the larger narratives in which a text or utterance is embedded in order to make an informed decision about how to handle names" (Baker: 127).

　　Combined with the above contents, we can explain it as Wu Xingguo makes use of the deconstruction of language function to transfer Beckett's language confusion. Language plays an important role in traditional literary creation. As a symbol system of the combination of signifier and signified, it carries the important function of conveying meaning. On the other hand, the absence of signifier inevitably leads to the absence of signified. Eugene Nida once pointed out two ways to make the dialogue more dramatic: one is witty verbal dialogue; the other is to make language lose its natural function, that is, to express meanings and exchange ideas. For the absurd play, since the verbal dialogue can no longer adapt to the new social and historical environment, it is bound to become the choice of literary creators that language loses its expressive function and highlights drama.

As a classic work of absurd drama, *waiting for Godot* is featured by this kind of language. On the one hand, the advanced language strategy and the unique character image design complement each other, and they jointly express the theme. It is the character digestion in the chaotic world. With the loss of the subjectivity and historicity of the characters, the main characters in the drama can neither actively think, judge, choose and act, nor can they grasp their own destiny. The performance of the characters on the stage has become a combination of instantaneous fragments, and they have been crushed by time and lose their integrity. Correspondingly, the dialogues between the characters in the play are full of endless nonsense without clue. Their language is not continuous and unified, let alone achieve self affirmation through language. It can be said that most of the dialogues in the play are illogical, and of course they cannot be used to express the abstract thoughts, emotions and impressions of the characters.

The shrinking and scattering of characters lead to the loss of name. The loss of name here does not mean that there is no name, but refers to the loss of the function referred to. After losing its name, people have been completely dispelled, and the foundation of language existence in traditional concepts has also been dispelled, and the status of language itself has become more and more prominent. It doesn't matter who is talking and What's the difference between who's talking. Wu Xingguo takes the framing method of labeling to rename these characters emphasizing the absurdity. "Where frame space allows them framing narratives in translation more latitude, translators, and to a lesser extent interpreter, can insert their own critical comments and glosses at various points" (Baker: 127). "Name" is no longer an indicator of a character with personality characteristics, but a symbol to mark characters and a tool for word games. All of this clearly illustrate translator's attitude towards the relationship between language and characters. To show the meaninglessness of human existence, language has lost the function of expressing meaning.

5.4 Repositioning of Participants

The translator can reposition the character and events through various linguistic means, such as person deixis, to encourage the participants to actively participate in the reconstruction of narrative. In the stage translation, Yi and Wu both adjust the relationship between the characters by means of repositioning of participants. Before checking the versions of Yi and Wu, we first introduce this fact that reposition the character and events can be constructed in two ways: in the discourse and in the paratexts.

The repositioning in the discourse means that to reposition the relationship between the participants, the translator can adjust almost all the text features. This can be explored by the examination of two theoretical versions. Yi Liming's interpretation of *Waiting for Godot* is more abundant. In particular, it is a bold stroke to reveal the identity of the characters and their relationship with each other. For example, Estragon and Vladimir that Beckett is actually using to represent the whole human race, that is, the human species. It can even be said that one represents men and the other represents women. Yi puts the following view in an interview "this can also be seen from the conversation between two people in the act II, because in the second act, two people are more like a couple fighting" (Zhang Yanyan: B1) . This kind of repositioning in the discourse show characters' relationship from this angle, which makes us find everything fresh and new.

In this book, this kind of identification involves the target readers from the point view of performance. It lies the fact that "time, space, deixis, dialect, register, use of epithets, and variety means of self—and other identification be to participants" (Baker: 132). The translator adjusts the text features. In some introductions and interpretations, we have read before, two people are called "two old vagabonds". Yi denies such a slightly "arbitrary" view, because the whole script has never said that these two people are vagabonds, and has never clearly indicated that they are very old. be that as it may, in the dialogue between Estragon and Vladimir, we know that they sleep in the "ditch" at night, so it's no wonder that people think they are tramps. In this regard, Yi also has his own opinion about the reposition of participants: "we all know that Beckett lived in a time shortly after the end of World War II, so I guess the 'ditch' here actually refers to the trench, and the state of these two people is actually the state of 'human like ghost'" (Zhang Yanyan: B1). "The 'ghost' here is the 'ghost' of the western concept. In the west, there are three states of human beings: one is living; the other is dead but not going to heaven; the third is going to heaven or going to hell. Ghost refers to the second state." As a matter of fact, "Estragon and Vladimir represent the first two states, and they will switch frequently throughout the script" (Zhang Yanyan: B1).

In addition, Yi also makes some adjustments to the relationship bond between the characters, which makes the people on the stage always relevant. Even this kind of repositioning produces the effect of the rigorous combination of the force and the reaction force required for the relationship between the characters in the traditional drama. Although in Yi's version, the "Gogo" and "Didi" on the stage are discussing some irrelevant or amusing topics, at least they're really talking, not talking to themselves. It can be seen in the process of translation, translators, editors and other participants work together to weaken, implement or change some narrative meanings in the original text or discourse. Just like Baker believes that "translation may be seen as a frame in its own right, whether in its liberal or metaphorical sense" (120).

This method is used more frequently and skillfully after Pozzo and Lucky boy come. We can see three and a half roles make the relationship more complex, and the purpose clearer. Although they also seem to be forgetful, they are really discussing how to deal with the "Lucky". All of these narrative translation adjustments can be demonstrated by "One aspect of relationality, a feature of narrativity discussed, concerns the way in which participants in any interaction are positioned, or position themselves, in relation to each other and to those outside the immediate event" (Baker: 147). The translator makes the relationship between characters separated from the framework of the original world. Therefore, the audience see that when the perspective of text or image only focuses on specific characters, specific scenes and specific environments, the world actually disappears, or is deliberately stripped and ignored by the creator, leaving only the part he wants to express around the spotlight on the stage. "Any change in the configuration of these positions inevitably alters the dynamics of the immediate as well as wider narratives in which they are woven" (Baker: 147).

A second way to reposition the participants is to use the repositioning in the paratexts. It shows that the translator encourages the characters and audience to actively participate in the reconstruction of narrative. French scholar Gérard Genette (1930—) first proposes the concept of "leparatexte". He calls the relationship between text and leparatext as "paratextuality", which is an important achievement of this series of boundary studies. In the preface of *Paratexts: Thresholds of interpretation*, Genette defines the concept of the paratexts. In a word, the materials around the literary works, which can adjust the relationship between the works and the readers, are paratexts which can make the text become the utterance, so as to succeed in revealing the content and process of human consciousness to the readers.

When it comes to Wu Xingguo's version, he adjusts the relationship between the characters by means of paratexts. There are many stage instructions of pause and silence in *Waiting for Godot*. At Beckett's time, these pause and silence also provide great opportunity for the actors to exert their creativity and create new performances. In Wu's version, when the stage ends quietly, drama lyrics are inserted, which are not in the original text. For example "Time is like flowing water tranquilly, and it cannot look for back again"（光阴似水，静悄悄）(Lu Jianying: 216). These opera librettos are all made up by Wu Xingguo. When two people in the play face loneliness, they can sing like this. There are many silent fragments in *Waiting for Godot*, Beckett deliberately takes away the plot and the dramatic conflict. If there is no story, no plot, how to put an actor on the stage?

After looking up a lot of materials about Beckett. Wu Xingguo's version is carried out from a different angle, which takes silence of paratext as an unlimited performance. To perform, Wu creates some new things like opera librettos as drama lyrics which can also be found in Chinese tradition. These new paratexts are inserted into the silence of paratext. This lie in the fact that there is no pause on the stage, just as there is no pause in life. If there is a pause, it is called death. Every pause doesn't have to be the same. We can't be deceived by the superficial meaning of the pause. We have to find it. Similarly, while Estragon and Vladimir are waiting for Godot under the tree, they are talking without naturalness. In the source text, Beckett writes stage instructions of silence. In the performance script, the silent theater rings out the play words: "life is precious, friendship is more valuable, life and death are determined by fate, why do you want to destroy your sword?（生命诚可贵，友情价更高，生死由命运，何须自残剑）"(WuTaiShangXia, 2015). These things, like the name of the play and the introduction of the story before the opening of the curtain, can arouse the interest and expectation of the audience. Jin Shijie（金士杰）shares the same opinions that "it's our duty to find out what's behind the word 'pause'. The writer has put a pause here, which does not mean that he has taken a rest. There must be something he hopes for, and he has turned it into a pause in a very rich way" (WuTaiShangXia, 2015). The paratext, especially the Beijing opera libretto can make the translator "appear". Although translation has traditionally been regarded as an "invisible" activity, and naturally the translator has become an "invisible" person. By studying the Beijing opera libretto, we can not only understand the translator's translation purpose, translation methods, translation motivation, and even their potential consciousness.

Furthermore, Wu Xingguo says, "after reading at least six versions of *Waiting for Godot*, I could understand what the play was talking about, and then translate it into a script again. What changed a lot was that I changed the Godot in the play into a Buddha" (WuTaiShangXia, 2015). He makes the repositioning of Godot. At the same time, He introduces the concept of Peking Opera into it. Wu Xingguo and Jin Shijie always throw things away from each other in the rehearsal field and agitate each other. For example, in the second half, there is a section of changing the hat between Estragon and Vladimir. Jin Shijie dances and demonstrates several angles and ways of losing his hat. Then he said, "when he comes to Wu Xingguo, he repositions it again. Wu Xingguo transforms it into a round line", "which is the concept of round in opera"(WuTaiShangXia, 2015). This repositioning of the "round" implies the aesthetic inertia of Chinese people by seeking images evoking the memories and emotions of collective experience. This kind of translation on account of this fact that "repositioning in translation can also influence the interplay between ontological and public narratives, resulting in a different level of visibility of the personal in the context of shared, collective experience" (Baker: 153). The repositioning in the paratexts is an important carrier to present the translation, the translator and the social context at that time. It constructs the meaning of the translation together with the source text. The paratext can even extend the life of the source text. In short, the paratext provides a "field" in which the text lives.

It is briefly summarized for this chapter in the following words, this book uses the Mona Baker's framework method to analyze the two versions for performance of *Waiting for Godot*. After emphasizing the narrative factors and translation framework methods contained in the original work, this book explores four types, namely temporal and spatial framing, selective appropriation, labelling and repositioning of participants. The proper use of these frame factors in drama translation shows that translation is a purposeful and conscious narrative. The narrative framework of translation is the means to achieve this end. No matter what translation strategy the drama translator chooses, their cumulative choices always produce effects that exceed the original text. Because the individual text narrative is not isolated from the big narrative circulating in any society.

Drama translation in particular deserves a mention. As a complex and unique literary type, it needs to consider many unstable factors in the process of translation, such as characteristic drama text, the balance between text and playability, and the relationship between dialogues and language. But if a theater text must be read differently, Bassnett wonders, then "does the theater translator translate the play text as a purely literary text or does he or she try to translate it with respect to its function within the complex system of the spectacle" (Bassnett: 119)? Because if translation only focuses on drama rather than performance, without director, stage and audience, then the real drama and dramatic narration are meaningless. In dramatic narratology, it is true that stage narration is far more important than dramatic text. Hence, as social actors, drama translators are responsible for the narratives they disseminate. They are responsible for the real-life consequences that give these narratives popularities and legitimacy. At the same time, this book also aims to integrate relevant theoretical knowledge of narratology to make drama translation more readable, performable, reflective and appreciative. It is expected to arouse people's attention to drama translation and provide a new perspective for the further development of drama translation.

VI The challenges faced by translators in adapting cultural nuances.

    Cultural nuances refer to the subtle differences in behavior, values, and beliefs that are unique to a particular culture. These can include aspects such as idioms, humor, body language, social norms, and even certain concepts that may not exist in other cultures. In the context of translation, understanding cultural nuances is of paramount importance. This is because language is deeply intertwined with culture, and words often carry connotations and associations that go beyond their literal meanings. A direct word-for-word translation might convey the basic message, but it may fail to capture the subtleties and richness of the original text.

    The author's choice of words, phrases, and expressions often reflects their cultural background and worldview. By capturing these nuances, translators can preserve the author's original intent and voice. An author's cultural background significantly influences their writing. It can shape the themes they explore, the characters they create, and the narrative techniques they use. A translator must have a deep understanding of this cultural context to accurately translate the work. For instance, when translating a Japanese novel into English, the translator needs to understand Japanese customs, traditions, and societal norms to accurately convey the author's intent. An author's worldview, or their perspective on life and the world around them, is often reflected in their work. This can be seen in the issues they choose to highlight, the opinions of their characters, and the resolutions they present. Translators need to grasp this worldview and ensure it is preserved in the translation. This might involve careful word choice and sentence structure to maintain the author's original tone and perspective. Every author has a unique voice, which can be seen in their writing style, their use of language, and the rhythm and flow of their sentences. Preserving this voice in a different language can be challenging but is essential to maintain the work's original feel and character. This might involve finding equivalent idioms, maintaining sentence rhythm, or even preserving intentional ambiguities. Cultural nuances, such as idioms, humor, and references to local customs or historical events, can be particularly challenging to translate. These elements are often deeply rooted in the source language's culture and may not have direct equivalents in the target language. Translators need to find creative solutions to convey these nuances, such as using footnotes to explain a cultural reference or finding an idiom in the target language that conveys a similar meaning. preserving the author's intent in translation is a complex task that requires linguistic proficiency, cultural understanding, and creative problem-solving skills. It's a delicate balancing act of staying true to the original work while making it accessible and engaging to a new audience.

Accurate translation of cultural nuances can help readers understand and appreciate the culture of the original text. This can foster empathy and cross-cultural understanding. This process involves more than just converting words from one language to another; it requires a deep understanding of both the source and target cultures. Every culture has its unique traditions, customs, and societal norms. These cultural contexts often influence the way ideas and emotions are expressed in language. A skilled translator must understand these contexts and accurately convey them in the target language. For example, a simple greeting in one culture might have different connotations in another, and the translator must choose the appropriate words to convey the intended meaning. Different cultures have different sensitivities and taboos. What is considered acceptable in one culture might be offensive in another. Translators need to be aware of these sensitivities and navigate them carefully to ensure the translation is culturally appropriate. By accurately translating cultural nuances, translators allow readers to gain insights into different cultures. This can foster empathy and promote cross-cultural understanding, helping to bridge cultural divides and promote global harmony.

6.1 Idiomatic Expressions

Idiomatic expressions are a fascinating aspect of language because they often convey meanings that cannot be deduced from their individual words. In translation theory, idioms present a unique challenge due to their cultural and linguistic specificity. When translating idioms, a literal word-for-word translation often does not work because the idiom's meaning is not contained in the individual words but in the entire expression as a cultural unit. Therefore, translators must find a balance between preserving the original expression's meaning and adapting it to fit the cultural context of the target language.

One approach is to use an equivalent idiom in the target language that carries the same meaning, even if the words are different. This strategy maintains the idiomatic nature of the expression while ensuring that the meaning is understood by the target audience. Another strategy is to paraphrase the idiom, explaining its meaning in more straightforward language. This can be useful when an equivalent idiom does not exist in the target language.

Mona Baker's classification of difficulties and strategies in translating idioms is a significant contribution to this field. She identifies socio-linguistic elements, cultural aspects, linguistic and stylistic considerations, and specific meta-lingual factors as important considerations in the translation process.

Every language has idioms and phrases that are deeply rooted in its culture. These expressions often don't have direct equivalents in other languages, making them difficult to translate. Idiomatic expressions are phrases or sentences that do not mean exactly what the words say. They have a figurative, rather than literal, meaning and are understood by native speakers of the language. Here are some examples: English: "Kick the bucket"—This phrase doesn't literally mean to kick a bucket. Instead, it's an idiomatic expression that means "to die." Spanish: "Estar en las nubes"—Literally translated, this means "to be in the clouds," but it's used to describe someone who is daydreaming or not paying attention. French: "Coûter les yeux de la tête"—This literally translates to "to cost the eyes of the head," but it's an idiomatic way to say something is very expensive. consider the English idiom "kick the bucket", which means "to die." If we were to translate this idiom literally into French, it would make no sense. However, the French idiom "casser sa pipe", which literally means "to break one's pipe", carries a similar meaning of dying. So, "kick the bucket" could be idiomatically translated into French as "casser sa pipe". Here are a few more examples of idiomatic translations:English idiom: "Bite the bullet" (Meaning: To face a difficult situation courageously);Spanish idiomatic translation: "Aguantar el chaparrón" (Literally: "Endure the downpour");English idiom: "The ball is in your court" (Meaning: It's up to you to make the next move);German idiomatic translation: "Der Ball liegt bei dir" (Literally: "The ball lies with you");English idiom: "Break a leg" (Meaning: Good luck);Italian idiomatic translation: "In bocca al lupo" (Literally: "In the mouth of the wolf")

Translating idiomatic expressions can be challenging because they often cannot be translated directly from one language to another. Instead, the translator must understand the figurative meaning of the expression in the source language and then find an equivalent expression in the target language that conveys the same meaning. This requires a deep understanding of both languages and cultures.

The Conceptual Metaphor Theory also provides insights into the translation of idioms, suggesting that understanding the underlying metaphors can help in finding culturally appropriate equivalents. The Conceptual Metaphor Theory (CMT), developed by George Lakoff and Mark Johnson, suggests that our understanding of abstract concepts is largely metaphorical and is based on our physical and cultural experiences. This theory is particularly useful in the translation of idioms because idioms are often grounded in metaphorical language.

For example, consider the English idiom "to grasp the concept," which implies understanding. In CMT, this is an application of the metaphor UNDERSTANDING IS GRASPING, where an abstract concept (understanding) is understood in terms of a physical action (grasping). When translating this idiom into another language, a translator would look for an idiom that conveys the same metaphor of understanding as a form of grasping or holding.

Here's another example: the idiom "spill the beans" means to reveal a secret. This idiom can be linked to the conceptual metaphor SECRETS ARE CONTAINED OBJECTS. When translating into another language, finding an idiom that equates secrets with a contained object that can be accidentally released would convey a similar metaphorical meaning.

CMT can also explain why some idioms are challenging to translate. For instance, the English idiom "kick the bucket," meaning to die, is based on a metaphor that may not exist in other cultures. Therefore, translators might have to find an idiom with a different metaphor that still conveys the concept of death in the target culture.

In Chinese, idioms (chengyu) are deeply rooted in history and culture. For example, the idiom "画蛇添足" (huà shé tiān zú), literally "to draw a snake and add feet," metaphorically means to overdo something or to ruin the effect by adding something superfluous. The metaphor here is that like a snake doesn't need feet, some actions do not require additional, unnecessary elements.

The use of CMT in idiom translation is not just about finding linguistic equivalents; it's about preserving the cognitive and cultural richness that idioms carry. By focusing on the underlying metaphors, translators can create translations that resonate with the target audience both linguistically and culturally.

Translating idiomatic expressions poses several challenges, primarily due to their deeply rooted cultural, linguistic, and contextual nuances. Here are some of the key challenges: cultural specificity, non-literal meaning, linguistic variation, loss of nuance, ambiguity, fixed expressions idioms colloquialisms, evolution over time and so on. Cultural specificity often contains cultural references that may not have equivalents in other cultures. This can make it difficult to find a translation that resonates with the target audience in the same way; The meaning of idioms usually does not align with the literal meaning of the words they contain. Translators must go beyond the words to grasp the figurative meaning and then convey it in another language; different languages may use different imagery or concepts to express similar ideas. This variation requires translators to not only translate words but also adapt the underlying concepts; Even when a close equivalent is found, subtle nuances of the original idiom may be lost, which can alter the impact or humor intended by the original expression; Idioms can be ambiguous, and without a clear understanding of the context in which they're used, their meaning can be misinterpreted, leading to incorrect translations; Some idioms are fixed expressions that resist changes in form. This rigidity can make it hard to adapt them to the grammatical and stylistic norms of the target language; Idioms are often colloquial and may include slang, making them even more challenging to translate for formal or international audiences; The meaning and usage of idioms can evolve over time within the source culture, which means translators need to be up-to-date with current usage to ensure accurate translation.

To overcome these challenges, translators employ various strategies such as finding an equivalent idiom in the target language, paraphrasing the meaning, or providing an explanation. The goal is to maintain the original expression's effect while making it accessible to the new audience.

In summary, the translation of idiomatic expressions is not just a linguistic exercise but also a cultural one. It requires a deep understanding of both the source and target languages, as well as their respective cultures, to achieve a translation that is both accurate and culturally sensitive.

6.2 Cultural References

Cultural references can indeed pose a significant challenge in translation. They are elements in the source text that refer to a specific aspect of the source culture, such as historical events, folklore, local customs, idioms, jokes, or even popular culture like movies, songs, and celebrities. These references are often easily understood by people familiar with the culture but can be confusing or meaningless to those who aren't.

Historical events often serve as a rich source of study for translation theory, as they provide insights into how translation has shaped and been shaped by the flow of time and culture. Translation theory examines the methods and approaches used to translate texts, including those that recount historical events, and it has evolved significantly over time.

In the context of historical events, translation theory can be applied to understand how narratives of these events are conveyed across different cultures and languages. For instance, the translation of key historical texts, such as the Bible or the works of ancient historians, has been subject to various translation theories and practices throughout history. These translations have not only made the texts accessible to a wider audience but have also influenced the interpretation and understanding of the events they describe.

The evolution of translation theory from prescriptive approaches, which focus on strict adherence to the source text, to more descriptive approaches, which consider the cultural and contextual elements of the target language, reflects the changing attitudes towards translation over time1. Descriptive approaches, such as the polysystem theory and the cultural turn, emphasize the importance of the target culture and the role translations play within it.

For example, the translation of the Homeric epics has changed over centuries, with each translation reflecting the linguistic and cultural norms of its time. Early translations might have focused on a word-for-word approach, while modern translations might prioritize readability and cultural relevance for contemporary audiences.

Moreover, the history of translation itself is a fascinating subject, with research focusing on language issues, literary issues, religious and philosophical issues, scientific interchange, and exploration and conquest. These aspects highlight how translation has been a pivotal tool in the dissemination of knowledge and ideas across different periods and societies. A text might refer to a specific historical event that is well-known in the source culture but not in others. For example, an English text might refer to "The Boston Tea Party," an event that has specific historical significance in the United States. A translator would need to find a way to convey the significance of this event to readers unfamiliar with U. S. history.

In summary, translation theory provides a framework for understanding the complexities involved in translating historical events. It helps us appreciate the nuances of language and culture that shape our perception of history and the role translation plays in bridging temporal and cultural divides.

Folklore and mythology play a crucial role in the translation of drama, as they are often deeply intertwined with the cultural and historical context of the original work. When translating dramatic texts that draw from these rich traditions, several factors must be considered to ensure that the essence of the original is preserved and communicated effectively to the target audience.

Folklore and mythology are embedded in the cultural fabric of a society. Translators must understand the cultural significance of the folklore and

VI   The challenges faced by translators in adapting cultural nuances.

---

mythological references in the drama to translate them meaningfully. For example, the translation of classical Greek and Latin drama, or works by Shakespeare, Corneille, and Racine, requires not just linguistic competence but also a deep understanding of the historical and cultural context in which these works were created. Drama is meant to be performed, so the translation must be speakable and adaptable for actors. This includes considering the rhythm, flow, and idiomatic expressions that are natural in the target language while still conveying the original's cultural nuances. Sometimes, direct translation of folklore or mythological references may not resonate with the target audience. In such cases, translators might adapt the reference to something more familiar to the target culture or provide additional context to make it understandable. References to folklore and mythology can be particularly challenging to translate. For instance, a text in Greek might refer to "opening Pandora's box," an idiom that comes from Greek mythology. Translators would need to either explain the myth or find an equivalent idiom in the target language. Rabindranath Tagore's plays often synthesize myths, legends, and folklores, presenting a vision that combines reality with dramatic elements. His use of symbols, illusions, and songs rooted in Indian culture requires careful translation to maintain their intended impact and meaning. In Korean dramas like "A Korean Odyssey" and "Bride of the Water God", folklore elements are central to the narrative. Translating such dramas involves not only the language but also the cultural beliefs and practices depicted through the folklore.

In essence, translating drama that incorporates folklore and mythology is a complex task that goes beyond linguistic translation. It involves a sensitive approach to cultural elements, ensuring that the translated work remains true to the spirit of the original while being accessible and engaging for the new audience.

VII The Future of Translation and Theatrical Adaptation

As we advance into the 21st century, the fields of translation and theatrical adaptation are undergoing significant transformations. The impact of globalization, technological advancements, and shifts in cultural dynamics are reshaping the way we approach these disciplines. This chapter delves into the academic perspectives on the future of translation and theatrical adaptation, examining the challenges and opportunities that lie ahead.

In translation the advent of artificial intelligence and machine learning has revolutionized the translation industry. Automated translation tools have become increasingly sophisticated, offering rapid and cost-effective solutions for language conversion. However, these technologies also raise concerns about the loss of nuance and cultural context. The future academic discourse will likely focus on the integration of human expertise with machine efficiency to preserve the subtleties of language and meaning.

Age Theatrical adaptation is no longer confined to the stage. With the rise of digital media, adaptations now extend to various platforms, from streaming services to virtual reality. Academics are exploring how these new mediums affect the adaptation process, particularly in terms of audience engagement and the

VII　The Future of Translation and Theatrical Adaptation

preservation of the original work's integrity. The challenge is to adapt not only the content but also the experience to fit the new medium.

Translation and adaptation are deeply rooted in cultural context. As the world becomes more interconnected, there is a growing need to understand and respect cultural differences. Future research will likely emphasize the role of translators and adaptors as cultural mediators who must navigate the complexities of intercultural communication. This includes addressing issues of cultural appropriation and representation.

The ethical dimensions of translation and adaptation are becoming increasingly prominent. Questions arise about the fidelity to the source material, the rights of the original creators, and the impact of adaptations on cultural heritage. Academics are calling for a more conscientious approach that considers the moral responsibilities of translating and adapting works, especially in an era where content can be rapidly disseminated and altered.

As the demand for skilled translators and adaptors grows, so does the need for specialized education and training. Academic institutions are developing curricula that combine linguistic proficiency with cultural literacy and technical skills. The future of these fields may see a greater emphasis on interdisciplinary studies, preparing professionals to meet the evolving demands of the global market.

Collaboration is key to the advancement of translation and theatrical adaptation. By fostering partnerships between academics, practitioners, and technology developers, the field can benefit from a diverse range of insights and innovations. This collaborative spirit is essential for addressing the complex challenges that come with translating and adapting content for a global audience.

The future of translation and theatrical adaptation is marked by both challenges and opportunities. As we navigate the complexities of a changing world, the academic community must remain at the forefront of exploring new methodologies, ethical frameworks, and collaborative models. By embracing innovation while honoring tradition, we can ensure that translation and adaptation continue to enrich our cultural landscape.

This overview provides a glimpse into the academic considerations for the future of translation and theatrical adaptation. It is a field that is constantly evolving, driven by the forces of change and the enduring power of language and storytelling. As we look ahead, it is clear that these disciplines will remain vital to our understanding and appreciation of the diverse narratives that shape our world.

7.1 The Evolution of Translation and Theatrical Adaptation

Translation and theatrical adaptation have a long history, dating back to ancient times when stories were translated and adapted to be shared across different cultures and societies. Over time, the methods and approaches to translation and adaptation have evolved, influenced by factors such as technological advancements, cultural shifts, and changes in societal values. For example, the invention of the printing press in the 15th century revolutionized translation by making written texts more widely available, while the rise of cinema in the 20th century opened new possibilities for theatrical adaptation.

In ancient times, stories were often translated and adapted to be shared across different cultures and societies. For instance, many of the Greek tragedies and comedies we are familiar with today were adaptations of older myths and legends. These adaptations allowed stories to cross cultural boundaries and be understood by different societies. Over time, the methods and approaches to translation and adaptation have evolved. This evolution has been influenced by various factors, including technological advancements, cultural shifts, and changes in societal values. For example, during the Middle Ages, the invention of the printing press revolutionized translation by making written texts more widely available. This not only increased the dissemination of translated works but also allowed for the standardization of languages, which further facilitated translation. The invention of the printing press in the 15th century was a major milestone. It not only made books more affordable and accessible but also allowed for the wider dissemination of translated works. This led to a greater exchange of ideas across different cultures and societies, fostering intellectual growth and cultural understanding. The rise of cinema in the 20th century opened new possibilities for theatrical adaptation. Plays could now be adapted into films, reaching a much larger audience. This also allowed for more creative freedom as filmmakers were not confined by the physical limitations of a theatre stage. For example, Shakespeare's plays have been adapted into numerous films, each bringing a unique interpretation and visual style to the classic texts. In the modern era, technological advancements continue to influence translation and theatrical adaptation. Digital technology has made translation tools more accessible, enabling more people to engage in translation. In the realm of theatrical adaptation, technologies such as augmented reality (AR) and virtual reality (VR) are being used to create immersive theatrical experiences, offering new ways to tell and experience stories.

In conclusion, the fields of translation and theatrical adaptation have a long history and have continually evolved over time. Influenced by technological advancements, cultural shifts, and societal changes, these fields continue to grow and innovate, offering new ways to share and experience stories across different cultures and societies.

7.2 Emerging Trends and Techniques

The future of translation and theatrical adaptation is a fascinating topic that intersects with various disciplines, including linguistics, cultural studies, and the performing arts. As we look ahead, we can anticipate several trends and developments in this field:

With the rise of artificial intelligence and machine learning, translation tools are becoming more sophisticated. This could lead to more accurate and nuanced translations of theatrical works, making them accessible to a wider audience. The advent of artificial intelligence (AI) and machine learning has revolutionized numerous fields, including translation and theatrical adaptation. These technologies have the potential to significantly enhance the accuracy and nuance of translations, thereby making theatrical works more accessible to a global audience. Automated translation software, such as Google Translate and DeepL, have already made significant strides in providing quick yet relatively accurate translations. These tools leverage AI algorithms to translate text from one language to another. However, they often struggle with handling culturally specific phrases or complex linguistic structures. This is where further advancements in AI could come into play. With the development of more sophisticated algorithms, these tools could potentially better understand and translate a variety of languages and dialects. This would not only improve the quality of translations but also make a wider range of theatrical works accessible to non-native speakers. In addition to enhancing translation, technological advancements could also transform the way theatrical performances are conducted and produced. For instance, virtual reality (VR) and augmented reality (AR) technologies can be used to create immersive theatrical experiences. By transporting audiences to different settings or allowing them to interact with the performance in novel ways, these technologies can significantly enhance storytelling and audience engagement.

VII The Future of Translation and Theatrical Adaptation

Furthermore, the digitization of scripts and the use of online rehearsal tools can make the process of producing a play more efficient and collaborative. With digital scripts, changes can be made and shared in real time, saving time and reducing the risk of miscommunication. Online rehearsal tools, on the other hand, can enable cast and crew members to rehearse together regardless of their physical location. This not only facilitates collaboration but also allows for a more flexible rehearsal schedule. In conclusion, technological advancements offer exciting new possibilities for the field of translation and theatrical adaptation. By improving the accuracy and nuance of translations, these advancements can make theatrical works more accessible to a global audience. Moreover, by transforming the way performances are conducted and produced, they can enhance storytelling and audience engagement. As we move forward, it will be exciting to see how these trends continue to shape the future of this field.

In our increasingly globalized world, cross-cultural collaborations in the field of theatrical adaptation are becoming more common. Globalization is fostering more international collaborations, which means that theatrical works are increasingly being adapted across cultural boundaries. This can involve not only language translation but also cultural adaptation to make the content relevant to different audiences. For instance, consider the adaptation of William Shakespeare's plays. While Shakespeare's works are originally in English, they have been translated and performed in numerous languages around the world. But the process involves more than just translating the text. The cultural context, historical setting, idioms, and even humor must be adapted so that the play resonates with the new audience.

One notable example is the Japanese adaptation of Shakespeare's "Macbeth" by renowned director Akira Kurosawa. In his film "Throne of Blood", Kurosawa reimagines the story in a feudal Japanese setting, complete with samurai warriors and a Noh theatre-inspired aesthetic. The dialogue is not a direct translation of Shakespeare's text; instead, it is rewritten to reflect the style and rhythm of the Japanese language. Another example is the South African adaptation of "Hamlet", called "Hamlet Hapgood", which sets the story in post-apartheid South Africa. The play uses the Xhosa language and incorporates South African cultural elements, making it deeply relevant to local audiences. These examples illustrate how cross-cultural collaborations can breathe new life into existing works, creating innovative and culturally rich experiences for audiences. As we move forward, we can expect to see more of these collaborations, driven by advancements in translation technology and a growing appreciation for cultural diversity in the arts.

Theatrical adaptations are no longer confined to the stage. We're seeing more plays being adapted into films, virtual reality experiences, and other digital formats. This trend is likely to continue, with translations playing a key role in making these works accessible globally. The realm of theatrical adaptations has expanded beyond the traditional stage, embracing the digital revolution. Plays are being adapted into various formats like films, virtual reality experiences, and other digital platforms, making them more accessible and engaging for a global audience. For instance, consider the adaptation of plays into films. This is a common practice that allows a wider audience to experience the story. A notable example is the film adaptation of the musical "Hamilton". Originally a stage play, it was filmed with the original cast and made available on a streaming platform, allowing people all over the world to experience the critically acclaimed production.

Virtual reality (VR) is another exciting avenue for theatrical adaptation. VR can create immersive theatrical experiences that transport the audience into the story's setting. For example, the Royal Shakespeare Company collaborated with digital agencies to create a VR adaptation of "The Tempest". The adaptation allowed audiences to interact with the performance in real-time, providing a unique and engaging experience.

Moreover, plays are also being adapted into video games and interactive experiences. These adaptations allow the audience to engage with the story actively, making choices that affect the narrative's outcome. An example of this is the video game adaptation of "The Lion in Winter", which allows players to step

VII The Future of Translation and Theatrical Adaptation

into the shoes of the characters and influence the story's outcome.

Translations play a crucial role in these adaptations. They ensure that these works are accessible to a global audience, breaking down language barriers. For instance, subtitles or dubbed versions allow non-native speakers to understand and appreciate these adaptations.

As technology continues to evolve, we can expect to see more innovative multimedia adaptations of theatrical works. These adaptations will not only make theatre more accessible but also enrich the audience's experience by leveraging the unique capabilities of each format.

There's a growing interest in creating hybrid forms of theatre that blend live performance with digital elements. Translation in this context may involve not just textual content but also multimedia components like subtitles, sign language, and audio descriptions. The advent of digital technology has opened up new possibilities for theatre, leading to the emergence of hybrid forms that blend live performance with digital elements. This innovative approach to theatre not only enhances the audience's experience but also expands the scope of storytelling. For instance, consider the use of digital projections in theatre. These can be used to create dynamic backdrops, add visual effects, or even interact with live performers. A notable example is the production of "The Curious Incident of the Dog in the Night-Time" by the National Theatre, which used digital projections to represent the protagonist's thought processes. Another form of hybrid theatre involves the use of live streaming. This allows performances to be broadcasted in real-time to audiences around the world, breaking down geographical barriers. For example, the National Theatre's "NT Live" program broadcasts live performances to cinemas worldwide, allowing international audiences to experience their productions.

Translation plays a crucial role in these hybrid forms of theatre. It involves not just the translation of textual content but also multimedia components. Subtitles, for instance, can make a performance accessible to non-native speakers or hard-of-hearing audiences. In some cases, subtitles can be creatively integrated into the digital elements of the performance, adding an extra layer of meaning. Sign language interpretation is another important aspect. Some productions feature sign language interpreters who translate the dialogue for deaf or hard-of-hearing audiences. In certain cases, sign language can be incorporated into the performance itself, as seen in Deaf West Theatre's productions. Audio descriptions are also used in theatre to make performances accessible to visually impaired audiences. These provide a verbal description of the visual elements of a performance, such as the setting, costumes, and non-verbal actions. With the rise of digital technology, audio descriptions can be delivered through personal devices, allowing for a more inclusive theatre experience. In conclusion, the rise of hybrid forms of theatre represents an exciting development in the field of theatrical adaptation. By blending live performance with digital elements, these forms offer enriched storytelling possibilities and make theatre more accessible to diverse audiences.

As the demand for translation and theatrical adaptation grows, there is an increasing need for education and training in this field. This has led to the development of more academic programs and workshops dedicated to teaching the skills needed for translating and adapting theatrical works. These educational opportunities are crucial for preparing future practitioners to meet the challenges and demands of this evolving field. For instance, many universities now offer courses and degrees in translation studies, providing students with a solid foundation in both theory and practice. These programs often cover a range of topics, from the basics of language translation to the complexities of cultural adaptation. Some programs may also offer specialized courses in theatrical translation, giving students the opportunity to study and practice this specific form of translation.

Workshops and seminars are another valuable educational resource. These often focus on practical skills and provide participants with hands-on experience. For example, a workshop might involve translating a short play and then staging a reading of the translated work. This allows participants to see the results of their translation efforts and receive feedback from peers and professionals in the field. The work of Phyllis Zatlin serves as a contemporary example of translation and theatrical adaptation. Zatlin has explored the translation of bilingual plays and the choice between subtitling and dubbing of films. Her insights into the practical aspects of translating for theatre and film provide valuable guidance for future practitioners in the field. Another key resource is the book "Translation and Adaptation in Theatre and Film" edited by Katja Krebs. This book offers a comprehensive exploration of the synergies between adaptation studies and translation studies. It discusses the impact of rewriting on cultural constructions and experiences, which is crucial for understanding the future of translation and theatrical adaptation.

These examples illustrate how the field is evolving and highlight the importance of considering both linguistic and cultural elements in the translation and adaptation process. As we move forward, the interplay between translation, adaptation, and performance will continue to shape the landscape of global theatre and film.

The academic landscape is continually evolving, with new trends and techniques emerging as scholars and researchers seek to push the boundaries of knowledge and innovation. Information Science (IS), a field at the intersection of data management, technology, and user behavior, has seen significant shifts in focus and methodology over the past decade. This evolution reflects the broader changes in our increasingly digital and interconnected world, and underscores the importance of interdisciplinary approaches in academia.

The field of theatre is increasingly recognizing the importance of accessibility, leading to a variety of initiatives aimed at making performances more inclusive for diverse audiences. These initiatives not only enhance the theatre-going experience for individuals with disabilities but also enrich the field as a whole by embracing a broader range of perspectives and experiences.

One common accessibility initiative is the use of sign language interpreters in performances. These interpreters translate the spoken dialogue into sign language, allowing deaf or hard-of-hearing audience members to follow along. Some theatres go a step further by incorporating sign language into the performance itself, creating a more integrated experience. For example, Deaf West Theatre in Los Angeles is known for its productions that seamlessly blend American Sign Language with spoken English, making their performances accessible to both deaf and hearing audiences. Audio descriptions are another important accessibility tool. These provide a verbal description of the visual elements of a performance, such as the setting, costumes, and non-verbal actions. Audio descriptions are typically provided through a personal listening device, allowing visually impaired audience members to understand and appreciate what's happening on stage. Captioning is also widely used to make performances more accessible. Captions display the dialogue and other relevant sounds in text form, helping deaf or hard-of-hearing individuals, as well as those who might struggle with understanding the language or accents used in the performance.

  In the realm of translation, accessibility can also involve developing scripts that are sensitive to cultural differences and inclusive of diverse perspectives. This means not only translating the language but also considering cultural nuances, idioms, and context. It could also involve adapting content to be more inclusive, such as by representing diverse characters or addressing themes relevant to different communities. For example, the play "I Was Most Alive with You" by Craig Lucas was written to be performed simultaneously in English and American Sign Language, with a cast of deaf and hearing actors. The play addresses themes of disability, addiction, and faith, offering a powerful example of how theatre can be made more accessible and inclusive through thoughtful translation and adaptation.

  These examples illustrate the growing emphasis on accessibility in theatre and the important role that translation plays in these efforts. As environmental awareness grows, many theatre companies are exploring ways to make their productions more sustainable. This shift towards sustainability involves a variety of practices, from the materials used in sets and costumes to the energy efficiency of lighting and sound systems. One common sustainability practice is the use of recycled or sustainable materials in set design. Instead of buying new materials for each production, some theatres are turning to recycled materials or sourcing from sustainable suppliers. For example, the set for Julie's Bicycle's production of "As You Like It" was made entirely from recycled and reclaimed materials. Costumes, too, can be made more sustainable. Some theatre companies are opting to rent or reuse costumes instead of buying new ones for each production. Others are choosing to source materials from ethical suppliers or use natural dyes. Energy-efficient lighting and sound systems are another important aspect of sustainable theatre. LED lights, for instance, use significantly less energy than traditional stage lights and can last much longer. Similarly, energy-efficient sound systems can reduce a theatre's overall energy consumption.

In addition to these practices, some theatre companies are also implementing broader sustainability initiatives. These might include recycling programs, composting food waste from concessions, or even installing solar panels to power their facilities. For example, the Oregon Shakespeare Festival has implemented a comprehensive sustainability program that includes recycling, composting, energy conservation, and sustainable procurement practices. Similarly, London's Arcola Theatre has become known as the world's first carbon-neutral theatre, thanks to its use of solar panels, LED lighting, and other sustainable practices. These examples illustrate the many ways in which theatre companies are working to reduce their environmental impact. As awareness of environmental issues continues to grow, we can expect to see even more innovative sustainability practices in the world of theatre. A growing trend in theatre is the move towards more interactive forms of performance, where the audience plays an active role. This shift is changing the traditional dynamics of theatre, creating more engaging and immersive experiences for audiences.

One form of this is immersive theatre, where the audience is not confined to their seats but can move around the performance space. In these productions, the boundary between the performers and the audience is blurred, and the audience is often directly involved in the action. A notable example of this is "Sleep No More", a production by Punchdrunk. In this immersive adaptation of Shakespeare's "Macbeth", audience members are free to explore the multi-story performance space, following characters and scenes at their own pace.

Another form of audience participation involves productions that invite the audience to participate in the storytelling process. This could involve voting on the outcome of the story, contributing ideas, or even becoming characters in the performance. For example, in "The Mystery of Edwin Drood", a musical based on Charles Dickens' unfinished novel, the audience votes on the ending of the story, choosing the identity of the murderer.

Interactive technology is also being used to facilitate audience participation. For instance, some productions use mobile apps or digital platforms to allow the audience to interact with the performance, such as voting on plot decisions or contributing to the dialogue.

These trends towards audience participation reflect a broader shift in the world of theatre and performance. As audiences seek more engaging and personalized experiences, theatre makers are finding innovative ways to involve the audience in the performance. This not only enhances the audience's experience but also opens up new possibilities for storytelling and performance. As the field of translation and adaptation evolves, so too does the nature of storytelling. We're seeing more experimental forms of theatre that challenge traditional narrative structures, as well as the use of technology to create new storytelling possibilities.

Experimental theatre often seeks to break away from traditional narrative structures and conventions. This can involve non-linear narratives, abstract themes, and unconventional use of space and time. For example, the works of playwrights like Samuel Beckett and Harold Pinter often eschew traditional narrative structures. Their plays often focus on existential themes and the human condition, expressed through abstract dialogue and unconventional plot structures. For instance, Beckett's "Waiting for Godot" is renowned for its minimal plot and repetitive dialogue, challenging traditional notions of storytelling by focusing on the human experience of waiting and the passage of time. Similarly, Harold Pinter, known for his 'Pinteresque' style, often leaves significant gaps in the narrative for the audience to fill in. His play "The Homecoming" is a prime example of this, with its ambiguous plot and characters that leave much to audience interpretation. On the other hand, technology is creating new possibilities for storytelling in theatre. Digital elements can be incorporated into live performances to create a multi-sensory experience. For example, the use of projections can add a visual layer to the performance, enhancing the storytelling with visual imagery. Moreover, technology is also enabling new forms of interactive and participatory theatre. Audiences can influence the outcome of the story in real-time using digital platforms or mobile apps. An example of this is the "Choose Your Own Adventure" style performances, where the audience votes on key plot decisions, creating a unique story in each performance.

VIII   Conclusion

Drama is considered to be a literary and a performing art, which explains the duality of its essence. Drama also has a duality of script because of literariness and performance. Both dualities determine the complexity of the drama translation. The translator should not only deal with the differences between the two languages and cultures, but also make clear the relationship between linguistic symbols and other dramatic symbols. Drama translation is complex, yet it is still feasible. Starting from the duality of drama, this book divides six Chinese versions of *Waiting for Godot* into two categories, four for literary analysis of reading and two for theatrical analysis. Accordingly, by using three theories, translators present an interpretation of six Chinese versions of *Waiting for Godot* from dialogue theory, rewriting theory and narratology. In what follows the book elucidates what the conclusions to be one after one.

To start with, when it comes to Bakhtin, dialogue and discourse mount into dominance and the dialogic thinking penetrates into all discourse. Four Chinese versions translated by Shi Xianrong, Liao Yuru, Yu Zhongxian and Qiu Gangjiang are relatively equivalent to the source text, while the four versions reflect the intention imposed by the author and the translator, thus creating a special kind of double-voice text. It is shown as serving two speakers' intentions: one is the intention of the original author; the other is the intention of the translator reflected.

Through a detailed double-voicedness examination, the book finds differences under the translators' intentions. Qiu's translation is characterized by its retaining absurdity and colloquialism. The retaining absurdity is embodied in the complete dismemberment of language. Shi's translation is characterized by its informative words. Shi's language is implicit and rhetorical. Limited by the performance time, each sentence is concise, but powerful, and can give information. Yu's translation is dynamic and performable. In the discussion of the characteristics of drama texts, the eloquence and performability have always been very important. Although the text of drama is written, the ultimate ownership of drama should be on the stage. Liao's translation is a parody of Beckett's style, and her translation is the most attentive in language imitation.

Furthermore, the book aims at finding out how the four translators are manipulated by ideology, poetics and patrons. when it comes to rewriting theory, translator's choice is operated from different dimensions, and it runs through the whole process of translation. The four Chinese versions of *Waiting for Godot* have made an adaptation in ideology, poetics and patronage. Shi's version in 1965 and Qiu's version in 1969 are greatly influenced by these three aspects, and the rewriting is obvious. In the 1960s, the first Chinese version gets translated by Shi Xianrong (1927—1993) in 1965. Owing to special political environment at that time, Shi makes quite a few deletions and alterations so that the version can be accepted. Yu's version in 2006 and Liao's version in 2008 are faithful to the source text due to social progress and political openness. Considering little about censorship, Liao focuses on the literary work itself when translating it. For the first time, it is translated by a female translator in 2008. This version is listed in the classical translated works for "National Science Council" in China's Taiwan. With the lapse of time, the content in the target text is more tolerant of diversity.

The language of Shi's translation is easy to understand, as he tries to make the reading effect of the target readers similar to that of the original readers. In most cases, the translator achieves his translation goals, balancing the target text and the original text and the target language ecology effectively, and making a greater contribution in the communicative dimension. At the same time, it is well received for its conciseness and neatness, enabling scholars to research the western classic play (Zhang: 39). Yu has made an outstanding effort to preserve the cultural information of the original text, and most of them choose the expression close to the author, that is, the expression of alienation, and try his best to preserve the cultural implication of the original text. Liao also introduces many western cultures involved in the play to Chinese readers through a large number of annotations, which makes the translated text closer to the original language ecology in terms of culture dimension. It is more conducive to readers' understanding and the spread of foreign cultures. In her translation, annotations account for almost one fifth of the text. her translation can be described as a collection of notes. This kind of translation is suitable for reading, but not for performing. Because actors have neither time nor place to comment when performing on stage.

Qiu Gangjian publishes his version in 1968 and it has characteristics of sexual explicitness in the sex scene. This version applies domestication to make his translation fluent and more acceptable to the readers. Proper use of domestication can make a drama resonate with both the target language audience and convey the ideological connotation of the source language script. Such as replacing the original dialect with the slang and dialect in the target language, and deleting the non-portable part rooted in the source language culture. Given the above, on the linguistic dimension, the four versions are close to the reader's language and easy to understand, which makes marvelous efforts for the target readers to read smoothly.

By analyzing different translators' works on *Waiting for Godot* in different periods, it can be seen that the choice of translation strategies embodies obvious characteristics of the times, and their translations are under the influence of the products of the mainstream culture the times. The translator does not translate in a vacuum. The translator's rewriting strategy and the translator's manipulation of all aspects of the original text are all influenced by other factors outside the text, such as ideology, cultural fashion and poetic ideas in a specific historical period. As the main way of cross-cultural communication, translation cannot be separated from the influence of ideology, so naturally, translation studies should also take ideology into account. Moreover, language is the carrier of culture, and it is not difficult to see the ideological intention behind the cultural information. The handling of cultural information is not only a matter of translation skills, but also a certain dominance of ideology in the process of cross-cultural communication. The formation of coexistence between foreign culture and native culture is artificially split, forming an unnecessary binary opposition pattern. Translation involves vocabulary, so it is necessary to break the discourse order of the source language and reorganize the cultural fragments. Either before or after reorganization, ideology is hidden in the cultural fragments. It is necessary to abandon ideological prejudice for advocating the coexistence of different cultures.

Finally, when it comes to narrative, scholars hold that drama translation research should not focus on whether drama translation is performable or not, but on how to make that drama performable. This is what this study focuses on. This book compares the two Chinese versions directed by Wu Xingguo and directed by Yi Liming by the framing methods. Yi's version first begins with the change of starting space. This version sets itself a leading space by choosing steel cross and mirror to replace the tree in the source text, which causes an unbalanced narrative effect. Second is about the influence of renaming, which successes in moulding the character vividly. Wu's version draws an analogy between God and Buddha, emphasize a function which moulds collective culture. It could be compressed as multiple interpretation embedded factors that are comprised of visible, sound and intangible narrative factor. All these factors work together consist of Beijing opera, Buddhist music, in order to mould vivid characters, enrich the main story and achieve multiple narrative effects making it performable. It is interpreted in the form of Peking Opera, full of oriental philosophical thinking and it is highly localized adaptation.

It can be seen that in addition to translation skills, the translator should be satisfied with the characteristics of performing arts and drama language on the stage. Translation is related to the main purpose of the drama, the development of the plot and performance effect. Therefore, the translation of drama for the purpose of stage performance can make the drama performer fully show the unique charm of drama, and highlight the difference between drama and other literary and artistic forms. Mona Baker's framing methods are sufficiently applied for drama translation from four methods like temporal and spatial framing, selective appropriation of textual material, framing by labeling and repositioning of participants. Through covering a case study by these methods in chapter four, this book emphasizes the significance of narrative factors figuring out how to make drama performable. Hence, embedded narrative factors are applied as one of the innovative points in this book. As argued earlier, because the translator of the drama text does not convey information to the audience directly, the translation of the script must go through a process of text conversion, stage conversion and drama communication involving translators, directors, actors and audiences.

Hence, the prerequisite of drama translation for the purpose of performance is that the translator must be familiar with the medium of theater. For a translator of drama works, besides mastering language skills and the ability to measure what is familiar to the audience and what is unfamiliar to the audience, he must also have a sense of drama. When translating drama works, the translator should direct his own translation in his mind while translating. These show that the translator's tasks are closely related to those of directors and actors. As luck would have it, the translators of these two versions are directors, which makes them performable. Accordingly, through the analysis, this book finds that narrative can be applied in the exploration of how to do performance-oriented translation of drama. Within its narrative framework, the discussions of drama translations can be more comprehensive and systematic, which advance the progress on developing a translation theory tailored to drama translation.

Taken together, the book examines the translated versions in the light of three different theories: the dialogism, the rewriting theory, and Baker's narrative theory. The three theories show internal cause, external cause and stage externality of drama translation studies. By comparing the translated versions in the three theories, six Chinese versions' characteristics can be clarified completely.

In essence, translating drama that incorporates folklore and mythology is a complex task that goes beyond linguistic translation. It involves a sensitive approach to cultural elements, ensuring that the translated work remains true to the spirit of the original while being accessible and engaging for the new audience.

The future of translation and theatrical adaptation is marked by both challenges and opportunities. As we navigate the complexities of a changing world, the academic community must remain at the forefront of exploring new methodologies, ethical frameworks, and collaborative models. By embracing innovation while honoring tradition, we can ensure that translation and adaptation continue to enrich our cultural landscape.

Bibliography

Books:

[1]Baker, Mona. *Translation and Conflict: A Narrative Account*. London: Routledge, 2018.

[2]Bakhtin, Mikhail. *"Problems of Dostoevsky's Poetics. (1963 ed.) Ed."* and Trans. by Caryl Emerson. Minneapolis: University of Minnesota Press, 1984.

[3]Barranger, Milly S. *Theatre: A Way of Seeing*. Boston: Cengage Learning, 2014.

[4]Beckett, Samuel. *Waiting For Godot*. New York: Grove Press, 2008.

[5]Booth, W. C. *The Rhetoric of Fiction*. Chicago & London: The University of Chicago Press, 1983.

[6]Crosthwaite, Paul. *Trauma, Postmodernism and the Aftermath of World War II*. New York: Palgrave Macmillan, 2009.

[7]Calhoun, C. J. *Social Theory and the Politics of Identity*. Cambridge: Blackwell, 1994.

[8]Eugene A, Nida and Charles R, Taber. *The Theory and Practice of Translation*. Shanghai：Shanghai Foreign Language Education Press, 2004.

[9]Fu Daobin. *Tang Bell: The Spiritual Prototype of Chinese Culture Oriental Press*. Beijing: Oriental Press, 1996.[傅道彬.晚唐钟声·中国文化的精神. 北京：东方出版社, 1996.]

Bibliography

[10]Frost, Robert. *Stopping By Woods on A Snowy Evening*. New York: Irwin & Company Limited, 1978.

[11]Genette, Gérard. *Paratexts: Thresholds of Interpretation*. No. 20. New York: Cambridge University Press, 1997.

[12]Gerald Prince. *The Form and Functioning of Narrative*. Beijing: Renmin University Press, 2013.

[13]Graver, Lawrence. *Waiting for Godot*. New York: Cambridge University Press, 1989.

[14]Haynes, J., & Knowlson, J. *Images of Beckett*. New York: Cambridge University Press, 2003.

[15]Hawthorne, Nathaniel, and Wilhelm Schmalenbach. *The Scarlet Letter*. London: Henry Frowde, 1903.

[16]Herman, David. *Storytelling and the Sciences of Mind*. Cambridge: MIT Press, 2013.

[17]Kelake, Huoerkuisite, & Yubing. *Mikhail Bakhtin: Mikhail Bakhtin*. Beijing: Renmin University Press, 2000.[克拉克, 霍尔奎斯特, &语冰. 米哈伊尔·巴赫金：米哈伊尔巴赫金. 北京：中国人民大学出版社, 2000.]

[18]Hermans, Theo, ed. *The Manipulation of Literature (Routledge Revivals): Studies in Literary Translation*. New York: Routledge, 2014.

[19]Kern, Edith. *Existential Thought and Fictional Technique: Kierkegaard, Sartre, Beckett*. New Haven and London: Yale University Press, 1970.

[20]Knowlson, J. *Damned to Fame: The life of Samuel Beckett*. London: Bloomsbury, 1997.

[21]Lawley, P. . *Waiting for Godot: Character Studies*. London: Continuum, 2008.

[22]Lu, Jianying. *Wu Xingguo's Contemporary Legend*. Taipei: World Culture, 2006.[卢健英.绝境萌芽：吴兴国的当代传奇. 台北：天下文化出版社, 2006.]

[23]Mark Shuttleworth, & Moira Cowie. *Dictionary of Translation Studies*. Shanghai：Shanghai Foreign Language Education Press, 2004.

[24]Maybin, Janet. *Language, Struggle and Voice: The Bakhtin/Volosinov Writings*. London: Sage, 2001.

[25]Mcdonald, & Ronan. *The Cambridge introduction to Samuel Beckett*. Cambridge: Cambridge University Press, 2006.

[26]Morrison, Toni. *Beloved*. New York: A Division of Random House, Inc., 2019.

[27]Metz, Christian. *Language and Cinema*. Vol. 26. Berlin & Boston: Walter de Gruyter, 2011.

[28]Nida, E. A. *Language, Culture, and Translating*. Shanghai: Shanghai Foreign Language Education Press, 1993.

[29]Prince, G. *A Dictionary of Narratology*. Lincoln & London: University of Nebraska press, 1987.

[30]Pirandello, Luigi. *Luigi Pirandello in the Theatre: A Documentary Record*. Vol. 3. London: Psychology Press, 1993.

[31]Qiu, Gang-jian et al. *Deng Dai Guo Tuo*. Taipei: Yuan Jing Press, 1992. [邱刚健.等待果陀. 台北：远景出版社，1992.]

[32]Saussure, Ferdinand de et al. *Course in General Linguistics*. New York: Columbia University Press, 2011.

[33]D Weissbort, and A. Eysteinsson. *Translation-Theory and Practice: A Historical Reader*. New York: Medium Aevum, 2006.

[34]Elam, Keir. *The Semiotics of Theatre and Drama*. London & New York: Routledge, 1980.

[35]Shang, Biwu. *Contemporary Western Narratology: Postclassical Perspectives*. Beijing: Ren Min Wen Xue Chu Ban She, 2014.[尚必武. 当代西方后经典叙事学研究. 北京：人民文学出版社，2014.]

[36]Steiner, George. *After Babel: Aspects of Language and Translation*. Oxford: Oxford University Press, 1975.

[37]Schleiermacher, Friedrich. *'On the Different Methods of Translating'*. Trans. Susan Bernofsky. In Venuti, Lawrence, ed.. *The Translation Studies Reader*. 2nd edn. New York and London: Routledge, 2004 (first published 1813).

[38]Voloshinov, Valentin Nikolaevich, and Michail M. Bachtin. *Marxism and the Philosophy of Language*. London: Harvard University Press, 1986.

[39]Whitman, Walt, and Karl Adalbert Preuschen. *Leaves Of Grass (1855)*. New York: Olms Presse, 1971.

[40]Shi Xianrong, Tu Zhen. *Drama Collection of the Absurd*. Shanghai: Shanghai Translation Publishing House, 1980.[施咸荣, 屠珍. 荒诞派戏剧集. 上海：上海译文出版社, 1980.]

[41]Shi, Xianrong. *Deng Dai Ge Duo*. Beijing: People's Literature Publishing House, 2002.[施咸荣. 等待戈多. 北京：人民文学出版社, 2002.]

[42]Tymoczko, & Maria. *Translation and Power*. Beijing: Foreign Language Teaching and Research Press, 2007.

[43]Wang Fuming. *Essays of Paradise Bookstore*. Zhengzhou: Elephant Publishing House, 2014.[王幅明. 天堂书屋随笔. 郑州：大象出版社, 2014.]

[44]Wang Hong. *Drama Stylistic Analysis: The Method of Discourse Analysis*. Shanghai：Shanghai Foreign Language Education Press, 2006.[王虹. 戏剧文体分析：话语分析的方法. 上海：上海外语教育出版社, 2006.]

[45]Wang Guowei, Fan Ya. *Words on The World*. Beijing：Beijing Book Co. Inc., 2019[王国维, 范雅. 人间词话. 北京：北京图书有限公司，2019.]

[46]Wang, Hongyin. *On the Criticism of Literary Translation*. Shanghai：*Shanghai Foreign Language Education Press*, 2006.[王宏印. 文学翻译批评论稿. 上海：上海外语教育出版社，2006.]

[47]Whitman, Walt, and Karl Adalbert Preuschen. *Leaves of Grass:(1855)*. New York: Olms, 1971.

[48]Worth, Katharine. *Waiting for Godot and Happy Days*. London: Macmillan International Higher Education, 1990.

[49]Yu, Zhongxian et al. *Deng Dai Ge Duo*. Changsha: Hunan Literature and Art Publishing House, 2006.[余中先.等待戈多. 长沙：湖南文艺出版社，2006.]

[50]Yuru Liao. *Deng Dai Guo Tuo, Zhong Ju*. Taipei: Lianjing Publishing House, 2008.[廖玉如.等待戈多.终局. 台北：联经出版社, 2008.]

[51]Zhang Nanfeng. *Polysystem Studies of Translation: Theory, Practice and*

Response. Changsha: Hunan People's Publishing House, 2012.[张南峰. 多元系统翻译研究：理论，实践与回应. 长沙：湖南人民出版社, 2012.]

Articles:

[1]Abel, Sam, and Martin Esslin. "The Field of Drama: How the Signs of Drama Create Meaning on Stage and Screen". *Theatre Journal*, vol 40, no. 3, 1988, p. 3-15. *JSTOR*, doi: 10.2307/3208347.

[2]Andre Lefevere, Swietlick, and Alain. "Translation, Rewriting, And the Manipulation of Literary Fame". *The Modern Language Journal*, vol 78, no. 2, 1994, p. 516-528. *Wiley*, doi: 10.2307/329049.

[3]Bassnett, Susan. "Translating For the Theatre: The Case Against Performability". *TTR: Traduction, Terminologie, Rédaction*, vol 4, no. 1, 1991, p. 99-111. *Consortium Erudit*, doi: 10.7202/037084ar.

[4]Bennett, W. Lance, and Murray Edelman. "Toward A New Political Narrative". *Journal Of Communication*, vol 35, no. 4, 1985, p. 156-171. *Oxford University Press (OUP)*, doi: 10.1111/j.1460-2466. 1985. tb02979. x. Accessed 15 June 2021.

[5]Baker, Mona. "Reframing Conflict in Translation". *Social Semiotics*, vol 17, no. 2, 2007, p. 151-169. *Informa UK Limited*, doi: 10.1080/10350330701311454.

[6]Castelán, Anabel. "Edwin Gentzler. Translation and Identity in The Americas, New Directions in Translation Theory". *Cadernos De Tradução*, vol 1, no. 29, 2012. *Universidade Federal De Santa Catarina (UFSC)*, doi: 10.5007/2175-7968.2012v1n29p176.

[7]Allison, Alexander W. "Adorno, Theodor. Minima Moralia: Reflections from Damaged Life. Trans. EFN Jephcott. London: Verso, 1978. ———. Negative Dialektik. Frankfurt am Main: Suhrkamp, 1973. ———. Notes to Literature. Vol 1. Trans. Shierry Weber Nicholson. New York: Columbia UP, 1991." *Active Romanticism: The Radical Impulse in Nineteenth-Century and Contemporary Poetic Practice* 4, 2015, p. 249.

[8]Bernstein, Cynthia, and Gerald Prince. "A Dictionary of Narratology".

Language, vol 65, no. 2, 1989, p. 436. *JSTOR*, doi: 10.2307/415368.

[9]Chen, Zengrong. "Translation Research and Communication of Absurd Drama in China". *Drama Literature*, no. 5, 2010, p. 15-19.[陈增荣. "荒诞派戏剧在中国的译介、研究与传播". 戏剧文学，(05)，2010, p. 15-19.]

[10]Cheng, Xiaomu. "True Acceptance of False Schools: A Journey to China of 'Absurd Drama'". *Drama (Journal of Central Academy of Drama)*, no. 1, 2017, p. 16-31.[程小牧. "虚假流派的真实接受：'荒诞派戏剧'的中国之旅". 戏剧（中央戏剧学院学报），(01)，2017，p. 16-31.]

[11]Chen, Ping. "On The Ternary Structure of Modern Chinese Time System". *Chinese Language,* no. 6, 1988, p. 401.[陈平. "论现代汉语时间系统的三元结构". 中国语文,（06），1988，p. 401.]

[12]Chu, Zexiang. "A Survey of The Spatial Adaptability of Verbs". *Chinese Language*, vol 4, 1998, p. 253-261.[储泽祥. "动词的空间适应性情况考察".中国语文,（04），1998，p. 253-261]

[13]Cui Chengde. "The Tragedy of Nothingness and Despair." *Foreign Literature Studies*, vol 3, 1985, p.69-75.[崔成德. "虚无与绝望的悲剧".外国文学研究,（03），1985，p. 69-75.]

[14]Danielle-Henri Barrou, & Meng Hua. "Imagology in the Sense of Comparative Literature." *Comparative Literature in China*, no.04, 1998, p. 79-90.[达尼埃尔-亨利·巴柔,& 孟华. "比较文学意义上的形象学". 中国比较文学（04），1998，p. 79-90.]

[15]Deng Di. "Translation in the Sense of Creation". *Shanghai Translation,* no.03，2017，p. 28-31.[邓笛. "创作意识下的翻译与翻译意识下的创作".上海翻译,（03），2017，p. 28-31.]

[16]Ding Yaozhan. "The" Avant-garde "Literature and Art of the Western World". *World Knowledge*, vol 09, 1964, p. 23-26.[丁耀瓒. "西方世界的'先锋派'文艺". 世界知识.（09），1964，p. 23-26.]

[17]Dong Hengyi. "The Degeneration of Dramatic Art-On the French 'Anti-Theatrical School'". *Frontline*, vol 08, 1963, p. 10-11.[董衡异. "戏剧艺术的堕落——谈法国'反戏剧派'". 前线,（08），1963，p. 10-11.]

[18]Zhongqiao, Duan. "Three Queries to Prof. Yu Wujin's Understanding Marx anew". *Academic Monthly*, vol1, 2006.[段忠桥."对俞吾金教授"重新理解马克思的"三点质疑".学术月刊,（01），2006.]

[19]Esslin, Martin. "The Theatre of The Absurd". *The Tulane Drama Review*, vol 4, no. 4, 1960, p. 3-15. JSTOR, doi: 10.2307/1124873.

[20]Eugene A. Nida, and Waterman, John T.. "Toward A Science of Translating: With Special Reference to Principles and Procedures Involved in Bible Translating". *Language*, vol 42, no. 1, 1966, p. 93. *JSTOR*, doi: 10.2307/411603.

[21]Feng Wei. "*Waiting for Godot* and Western Comedy Tradition". *Foreign Literature Review*, vol 116, no.4, 2015, p. 173-186.[冯伟."《等待戈多》与西方喜剧传统".外国文学评论,4, 2015, p. 173-186.]

[22]Fludernik, Monika et al. "Narratology in Context". *Poetics Today*, vol 14, no. 4, 1993, p. 727-732. JSTOR, doi: 10.2307/3301102.

[23]Head, Brian W. *Politics and Philosophy in the Thought of Destutt de Tracy*. Vol. 29. Routledge, 2019.

[24]He, Shaobin. "Translation As Rewriting: A Study of and Lefevere's Notion of Translation". *Journal of PLA University of Foreign Languages*, vol 028 no.05, 2005, p. 66-71+108.[何绍斌."作为文学'改写'形式的翻译——Andre Lefevere翻译思想研究".解放军外国语学院学报, no.05, 2005, p. 66-71+108]

[25]Nesbet, Anne, and Michael Holquist. "Dialogism. Bakhtin And His World". *The Slavic and East European Journal*, vol 37, no. 1, 1993, p. 69. JSTOR, doi: 10.2307/308638.

[26]Hong, Zengliu. "*Waiting for Godot*: a High Degree of Unity of Language Form and Content". *Foreign Languages,* no.3, 1996, p. 30-33.[洪增流."《等待戈多》——语言形式和内容的高度统一".外国语（上海外国语大学学报），（03），1996, p. 30-33.]

[27]Jakobson, Roman. "4.2 Closing Statement: Linguistics and Poetics (1960)." *The Lyric Theory Reader: A Critical Anthology*, 2014, p. 570-579.

[28]Gilroy, James P. et al. "Waiting for Death: The Philosophical Significance of Beckett's 'En Attendant Godot'". *Rocky Mountain Review of Language and Literature*, vol 34, no. 4, 1980, p. 25. *JSTOR*, doi: 10.2307/1347411.

[29]Jia, Liting. "Language Characteristic in Waiting for Godot". *Journal of Changchun Normal University*, vol 28, no. 01, 2009, p. 133-135.[贾丽婷."《等待戈多》的语言特色".长春师范学院学报（人文社会科学版），（01），2009，p. 133-135.]

[30]Jin, Sifeng. "The Absurd Drama and the Chinese absurd drama". *Foreign Literature Studies*, no. 04, 1989, p. 122-129.[金嗣峰."荒诞派戏剧和中国的荒诞剧".外国文学研究，（04），1989，p. 122-129.]

[31]Liang, Benbin. "Dialogue features in Waiting for Godot". *Movie Literature,* vol 514, no. 13, 2010, p. 97-98.[梁本彬."《等待戈多》的对话特色".电影文学，（13），2010，p. 97-98.]

[32]Lin Ping. "On The Contribution and Limitation of Translation Rewriting Theory". *Journal of Changjiang Normal University*, vol 29, no. 01, 2013, p. 88-91.[林萍.翻译改写理论的贡献与局限评说.长江师范学院学报，29（01），2013，p. 88-91.]

[33]Liu Xiuyu. "Acceptance of Beckett's Plays in China". *Literary Contention*, no. *07,* 2013, p. 142-144.[刘秀玉."贝克特戏剧的中国接受".文艺争鸣，（07），2013, p. 142-144.]

[34]Iser, W. "What Is Literary Anthropology? The Difference between Explanatory and Exploratory Fictions". *Second Texts*, vol *25,* 2006, p.25.

[35]Lu Dan. "Overlap·Parallel·Cross——Some Thoughts on O'Neill and Beckett's Plays." *Journal of Jianghan University (Social Science Edition)*, vol 02, 1985, p. 68-71.[卢丹."重叠·平行·交叉——关于奥尼尔与贝克特剧作的点滴思考".江汉大学学报（社会科学版），（02），1985，p. 68-71.]

[36]Liu, Aiying. "The Construction and Development of Beckett's English Criticism". *Foreign Literature Review*, no. 01, 2006, p. 138-146.[刘爱英."贝克特英语批评的建构与发展".外国文学评论，（01），2006，p. 138-146]

[37]Luo, Xuanming. "Ideology and Literary Translation: on Liang Qichao's

translation practice Journal of Tsinghua University". *Qichao's Translation Practice Journal of Tsinghua University: Philosophy and Social Sciences,* no. 01, 2006, p. 46-52.[罗选民."意识形态与文学翻译——论梁启超的翻译实践".清华大学学报:哲学社会科学版1,2006,p. 46-52.]

[38]Lv, Shuxiang. "Study on Grammar through Contrast". *Language Teaching and Research,* no. 02, 1992, p. 5-19.[吕叔湘."通过对比研究语法".语言教学与研究,(02),1992,p. 5-19.]

[39]Somers, Margaret R. "Narrativity, Narrative Identity, And Social Action: Rethinking English Working-Class Formation". *Social Science History,* vol 16, no. 4, 1992, p. 591-630. *JSTOR,* doi: 10.2307/1171314.

[40]Malone, Joseph L., and Mary Snell-Hornby. "Translation Studies: An Integrated Approach". *Language,* vol 67, no. 1, 1991, p. 197. *JSTOR,* doi: 10.2307/415587.

[41]Ni, Xiuhua. "Translation: A Cultural and Political Act-An Analysis of the Phenomenon of Chinese Translation of 'The Gadfly' in the 1950s". no. 4, *Comparative Literature in China,* 2005, p.116.[倪秀华."翻译:一种文化政治行为——20世纪50年代中国译介《牛虻》之现象透析".中国比较文学,(02),2005,p. 116.]

[42]Paloposki, Outi. "The Translator's Footprints." *Translators' Agency.* Tampereen Yliopistopaino, 2010, p. 86-107.

[43]Ran, Dongping. "On Narrative Rhythm of Western Modernist Drama". *Foreign Languages Research,* no.06, 2009, p. 96-100.[冉东平."西方现代派戏剧的叙事节奏".外语研究,(06),2009,p. 96-100]

[44]Shlesinger, Miriam, et al. "Markers of Translator Gender: Do They Really Matter?" *Copenhagen Studies in Language,* vol 38 .2009, p. 138-198.

[45]Shu, Xiaomei. "A Discussion on the Time and Space Structure in Beckett's Dramas." *Foreign Literature Studies,* no.02, 1997, p. 105-109.[舒笑梅."试论贝克特戏剧作品中的时空结构".外国文学研究,(02),1997,p. 105-109.]

[46]Shu, Xiaomei. "Poetic, Symmetrical and Absurd" —the Main Features

of the Dramatic Language in Beckett's *Waiting for Godot*". *Foreign Literature Studies*, no.01, 1998, p.56-59.[舒笑梅."诗化·对称·荒诞——贝克特《等待戈多》戏剧语言的主要特征".外国文学研究,（01）,1998, p. 56-59]

[47]Somers, M. R., and Gibson, G. D.. "Reclaiming the Epistemological Other: Narrative and the Social Constitution of Identity". *Crso Working Paper,* 2007.

[48]Song, C. X.. "On the Religious Spirit of Bakhtin's Carnival Theory". *Journal of Henan Normal University(philosop)*, vol *129*, no.2, 2008, p. 52-56.[宋春香."论巴赫金狂欢理论的宗教精神诉求".河南师范大学学报（哲学社会科学版）,（02）, 2008, p. 52-56.]

[49]Song, J. . "A New Breakthrough in Studies of Foreign Drama: A Review of Translation and Studies of Foreign Drama in New China". *Shandong Foreign Languages Teaching Journal*, no.1，2019, p. 130-133.[宋杰."外国戏剧研究新突破——《新中国外国戏剧的翻译与研究》述评".山东外语教学,（01）, 2019, p. 130-133.]

[50]Suchy, P. A. "When Worlds Collide: The Stage Direction as Utterance". *Journal Of Dramatic Theory & Criticism*, vol *6,* 1991.

[51]Sun Yu and Wang Tianhao. "A Semiotic Interpretation of *Waiting for Godot*". *Chinese Journal (Foreign Language Education and Teaching)*, no. 9, 2012, p. 26-27+134[孙宇，王天昊."《等待戈多》符码的戏剧符号学阐释".语文学刊（外语教育教学）,（09）, 2012, p. 26-27+134]

[52]Tong, Xiaoyan. "Conversational Relevance and Absurdity in *Waiting for Godot*". *Journal of Huainan Normal University*, no. 4, 2010, p. 64-66.[童晓燕."《等待戈多》中的会话关联性与荒诞主题".淮南师范学院学报,（04）, 2010, p. 64-66.]

[53]Tsimikas, Sotirios, and Gregor Leibundgut. "Post-Thienopyridine Platelet Response, Cardiovascular Outcomes, And Personalized Therapy". *JACC: Cardiovascular Interventions*, vol 3, no. 6, 2010, p. 657-659. *Elsevier BV*, doi: 10.1016/j. jcin.2010.03.006.

[54]Wang, Hongbin. "The Structure of the Number Name after the 'You' in

the 'You-Word Sentence'." *Journal of Ludong University (Philosophy and Social Sciences Edition)*, vol 000, no.02, 2000, p. 39-44.[王红斌."'有字句'中'有'后面的数量名结构".鲁东大学学报（哲学社会科学版），（02），2000，p. 39-44.]

[55]Wang, Yanling. "Pursuing and Waiting: A Comparison between "Passing by" and "Waiting for Godot". *Journal of Tianjin Normal University (Social Science Edition)*, no.04, 1987, p.94-97.[王艳玲."追寻与等待——《过客》与《等待戈多》之比较".天津师范大学学报（社科版），（04），1987，p. 94-97.]

[56]Wang, Yangwen and Tian, Debei. "A Review of Beckett Studies in China". *Jianghuai Forum,* vol 000, no.006, 2010, p. 185-189.[汪杨文，田德蓓."中国贝克特研究综述".江淮论坛，（006），2010，p. 185-189]

[57]Wang, S. "On Waiting in *Waiting for Godot*". *Foreign Literature Studies*, 2005, p. 88-92+174.

[58]Weber, Samuel. "A Touch of Translation: On Walter Benjamin's 'Task of the Translator.'." *Nation, Language, and the Ethics of Translation*, vol 10, 2005, p. 65.

[59]WEI, Qing-guang. "The Manipulation by Patronage on Translation". *Journal of Tianjin Foreign Studies University,* vol 13, no. 3, 2006, p. 38-41.[魏清光."赞助人对译介活动的操纵".天津外国语学院学报，（03），2006，p. 38-41]

[60]Yi, Yang. "An Interpretation of Chinese Narratology from Cultural Perspective". *Comparative Literature: East & West*, vol 3, no. 1, 2001, p. 37. *Informa UK Limited*, doi: 10.1080/25723618.2001.12015286.

[61]Yu, Fengbao. "Insight into the Past and Guide the Future: Reading Translation and Research of Foreign Drama in New China". *Si Chuan Xi Jv*, no. 7, 2018, p. 7-10.[于凤保."洞察往昔导引未来的学术史著作——读《新中国外国戏剧的翻译与研究》".四川戏剧，（07），2018，p. 7-10.]

[62]Zhang, Guogong and Gao, Junkai. "Professional Reading of Applied Literature in Literary Editing--Taking People's Literature Press as An Example". *Modern Publication*, vol 28, 2021, p. 24.[张国功，高俊凯."《应用文学在文学编辑中的专业阅读——以人民文学出版社为例》".现代出版第28卷，2021，p.

24.]

[63]Zhang, Helong. "The Samuel Beckett Studies in China". *Foreign Literatures*, vol 30, no.3, 2010, p. 37-45.[张和龙. "国内贝克特研究评述". 国外文学,（03）, 2010, p. 37-45]

[64]Zhang, Yanyan. "Waiting For Godot Points to Where We Are Going". *Beijing Youth Daily*, no. 2019-07/15, 2019, B1, Accessed 16 June 2021.[张艳艳. "《等待戈多》指向的是我们人类将去向何方". 北京青年报，2019-07/15, 2019, B1, 查阅日期：2021年6月16日.]

[65]Zheng, Hai-tao and Zhao, xing. "Dusk Is the Most Difficult Pastime--The Cultural Mechanism of The Formation of Dusk Image and Its Evolution from Pre Qin to Tang Dynasty". *Journal of China West Normal University*, no.2, 2008, p. 5-10.[郑海涛, 赵欣. "最难消遣是黄昏——黄昏意象生成的文化机制及其先秦至唐代的嬗变". 西华师范大学学报,（02）, 2008, p. 5]

[66]Zhu, Xuefeng. "Spatiotemporal Poetics of Beckett's Later Plays". *Foreign literature review*, vol 100, no.4, 2011, p. 124-136.[朱雪峰. "贝克特后期戏剧的时空体诗学外国文学评论".（04）, 2011, p. 124-136.]

Internet:

[1]Lv, Xueping. "Comment on Contemporary Legendary Theater *Waiting for Godot*-Life Is a Hopeless Waiting". https://www.sohu.com/a/332704404_100004574. 2019.[吕学平. "评·当代传奇剧场·《等待果陀》| 人生，一场没有希望的等待". https://www.sohu.com/a/332704404_100004574. 2019.]

[2]Shen, Dan. "Booth's 'The Rhetoric of Fiction' and China's Critical Context". *Narrative*, vol. 15, no. 2, 2007, p. 167–186. *JSTOR*, www.jstor.org/stable/30219249. Accessed 13 June 2021.

[3]WuTaiShangXia. "We Should Believe in A Kind of Person Who Is Called Clown-Jin Shijie on *Waiting for Guo Tuo*". https://www.biosmonthly.com/article/6318. 2015.[舞台上下. "我們要相信一種人，這種人叫小丑——金士傑談《等待果陀》". https://www.biosmonthly.com/article/6318. 2015.]

[4]Zhao, Zhenjiang. "Qiu Gangjian Went Too Early, If He Compiles 'The Golden Age', The Box Office Will at Least Triple". https://www. thepaper. cn/newsDetail_forward_1281675. Accessed 10 June 2021.[赵振江."邱刚健走得太早,如果他编《黄金时代》,票房至少翻三倍". https://www. thepaper. cn/newsDetail_forward_1281675. Accessed 10 June 2021.]

Phd. Book:

[1]Han Jia. "A Study on the Intersubjectivity of Literary Translation from the Perspective of Bakhtin's Dialogue Theory". Phd. Book: *Shandong University*, 2007.[韩佳."巴赫金对话理论视角下的文学翻译主体间性研究". 山东大学, 2007.]

[2]Han Jin. "On the Chinese Translation of Jiayin's Biography from the Perspective of Narratology". Phd. Book: *Beijing Foreign Studies University*, 2017. [韩 金."从叙事学角度看《迦茵(因)小传》的中文翻译". 北京:北京外国语大学, 2017.]

[3]Cronin, Anya M. "The reflection of the Wastelands of *Waiting for Godot* and Endgame in Electronic Media". Phd. Book: *Cronin Rowan University*, 2008.

[4]Qiu Jun. "Dialogic Analysis in Drama Translation". Phd. Book: *Medical Interpretation Hunan University*, 2012.

Appendix

Appendix I

Table of Annotation in Four Chinese Versions (Chinese)

Yu	Shi	Qiu	Liao
16 annotations	16 annotations	9 annotations	47 annotations
1) 241 你一定跟芝麻菜混淆了（法国监狱的名称）	1) 巴黎塔的解释，高三百米4	1) 38 Atlas 希腊神话双手擎天的神。宙比特。	1) 原文Nothing to be done.此句在劇中一再出現，有「不必做」或是「沒事做」並存之意，中文難以表達，做不「了」較貼近原意。

· 213 ·

续表

Yu 16 annotations	Shi 16 annotations	Qiu 9 annotations	Liao 47 annotations
2) 249 上吊，文字游戏	2) 希腊神话的神，受双肩接天的惩罚30	2) 41 四人都戴圆形高帽(Bowler)	2) 貝克特常用語意模糊或語帶雙關的句子，此爲一例。原文The same as usual 意指打的人數，但也可強調果果被打的次數，因此譯文不刻意把「人」譯出來。
3) 257 关于戈多的称呼（还没有，法语中本来要连读的	3) 希腊神话里的众神的领袖30	3) 43 英国制，名烟斗商标	3) 按《舊約聖經.箴言》13: 12:「所盼望的延遲未得，令人心憂……」原文是"Hope deferred maketh the heart sick."但是作者在此刻意讓維拉迪米爾忘記經文里的「心憂」(heart)這个字，而有所隱喻。
4) P275 阿特拉斯 朱的儿子（希腊神话）	4) 四个登场人物都带着礼帽——原注32	4) 44 潘，希腊神话中半人半羊之牧神	4) 維拉迪米爾指的是希望，但是貝克特在此句裡不刻意說明，因此譯文也故意省略。
5) P278 所有的这些人物都带着圆顶礼帽	5) 生产石南烟斗的著名工厂34	5) 46 原文字Black，是倒霉，晦气之意，与后一句是文间语	5) Repentend倾向于宗教上的"忏悔"之意，因而舍"后悔"的译文。
6) 281 英语版本 丢了我的凯普——生产石楠烟斗的工厂的名称	6) 潘——希腊神话里的山林之神35	6) 51 Frandolo, 创始于法国Provence的一种团体舞	6) Our Savour 就整齣戲而言，意指這對流浪漢的救主，但在此意指耶穌，因此譯爲救世主較妥當。

续表

Yu 16 annotations	Shi 16 annotations	Qiu 9 annotations	Liao 47 annotations
7) 282 拉住，忍住，文字游戏 忍住大小便	7) 卡图勒斯——公元前罗马抒情诗人37	7) 51 Brawl,一种古老的法国民间舞蹈	7) Weeping有低泣和枝葉垂下之意：在此可見貝克特用字的巧意，然而對譯者是一大挑戰。
8) 283 潘神是希腊神话中的之神。	8)（向佛拉基米尔）原文皆为埃斯特拉冈，显然有误，根据1952年子夜出版社法文改正38	8) 121 Abel 见到创世纪第四章	8) part和後文depart都有分和分手之意，譯文抹後者，乃因這對流浪漢的關係既像情人又像朋友
9) 285 加图鲁斯( )公元前87——前54)拉丁诗人	9)（向佛拉基米尔）原文皆为38	9) 121 Cain 见到创世纪第四章	9) 曼陀羅草（風茄）是《聖經》雅歌提及用來調情的植物，跟上文的勃起產生關聯。
10) 294 米兰达是莎士比亚暴风雨的女主人公	10) 密兰达，莎士比亚的女主人公		10) 有参与之意
11) 322 我敢把我的手放在火上 注释：意思是敢于发誓	11) 12)十九世纪俄国著名无线电学家44		11) 希臘神話，比喻身重的人。
12) 322 鲁西永是法国一地	12) 十九世纪英国著名探险家44		12) 罗马神话中的宙斯神

· 215 ·

续表

Yu 16 annotations	Shi 16 annotations	Qiu 9 annotations	Liao 47 annotations
13) 354 阿列日是法国的一个省	13）塞缪尔约翰逊 45 英国文学家(1709—1784), 第一部英国字典的编纂者		13) 维拉迪米一副没劲且语意模糊的说出一串连音。
14) 358 这是整个人类（译者说话）备注：亚伯和该隐是全体人类的祖先，所以说是整个人类	14）康纳马拉 45 爱尔兰西部靠海的山区		14) 英国名牌烟斗
15) 拉丁文，回忆过去的美好时光	15) 68 法文，你要什么		15) Subside有冷静、减弱和下沉之意，此爲雙語，和下一句互爲意指。
16) 363 拉普郎什，有舞台的意思	16）拉丁文；回忆过去的快乐时光		16)Pan牧神是宙斯之子，羊犄角、羊腿、羊，留獸的痕，帶著貪婪.欲望.情欲等官能的特点。
			17) Black 译成阴影，乃指迪迪对时间流逝的缓慢而增加等待的焦虑。
			18)法文Tres bon 意即很棒之意。此剧由贝克特亲自翻译成英文，但他保留少数法文字，后文仍可见几个例子

续表

Yu 16 annotations	Shi 16 annotations	Qiu 9 annotations	Liao 47 annotations
			19) The farandole;源於法国的尼斯,是一種多人協力一起跳的舞。舞者手牽著手隨著節拍跳躍,用一双脚下重拍,單站立時左右相互交換位置,用收輕拍。
			20) The fling:蘇格蘭舞。關於舞有兩種説法。有人認爲這是蘇蘭人打仗使後,慶祝戰爭胜利所跳的戰舞;另外一些人認爲是打仗前,用來在戰甲上跳的舞。根據後者説法,舞者起舞時繞著戰甲上的突刺打,同時指打拍子。
			21) The barwl:原名是branle,16世纪的法國舞蹈,後傳到英國以及蘇蘭而被稱爲brail。這種舞是给情侶跳的;他們排成圓圈或是成一條練,主要動作是橫向移動。
			22) The jig:愛爾蘭民俗舞蹈。jig分很多種,通常以6/8拍寫成。常見的jig是以一個八的作爲基調,重一次,然後進行下一個八拍的動作。
			23) The fandango;西班牙佛朗明奇舞的一種。大方登戈舞由情侶進行熱情對舞,一間始節奏緩慢,但是隨箸舞曲進行,節奏會逐漸快。小方登戈舞則是輕快活潑的舞,較適合慶典宴會。
			24) The horpipe:絶大部分用拍子寫成,通常是水手跳的民俗舞蹈,發明於18世紀,盛行於19世紀。

续表

Yu	Shi	Qiu	Liao
16 annotations	16 annotations	9 annotations	47 annotations
			25) The Hard Stool 是一種板凳之舞，但也有便秘之意。因此句大寫，是专有名詞，並且由嚴肅的迪迪说出.此取前者之意。
			26) qua qua qua qua 是拉丁文qua的重複字，等於英文的"as",中文的「以」或"当"。
			27) apathia、athambia和aphasia原爲希臘文，是冷漠、冷静和失语之意。
			28) Miranda是莎剧《暴风雨》的男主角米蘭公爵普洛士丕之女。
			29) fartov是放屁之意,Belcher是骂人的話，以大寫呈現，爲專有名詞，因此直接译爲「花」和「败车兒」，帶有戲謔之意。
			30) Conating有努力、渴望和策划之意，而貝克特取此字乃爲配合前文其他運勤名稱的尾ing,如:running,cycling,swimming,flying,floating,riding,gliding。此字介於各項运动項目之間，卻非运动名稱，乃是戲仿文字,此譯爲考努力。
			31) Feckham,Peckham,Fulham和Clapham後三者是地名，位於倫敦近郊。首字是作者探和後三字音的文字，就像上兩個注解所談的字，也是作者刻意之的文字戲仿。

Appendix

续表

Yu	Shi	Qiu	Liao
16 annotations	16 annotations	9 annotations	47 annotations
			32) Bishop Berkeley 英国人，1685年生於愛蘭。1734年被任命爲愛蘭罗因教區的主教，提倡唯心論。
			33) 拉丁文per caput是英文的per person，中文的「每一個人」。
			34) 法文 a dieu是英文的to God,亦即再見之意。在此三人皆講法文，因此探用較典雅的「告別」。
			35) 這暗指舊約<創世紀·第四章>亞伯和隱的故事。亞伯和該隱是亞当和夏娃偷吃禁果所生之子，該隱嫉其兄亞伯受上帝恩寵而殺兄。男孩的哥哥被打意即該隱被罰之意，此乃呼應前文迪迪所談的故事，一個小偷一被救的五五比例。亞伯和該隱的名字於後文將再度出現，意指全人类。
			36) 仓库的上层楼
			37) Pale for weariness取自英國浪漫時期詩人雪萊(Percy B. Shelley)的詩 "Art thou pale for weariness."
			38) The Rhone 是德国境内的一条河。
			39) 法文Que voulez-vous.等於英文的What do you want?中文的"你要什么?"
			40) Curate是牧師助理，有插手許多事之意，在此是罵人的，又爲了配合上一句「阴沟鼠」三個字，因此譯爲「管家婆」。

· 219 ·

续表

Yu 16 annotations	Shi 16 annotations	Qiu 9 annotations	Liao 47 annotations
			41) 這几句罵人的話，都刻意押韵。迪迪和果果比賽誰能在最短時間內找到既能罵對方，又符合上一句的韵，誰就贏了。迪迪罵出cretin（白痴），果果馬上接著crritc(批——批评家)不但符合上一句的韵，也找到特殊的罵人話，因此迪迪一副被擊敗的樣子。
			42) 位于法国和西班牙之间。
			43) repertory是定幕劇，在口語上不易聽懂，因此改爲「節目」。
			44) Caryatids是古典建築里的支撑物，雕有神像，即俗稱的「女像柱」。采「柱子」之譯，乃是爲了口語上的方便。
			45) Memoria praeteritorum bonorum是拉丁谚语。
			46) Exactly用於回答時是指完全正確，這里英文雙關語難以表达，因此重複前一句的「究竟」。
			47) Fair若形容毛髮乃指金色，但顾及一般説法，仍譯白色鬍子，可呼應幸运獨白里的上帝形象。

Appendix II

Table of Annotations in Four Chinese Versions (translated by author)

Yu	Shi	Qiu	Liao
16 annotations	**16 annotations**	**9 annotations**	**47 annotations**
1) You must have confused with sesame vegetables (the name of the French prison). P241	1) The interpretation of the Paris Tower, 300 meters high. P4	1) Atlas, The God holding the sky in both hands in Greek mythology. P38	1) "Nothing to be done". This sentence appears repeatedly in the play. There is no coexisting meaning "don't have to" and "have nothing to do". It is difficult to express in Chinese, "be unable to do" is "closer to the original intention.
2) hanging, word game. P249	2) Atlas, The God holding the sky in both hands in Greek mythology. P30	2) All four wear round high hats (Bowler). P41	2) Beckett often uses sentences with vague meanings or puns. For example: "the same as usual" refers to the number of people beaten, but can also refer to the beaten times, so the translation does not deliberately translate "people" out.
3) About Godot's name (not yet, in French would have been read in succession). P257	3) The leader of the gods in Greek mythology. P30	3) British famous pipe trademark. P43	3) According to the *Old Testament.* Proverbs 13: 12: "The delay that is expected is not known; it is worrying...The original text is" Hope deferred maketh the heart sick." But here the author deliberately lets Vera Dimir forget the word "heart" of the scriptures, and it is translated metaphorically.

续表

Yu 16 annotations	Shi 16 annotations	Qiu 9 annotations	Liao 47 annotations
4) Atlas Zhu's son (Greek mythology). P275	4) All four debuting characters wear a hat that goes with formal dress. P32	4) Pan, half-man and half-sheep shepherd god in Greek mythology. P44	4) Vila Demir is referring to hope, but Beckett does not mean to say it clearly, so the translation is also deliberately omitted.
5) All of these characters wear dome hats. P278	5) Famous factory for the production of Shinan pipe. P34	5) The original word "Black", is hapless, obscure, with the latter sentence is the interwoven language. P46	5) "Representend" tends to mean "repentance" in religion, therefore give up the translation of "regret".
6) English version "lost my Cape"—the name of the factory that makes pipes. P281	6) Pan—the god of the mountains and forests in Greek mythology. P35	6) Francolo, a group dance founded in Provence, France. P51	6) In the case of the whole play, Our Savour means the Savior of the tramp, but in this case, it means Jesus, so it is more appropriate to translate as the Savior.
7) pull, hold back, word game. P282	7) Cartulus—a lyric poet of Rome B. C. P37	7)51 Brawl, an ancient French folk dance. P51	7) Weeping has a low sob and a leafy meaning: here you can see Beckett's cleverness in words, but it is a challenge for the translator.

· 222 ·

Appendix

续表

Yu 16 annotations	Shi 16 annotations	Qiu 9 annotations	Liao 47 annotations
8) Pan is one of gods of Greek mythology. P283	8)(to Vladimir) the original text is Estragon, which is obviously wrong. It is corrected according to the French language of midnight press in 1952. P38	8) Abel sees Genesis 4. P121	8) Part and the later depart have the meaning of separation and break-up, the translation erases the latter, because the relationship between the tramps is like a lover and a friend.
9) Gaturus A Latin poet (87-54 BC). P285	9)(to Vladimir). P38	9) Cain sees Genesis 4. P121	9) Mandala grass (wind eggplant) is a biblical anthem that refers to plants used for flirting, which is associated with the erection of the text.
10) Miranda is the heroine of Shakespeare's *The Tempest*. P294	10)Milanda, Shakespeare's heroine.		10) There is a sense of participation.
11) I dare put my hand on the fire Note: It means swearing. P322	11) A famous Russian radiographer in the 19th century. P44		11) Greek mythology, It's a metaphor for a heavy person.
12) Rousey is a French place. P322	12)Famous British explorer of the nineteenth century. P44		12) The God of Zeus in the Roman gods.

续表

Yu 16 annotations	Shi 16 annotations	Qiu 9 annotations	Liao 47 annotations
13) Alej is a province of France. P354	13) Samuel Johnson, English Writer (1709—1784), author of the first English dictionary. P45		13) Veradimi says a string of conjoined sounds in a boring and vague tone.
14) This is the whole human note: Abel and the Cain are the ancestors of all mankind, so it is the whole human race. P358	14) Connacht Mara, The mountains of western Ireland by the sea. P45		14) British brand-name pipe.
15) Latin, Memories of the good old days. P363	15) French: what do you want. P68		15) Subside has a cool, weak and sinking meaning, which is a pun and means to each other in the next sentence.
16) Raprangsh, with stage meaning. P363	16) Latin: Memories of the good old days		16) Pan is the son of Zeus, sheep horns, legs, sheep, leaving traces of animals, with the characteristics of greed, desire, lust and other functions.
			17) Black is translated into shadows. Shadow refers to Didi's anxiety about the increase of waiting due to the slow passage of time.

续表

Yu	Shi	Qiu	Liao
16 annotations	16 annotations	9 annotations	47 annotations
			18) French Tres bon means great. The play was personally translated into English by Beckett, but he retained a small number of French characters, and several examples can still be seen later.
			19) The farandole; From nice, France. It is a kind of dance that many people dance together. The dancers hold hands and jump with the beat. They use a pair of feet to remake. When they stand alone, they exchange positions with each other and use the close tap.
			20) There are two versions of this dance. Some people think that it is a kind of war dance performed by the Sulans to celebrate the victory of the war; Others recognized it as a dance used to demon and dance on armor before a war. Other people think it's used to dance on the armor before the war. According to the latter, when dancing, the dancers beat around the spike on the armor, and at the same time, they beat time.

续表

Yu 16 annotations	Shi 16 annotations	Qiu 9 annotations	Liao 47 annotations
			21) The barwl: originally known as branle, it was a French dance in the 16th century, and later spread to England and Suran and was called brail; They form a circle or a line, and their main action is to move horizontally.
			22) The jig: Irish Folk Dance. Jig is divided into many kinds, usually written in 6/8 pats. The common jig is to set the tone with an eight, repeat it again, and then perform the next eight beats.
			23) The fandango; A kind of Spanish Flaminch dance. The generous Dengo dance is performed passionately by a couple, one with a slow start, but with the dance, the rhythm will gradually fast. Small Fangango dance is a light and lively dance, more suitable for the celebration banquet.
			24) The horpipe: most of the dance is written with beats, usually a folk dance by sailors, invented in the 18th century and popular in the 19th century.

Appendix

续表

Yu	Shi	Qiu	Liao
16 annotations	16 annotations	9 annotations	47 annotations
			25) The Hard Stool is a bench dance, but it also has constipation. The sentence is capitalized, so it is a proper noun. And the song is said by the serious Didi said. This is the meaning of the former.
			26) Qua qua qua is a repetition of Latin qua, equivalent to "as" in English and "Yi" or "Dang" in Chinese.
			27) Apathia, athambia and aphasia are originally Greek, which means indifference, calmness and aphasia.
			28) Miranda is the daughter of the Prince of Prospero, the hero of Shakespeare's drama *The Tempest*.
			29) Fartov means farting, Belcher means swearing, which is presented in capital. It is a proper noun, so it is directly translated as "花" (huā) and "败车儿" (bài chēr), which means joking.

· 227 ·

续表

Yu	Shi	Qiu	Liao
16 annotations	**16 annotations**	**9 annotations**	**47 annotations**
			30) "Conating" means striving, longing and planning. Beckett uses this word to match the ending of other names of "running, cycling, swimming, flying, floating, riding, gliding" in the previous article. This word is between various sports, but it is not a name of sports. It is parody. Here it is translated as "考努力".
			31) Feckham, Peckham, Fulham and Clapham, the last three are place names, located in the outskirts of London. The first word is the author's words to explore the last three characters. Just like the words mentioned in the last two notes, it is also the author's deliberate parody of words.
			32) Bishop Berkeley, an Englishman, was born in Ellen in 1685. In 1734, he was appointed bishop of Ellen rowing, advocating idealism.
			33) Latin "per caput" is "per person" in English and "everyone" in Chinese.

续表

Yu	Shi	Qiu	Liao
16 annotations	16 annotations	9 annotations	47 annotations
			34) French "a Dieu" is the English word "to God", which means goodbye. All three of them speak French here, because they use the more elegant "goodbye".
			35) This implies the story of Abel and Cain in the *Old Testament* (Genesis 4). Abel and Cain are the sons of Adam and Eve who ate the forbidden fruit secretly. Cain is jealous that his brother Abel because of God's favor and he killed his brother. The beating of the boy's brother means that Cain was punished. This is in line with what Didi said earlier, the ratio of a thief who was rescued is five to five. The names of Abel and Cain will appear again later. It means all mankind.
			36) The upper floor of the warehouse.
			37) Pale for weariness is taken from the poem "Art thou for pale weariness" by Percy B. Shelley.
			38) The Rhone is a river in Germany.

续表

Yu	Shi	Qiu	Liao
16 annotations	**16 annotations**	**9 annotations**	**47 annotations**
			39) French "Que voulez-vous" is like" what do you want" in English? Chinese "What do you want（你要什么）?"
			40) Curate is a clergyman's assistant. He means to meddle in many things. In comparison, he is abusive. In order to match the three words "sewer rat", he translates it as "housekeeper".
			41) These words are deliberately rhymed. In the competition between Didi and Gogo, who can find the one scold each other in the shortest time, but also conform to the rhyme of the previous sentence, who will win. Didi scolded cretin, and Gogo immediately followed by crritc, which not only conformed to the rhyme of the previous sentence, but also found a special curse, so Didi looked defeated.
			42) Located between France and Spain.

续表

Yu	Shi	Qiu	Liao
16 annotations	**16 annotations**	**9 annotations**	**47 annotations**
			43) Repertory is a set-up play that is not easy to understand in spoken English and it is changed to "program".
			44) Caryatids is the support of classical architecture, carved with the image of divine, which is commonly known as "female statue column". The translation of "column" is for oral convenience.
			45) Memoria Praeteritorum bonorum is a Latin proverb.
			46) "Exactly" is used to mean "exactly". It is difficult to express English pun here, so repeat "exactly" in the previous sentence.
			47) Fair, if it is used to describe hair, it means golden, but considering the general saying, it is translated with white beard, which can echo the image of God in Lucky monologue.